WATERY GRAVE

WATERY GRAVE

METAL LEGION™ BOOK FIVE

CH GIDEON   CALEB WACHTER   CRAIG MARTELLE

DISRUPTIVE IMAGINATION

LMBPN Publishing
PMB 196, 2540 South Maryland Pkwy
Las Vegas, NV 89109

First US edition, February 2019
Print ISBN: 978-1-64202-440-1

DEDICATION

We can't write without those who support us. On the home front, we thank you for being there for us.

We wouldn't be able to do this for a living if it weren't for our readers. We thank you for reading our books.

WATERY GRAVE TEAM

Thanks to our Beta Readers

Micky Cocker, James Caplan, Kelly O'Donnell, and John Ashmore

Thanks to the JIT Readers

Micky Cocker
Peter Manis
Misty Roa
Crystal Wren
Jeff Eaton
John Ashmore
Paul Westman

If I've missed anyone, please let me know!

Editing services provided by LKJ Bookmakers www. lkjbooks.com

PROLOGUE: MAINTAINING TEMPO

"Stop that," Colonel Jenkins insisted of his Brigade XO, Major Xi Bao, whose constant fidgeting with her uniform was starting to get on his nerves. Waiting outside one of the most recognizable war rooms in the Terran Armed Forces was trying at the best of times. It reminded him too much of the boards of inquiry and his court-martial. It was like waiting for his own funeral. Every time. "You'll be fine. Just keep your mouth shut unless someone orders you to open it."

"Thanks for the vote of confidence, boss," Xi quipped, slicing him a glare that caused Colonel Moon to chuckle uncharacteristically. He must have been nervous, too. "I wonder what's taking them so long?" she muttered, but she mercifully ceased fussing with her uniform, which fit as if she were born to be the TAF poster child.

"The general's better at this part than any of us will ever be," Colonel Moon observed matter-of-factly.

"We've been waiting for *two hours*," Xi hissed.

"He's got his reasons," Jenkins soothed, although he too was beginning to wonder what could be taking so long.

A few minutes later, the doors finally opened and a Terran Fleet Lieutenant beckoned. "The admiral will see you now."

The trio of Terran Armor Corps officers formed a file with Moon at the head and Xi at the rear and proceeded down the short hallway leading to the war room.

The Scabbard.

Named for its shape, it was long and slender with opposing lines of fifty seats on either side of the narrow metal blade-shaped table. The Scabbard had been home to some of the most important wartime meetings in Terran history. There was no declared territory here. No branch claimed ownership of any given seat or portion of the table. The Scabbard was meant to do precisely what it sounded like: contain the mightiest weapon in the Terran Armed Forces until it was needed to strike.

At the far end of the room, twenty-some seats were occupied, and Jenkins took note that only one of the Republic's military branches was represented: Fleet.

The top-ranking Fleet officer sent a steely glare Jenkins' way as he, Moon, and Xi approached General Pushkin's side of the table, opposite Fleet's.

"Colonel Moon, Colonel Jenkins," Admiral Wallace stiffly stated. "Major Bao. Before we begin, I'd like to clear up a certain matter in the interest of transparency."

Jenkins suspected what was coming and kept eye contact with the admiral as the other man's gaze flicked between Moon and Jenkins.

"I don't like being lied to, gentlemen," Wallace said bluntly, "and that was precisely what happened during our last dialogue. The so-called 'joint operation' my *former* Intelligence Officer," he turned a hard look Pushkin's way, while the Metal Legion's foremost officer remained as calm as ever, "described was pure fantasy. But even I can admit," he continued sourly, "that sometimes deception is essential to an ongoing operation's success.

However," his voice hardened, "don't think you can hide behind General Akinouye's name or Admiral Zhao's good graces should you flout your sworn duties as Terran servicemen in the future. Do I make myself clear?"

"As a Solarian's conscience, Admiral," Colonel Moon replied with surprising flair and good humor, nearly causing Jenkins to break into a smile.

Wallace gave Moon a withering look before turning his attention to the woman seated beside him. "This is Lieutenant Commander Ulbricht of the New American Navy." The middle-aged seagoing woman nodded deferentially as Wallace continued, "Let's cut to it. The Vorr need our help, and we've convened this meeting to address which branches of the Terran Armed Forces will participate in the op."

Moon, Jenkins, and Xi seated themselves to General Pushkin's left while Admiral Wallace pulled up a holographic image of a bleak-looking world, the majority of which was covered in dark gray rock. The planet's visual monotony was broken only by a handful of tiny oceans, and before Jenkins could identify it from memory he heard Xi to his left ask, "VX-0978?"

"That's right, Major," Wallace confirmed. "This is a world in Vorr space where our aquatic friends appear to have uncovered some sort of archeological site. They were in the process of excavating it when a Jemmin gatecrasher," the holo-image of the planet was replaced by one of the most terrifying warships in Nexus space, "broke through the Vorr line at the Nexus and made straight for this world. The Vorr pursued and ultimately destroyed the gatecrasher, but not before it neutralized nearly every piece of Vorr military hardware in the star system. The Vorr have thus far been unable to extricate themselves from their ongoing battle for the Nexus and divert assets to VX-0978. Of concern and interest to Fleet, they've found that Jemmin's targeting systems preferentially bracket ships bearing the necessary equipment to go down and extract the artifacts and other materials the Vorr have been digging up, which we'll refer to in this brief as the 'Pearl.'"

"How many Jemmin forces remain in orbit over the Pearl, Admiral?" Jenkins asked

"Unknown," Wallace replied flatly. "At last count, there were at least a dozen fighters and one nearly-hulked Jemmin warship in overwatch of the dig site. Since the gatecrasher was destroyed, no traffic has gone into or out of the Pearl's system. We've independently verified the Nexus-side has been clear since the Vorr Fleet returned, but the Vorr have restricted our people from moving in survey teams to the site."

"They don't want us poking around for ourselves," Moon mused.

"That'd be the smart guess," Wallace agreed. "Jemmin's got a hard-on for this world, people, and it's only a matter of time before anything of value on the Pearl is destroyed by whatever Jemmin forces remain there. The Vorr have given us an insertion window in three days' time, but we have to keep the force small. To wit, no more than two ships, neither of which can be larger than a cruiser, can go to the Pearl. Let me be blunt: this mission is tailor-made for the Terran Marines," Wallace continued smugly, drawing a soft snort from General Pushkin and causing the admiral to adopt a muted look of irritation. "But Commander Ulbricht made the radical suggestion of using TAC supporting elements instead. After consulting with my staff, I thought it would be prudent to hear Armor Corps' take on the situation before making a decision."

Pushkin leaned forward confidently. "The Metal Legion is prepared to go where others can't or won't. This is nothing unusual to us."

"I'm more concerned," Colonel Moon interjected, "about

the mission profile. If I remember my latest org charts, Commander Ulbricht is assigned to the Submarine Recovery team of the American Navy's Third Fleet. Is that correct, Commander?"

Ulbricht nodded approvingly. "It is, Colonel."

"Which means," Jenkins continued, his brow lowering in contemplation, "that we're talking about dropping deep-dive submarines from orbit...in a can?" He'd never read about anything like this being attempted in Terran Armed Forces history. Usually subs, in the rare events during which they were needed, would be lowered from orbit on the tethered platforms normally used to retrieve mechs or other bulky assets from a planet's surface. But a combat drop of *submarines*?

It was completely unheard of.

"Obviously conveying them to the dig site will require heavy haulers similar to those we used in Brick Top," Pushkin said dismissively. "Submarines are delicate, yes, but no more so than a tunnel-boring laser."

"My hardware's less delicate than you might imagine." Commander Ulbricht smirked, and Jenkins wasn't entirely sure if the sexual innuendo had been intentional. Judging from Pushkin's boyish grin, it had.

But Admiral Wallace was in no mood for games.

"Fleet assets could drop the subs, along with Marine escorts and fixed defensive systems." Wallace scowled. "And our people could deep-dive alongside the subs to ensure ongoing security. Frankly, it's this particular lack of submarine assets that gives me pause in handing this op over to TAC, but the only warships we've got that are capable of carrying out this mission in the allotted timetable fall outside the mission parameters. The smallest drop-capable ship that can deploy in time is the battlecruiser *Yamato*."

"That's Fleet for you." Pushkin chuckled. "All hammers and

no scalpels."

"Size matters, General," Moon said under his breath, but loud enough for all to hear. Wallace raised his hand to let the others know that he'd had enough.

Ulbricht smoothly filled the silence. "I've got three deep-dive-capable retrieval vehicles, each of which is armed with standard defensive weaponry. The Vorr have erected a robust underwater defensive system and given us the passcodes to permit us access to the dig site, so once we arrive, we should be safe to complete the dig and extract the packages. But we'll need a land escort to get there, and I'd prefer to bring along a few more vehicles or possibly even Marines to provide extra fire support during extraction."

"Caulk and weld..." Xi muttered, drawing looks of approval from Jenkins and Moon.

"Say that again, Major?" Admiral Wallace asked tightly, his eyes having not wavered from Pushkin following the other man's slur against Fleet.

"Non-Legion personnel could be forgiven," Xi explained with a hint of smugness that simultaneously amused and concerned Jenkins, "for being unaware of the fact that over seventy percent of mechs in the Metal Legion are, with minor modifications such as a hundred liters of caulk and about thirty meters of fresh weld, capable of carrying out tactical submarine operations at depths around those in this mission brief."

"Legion vehicles," Colonel Moon continued easily, "are, for the most part, positively buoyant by design. Some, like the old Scorpion-class, are even designed for the modular attachment of underwater weapons, drives, and buoyancy systems to facilitate submerged maneuverability."

"The Recon mechs and some of the older, track-based heavies sink like rocks." Jenkins nodded in agreement as Admiral Wallace's expression changed to mixed bewilderment and approval. "But the Terran Armor Corps had operations like this one in mind when it was formed. It's just that the colonial Navies have been so good at their jobs that we haven't had much need to test the capability."

"*We go where others can't or won't...and everywhere we've held*," General Pushkin rhythmically intoned the old Metalhead poem, supposedly penned by General Akinouye himself when he was a lieutenant. "*On land or sea, you'll die the same...we need but caulk and weld.*"

Admiral Wallace pursed his lips and fixed his gaze on the wall as Pushkin finished the poem, which was likely known by just a handful of Metalheads. For the first time in Jenkins' experience with Wallace, the admiral was at a complete loss for words.

Jenkins, Moon, and Xi looked at each other in silent approval before declaring with a united voice, "Metal never dies."

Colonel Jenkins added, in case anyone at the table was unclear what they meant, "My mechs will successfully complete the mission. All you have to do is get us there."

<hr />

The quartet of officers quickly returned to TAC HQ and were mostly silent en route. Conveyed by a heavily armored aircar with an escort of Metal Legion aerospace fighters, Xi felt decidedly uneasy during the trip. It was difficult to ignore the strong precautions General Pushkin had taken to safeguard their trip, which suggested two things that unnerved Xi.

First, that there was a legitimate chance the Terran Armor Corps had enemies on New America who might take action against them. In principle, this wasn't something that overly concerned her, but the reality of wondering whether a surface-to-air missile might be lurking in their flight path was far from a welcome experience.

The more daunting revelation was that even as the lowest-ranking member of the group, the newly-minted major was a valuable enough asset to the Metal Legion that she was worth protecting.

Just two years earlier, Xi Bao had been a Tier One felon serving a multi-decade prison sentence for data theft and other virtual crimes. She was considered so dangerous that she had been confined to an eight-by-ten concrete box and deprived of access to outside communication devices. But now she was apparently considered so important to Terran security that a quartet of Viper aerospace fighters flew an offset diamond escort of her aircar.

I've just traded one locked box for another, she mused.

She left those thoughts behind as the aircar descended to TAC HQ, and soon the quartet found themselves in the central transit space of the Metal Legion's headquarters.

"I'll be blunt," Pushkin said after they reached the safety of Legion HQ and the doors had closed behind them. "This is an important operation, perhaps more important than Brick Top."

Xi's brow furrowed. "But Jem..." she started, referring to the entity intelligence who was a critical ally in the fight against Jemmin. "How so, General?"

"Colonel Jenkins was right about Admiral Zhao. He is a good man." Pushkin sighed as he assumed the head position at the war room's central table. "But he also views Armor Corps as a rival to be contended with, not an obstacle to be removed...or even a friend to be assisted during a time of need. It is my belief that Admiral Zhao has an eye on the highest political offices, and that he intends to use the Metal Legion as leverage to acquire the position he seeks."

"You think he wants to be President?" Jenkins asked in

surprise.

"Doubtful," Pushkin allowed. "At least, not yet. The court-martial you two underwent was anything but ordinary. It was theater, and well-done theater at that," he admitted. "There is nothing that expressly prohibits an active-duty Terran officer from pursuing political office, although it is rarely done for too many reasons to mention. The point is that he is testing the waters by seeing just how much influence he can muster. He knew the positive sentiment regarding being freed from alien control had value. He came through as a hero. So far, he has managed to manipulate the Fleet shipyards into doing precisely what he said they would: refitting a handful of our mothballed hulls. But it's *how* he's doing it, and more specifically, which ships he's picking, that shows something more than what we see on the surface."

A holographic image sprang to life above the table before them, and Xi knew instantly what was represented there. "The *Vercingetorix*."

"You know your hulls, Major," Pushkin said dryly, "but do you know your history as well?"

Xi cocked her head contemplatively. "Vercingetorix was a warlord who harassed Roman supply lines with hit-and-run tactics, relying almost exclusively on light cavalry. He was one of the most successful antagonists of Rome in his day."

"Yes, yes." Pushkin waved a hand dismissively. "It's not his peak that Zhao wants you to focus on, but his end."

Xi's brows lowered as she recalled that particular bit of history. "Vercingetorix took refuge in a fortress on a peak while Julius Caesar led his army to the foot of that hill. Vercingetorix relied on the fortress's walls, his cavalry's fast-strike capability, and the fact that he was in friendly territory where he could call on allies for assistance for security. Caesar outflanked him, however, by having his engineers build a double ring of siege walls: one facing the fortress to besiege it, and the other facing outward to repel Vercingetorix's reinforcements."

"It's a cleverly-delivered message," Colonel Moon grunted. "Maybe *too* clever."

"And an important message in itself," Jenkins agreed heavily.

Xi nodded slowly in comprehension. "No matter how safe you think you are, there's always a way to bring you down."

Pushkin nodded knowingly. "Had Vercingetorix acted faster to call for reinforcements, he could have fought Caesar off or, at the very least, secured a withdrawal from the site of his eventual defeat. But he was confident in the strength of his position and grew complacent."

"Admiral Zhao is warning us not to be complacent?" Jenkins asked uncertainly.

"Perhaps," Pushkin allowed. "And if so, he is also building a double ring of siege walls around us. Right now, we need Fleet support to get our ships online, and we need ongoing Republic funding to continue operating, let alone expanding as we must if we intend to keep our feet beneath us as an independent branch of the Terran Armed Forces. On the surface, the Metal Legion appears to be ascending, with support flowing in at record rates and more material assets in inventory than we've had in decades. But in reality, our options have never been fewer, and those who hold our purse strings are acutely aware of that fact. To address this weakness, I have arranged for...let's call it a 'diplomatic observer' to accompany you on Operation Watery Grave."

"Great name, that," Colonel Moon deadpanned.

"We dance to our own beat, Colonel." Pushkin chuckled. "The observer will require ongoing access to the operation's commander, which is you, Colonel Jenkins."

Xi felt a wave of relief wash over her that she wouldn't be

housing the "observer." Ms. Samuels had been surprisingly helpful during Operation Frozen Fire, but having her aboard had kept Xi on edge throughout the op. As a newly-made field officer whose duty would include overseeing a command of her own rather than serving exclusively as XO to Colonel Jenkins, Xi knew that she needed all of her attention to be on the job at hand and not dedicated to babysitting this person.

"Who is the observer?" Jenkins asked measuredly, making clear he was no happier about having someone aboard his mech than Xi had been about Ms. Samuels being aboard hers.

"Her name is Alice," Pushkin replied, causing Jenkins' brow to rise in surprise. "You have already met."

"The Solarian delegate who interrogated me?" Jenkins asked in confusion.

"Indeed." Pushkin nodded. "They were impressed by your conduct in Operation Antivenom, and would like a more..." his lips twisted into a smirk, "intimate view of how the Legion operates. Given our situation," he gestured to the *Vercingetorix's* silently rotating image before them, "I think it's prudent to make certain concessions in the interests of securing financial and material support. In fact, two of the vehicles I've approved for this op's roster were recently donated by Sol. Still, while Sol-Terran relations have improved following Antivenom, it would be wise to keep this observer at arm's length as much as possible."

"That's difficult to do in the cabin of a command mech, General," Jenkins said irritably.

Pushkin splayed his hands as wide as the grin on his face. "Improvisation is in every Metalhead's blood, Colonel. I'm sure you'll manage."

"Yes, sir," Colonel Jenkins acknowledged without elaboration.

"We need the support, Lee," Colonel Moon said gravely.

"And they requested you by name to serve as their liaison."

"Did they say why?" Jenkins asked, his demeanor softening at hearing that last bit.

"Not really." Moon shook his head. "But our list of options is limited. Expanding that list is key to securing the Legion's future."

"Understood," Jenkins said after a brief delay, during which time his stormy expression cleared significantly. "We'll get the job done. And while I think we can all agree I'm no diplomat, I'll do what I can."

"Good." Pushkin nodded approvingly. "Besides the *Vercingetorix*, which is capable of deploying one company of Cruiser-grade or lighter mechs, the *Red Hare* stands ready to contribute to this mission. It is my recommendation that Colonel Jenkins assumes operational command of Clover Battalion elements deployed from the *Red Hare*, while Major Xi commands the *Vercingetorix* company, which will include the heavy haulers tasked with conducting American Navy elements to the dig site."

Xi felt a thrill at hearing the general's acknowledgment of her command.

"I concur," Colonel Jenkins agreed. "I've already spoken with Captain Chao, and he'll serve as my XO in Clover. The Han Colonial Guard transfers will respect him, and he'll be able to help facilitate their integration into the Metal Legion."

"Good." Pushkin nodded approvingly before turning to Xi. "Have you assembled a roster, Major?"

"I have," Xi agreed. "Given the operational requirements and my command's role in it, Captain Koch will be my XO. He will oversee ground HQ while I lead an escort platoon to accompany Commander Ulbricht's retrieval team to the underwater dig site."

"Captain Koch?" Pushkin asked skeptically. "Why not

Captain Winters? He has the tactical experience and organizational talents, whereas Captain Koch's combat duties are limited since he has primarily operated support vehicles."

"Captain Winters," Xi explained, feeling more than a little uncertain as she explained her rationale, "is still recovering from wounds sustained on Luna, General. And it is my opinion that his organizational talents would be better deployed here at HQ to help assess the increasing number of inter-branch transfers we've received since Antivenom. Captain Koch's tactical experience may be limited, but he knows the equipment and has more combat experience than Captain Winters, and my command will likely be a supportive one during this deployment. Koch is the support specialist, General, and I have no experience in that department, so his expertise will be invaluable to me."

Pushkin ominously drummed his fingers on the table, flitting a glance to Colonel Moon and another to Colonel Jenkins before he broke out into his trademark grin. "An excellent use of personnel and equipment, Major," the general congratulated her. "I agree. Captain Winters will be more valuable here than on the Pearl, and Captain Koch is the ideal candidate to serve as your XO."

Xi felt like sighing in relief but refrained from doing so as the general continued, "Colonel Jenkins will have operational command of the mission. Colonel Moon will serve as commanding officer of the *Vercingetorix,* and has already received my approval for the ship's crew transfers and new command staff. The *Red Hare* is provisioned and ready to deploy, while the *Vercingetorix* arrives in thirty-one hours and will require all Legion assets to be transferred aboard at that time. I expect to have finalized rosters on my desk by then. Dismissed."

"Yes, sir!" the trio replied, and just like that, the Metal Legion was riding back into the fire.

1

MUSTER

"Ok, Nugget," Xi muttered as she booted up the tactical simulator for the thirtieth time that day, "let's see what you've got."

The neural link that normally connected a mech Jock to her vehicle went live as the tactical simulator sprang to life with a flood of signals. To an untrained pilot, the signals would feel every bit as real as the genuine article, but Xi had spent enough time in the pilot's chair to know the difference.

The simulations she had set up for this round of assessments were two-way, meaning the fog of war affected not only the aspiring Jock she was testing, but they also blinded Xi to the tactical variables.

The type of mission had been decided by the applicant (in this case, a convoy-protection op) while other variables were up to Xi (she had thus far chosen to use random equipment malfunctions on both the applicant's mech and her own).

Xi had spent *thousands* of hours in the simulator during her early induction into then-Commander Jenkins' Jock-training program. She had actually fallen asleep inside the simulator on a handful of occasions when sixty-hour-plus stints overcame her neurological system's ability to cope.

The first feedback came through her virtual Warlock-class mech's sensors, and there was no immediate sign of the convoy. The terrain was broken, a variety of canyons and plateaus dotting the landscape, so Xi prepped a delayed-launch recon drone and left it on the ground while guiding her vehicle to a nearby plateau.

The Warlock was a humanoid Cruiser-grade mech possessing significant advantages in both armor and speed, paired with an underwhelming arsenal of just one SRM launcher, a pair of chain guns, and a heavy plasma cannon. The design was deeply flawed. It presented a variety of tactical weaknesses a savvy Jock could potentially exploit, but thus far all sixteen of the applicants had failed to take sufficient advantage of those weaknesses to emerge victorious from the simulation.

She moved her mech to relative safety beside the nearby plateau and activated the drone she had left on the ground. It shot skyward, feeding telemetry back to her for several seconds before an airburst artillery shell reduced it to a cloud of wreckage that fluttered back to the surface.

"Rookie." Xi scowled disapprovingly as she plotted the source of the shell. It was on the far side of the next plateau over to the west, which meant Xi had a clear line of approach that would give her an ideal firing arc no matter which direction the convoy headed. "All too easy..." She grunted while directing her Warlock mech to an ideal firing position.

Sure enough, the convoy emerged from the northern edge of the plateau just as she had expected it would. That meant the Nugget was likely to try an attack from the south, so while Xi kept her plasma cannon trained north, she primed her SRMs and locked their targeting sensors on the southern edge.

A Scorpion-class mech soon emerged from concealment on the southern edge, and Xi loosed eight SRMs from their launchers. Using a risky technique, she actually fired the missiles before acquiring positive target lock, but then forwarded the targeting data to the missiles in-flight (after disabling their remote lockouts), which caused them to converge on the target vehicle half a second faster than if they had been launched traditionally.

It was a stupid, overly-ballsy maneuver a savvy Jock could potentially use against Xi by disrupting the missiles with a jamming field, or possibly even by ejecting a cloud of chaff.

Unfortunately for this particular Nugget, neither technique was employed in time.

Five of the eight SRMs struck home, scratching both of the Scorpion's missile launchers and one of its fifteen-kilo mains. Xi's scowl deepened as she turned the plasma cannon toward the battered mech, which sent an HE shell whistling through the air toward Xi's position. But Xi had already evacuated that spot in a classic lateral displacement maneuver (another move the Nugget could have capitalized on but failed to).

The Nugget's shell still landed danger-close, showering Xi's mech with a spray of debris and triggering an auto-shutdown of the SRM launcher. As the Warlock's plasma cannon thrummed to life, it was clear who would win this particular engagement.

The cannon whumped, with its recoil driving the Warlock's reinforced feet deep into the dusty terrain of the virtual battle-field. In a ponderous, arcing trajectory, the plasma projectile soared toward the beleaguered Scorpion, which it soon enveloped in a blue-white inferno that annihilated the applicant's vehicle.

All told, it was a thoroughly mediocre performance by the Nugget, and Xi was nowhere near pleased with the outcome of the day's interviews.

"I'd say 'better luck next time,' Nugget," Xi quipped over the simulator's built-in cross-talk system after the simulation had ended following the Scorpion's obliteration, "but Metalheads don't get 'next times.' Send in the next wannabe." She sighed in frustration, wondering if she had been quite so pathetic during her early training.

"Yes, ma'am," the other woman replied sourly.

A few minutes later, the system went live as the day's final applicant jacked in. This entire group of wannabe Jocks was already equipped with neural linkage implants, either due to having transferred from another branch where such implants were employed or, in the case of these last two, having come from private piloting service backgrounds.

"All right, Nugget," she muttered, "let's see if *you* can do more than turn yourself into a smoking crater."

The parameters came back identical to the last one, with a convoy protection mission chosen by the applicant and random system failures chosen by Xi. Xi's virtual Warlock-grade mech filled her senses with feedback via the neural link, and she was more than a little surprised to find that the terrain was, in fact, identical to that of the last op.

For this evaluation, there were only twelve maps from which the system randomly chose battlefield terrain. Thus, it wasn't all that surprising that the system doubled up on a map in successive packages.

But the fact that Xi's Warlock was positioned in an identical spot to the last simulation was more than enough to make silent alarms go off between her ears.

"So you're a cheater?" Xi quipped as she prepped another delayed-launch drone, just as she had done in the previous simulation. "Interesting..."

She waited on the time-delayed drone for an additional four seconds compared to last time before sending it skyward, and this time no artillery shell struck it from the sky. Instead, a single anti-missile rocket successfully intercepted it while the rocket's author hunkered down and out of view behind the same plateau that had shielded the previous convoy from view.

"Better..." she grudgingly allowed while taking a nearly-identical path to the plateau as the one she had taken the previous time. She considered storming the southern edge at flank speed but ultimately decided against it since the distance was likely too great to cover before the Nugget made his move.

She kept her missiles primed, this time aimed at the northern rim of the plateau while her plasma cannon was fixed on the southern edge. The cannon was pre-primed (a dangerous condition, since a direct hit could cook the bolt off in its launcher, annihilating her mech outright) so that at the first flicker of movement from either direction, she could engage the enemy mech with enough firepower to effectively end the engagement just as she had done in the previous simulation.

That flicker of movement came from the south, just as before, and with disappointment, she launched the plasma cannon's primed projectile at the southern rim. The bolt sailed through the air, and her pre-primed SRMs loosed toward the northern rim even before the plasma bolt touched down.

But in the split-second between those weapons' firing, she realized what the Nugget had done by sending decoy vehicles from the convoy to the southern and northern rims in order to draw her fire. She barely managed to swerve her mech aside in time to avoid being totally annihilated by the inbound capital-grade railgun strike that tore *through* the center of the soft, earthy plateau and engaged the very spot she had stood a tenth of a second earlier.

"So you want to play rough?" she shouted as her Warlock's left arm (bearing the mech's plasma cannon) was blown completely off at the shoulder, causing her mech to crash to the soft dirt to her right. Scrambling as fast as a downed one-armed humanoid mech could manage, Xi was actually able to right her vehicle in less than thirty seconds. It was nothing short of a miracle, requiring ace-level Jock skills to accomplish by *any* measure.

As she righted her vehicle, she knew that another railgun strike was imminent. Loading her SRMs into the fortunately still-functional launcher, Xi stormed toward the northern rim of the plateau as fast as her mech's legs could carry her. Reaching a top speed of ninety kph, she sent another drone skyward and was rewarded with a glimmer of telemetry before it, too, was torn down by the virtual clone of Gunslinger's mech, the *Sam Kolt*.

The Nugget's capital-grade railgun roared a second time, sending tons of dirt in a wave away from the impact, tearing a ten-meter-wide ravine into the plateau's soft center and missing Xi's sprinting Warlock by a full five meters.

At that point, despite half of Xi's systems running with critical damage, it was all over but the crying for the Nugget.

Xi continued her sprint but adjusted course to go through the freshly-made path provided by the Nugget's bold railgun strike. He would need a full sixty seconds to even attempt firing again, and that was more than enough time for her to end his hopes and dreams of cracking her goose egg in the day's loss column.

"Close," she snarled, gaining positive target lock with her SRMs as the Nugget slowly moved his mech up into a humanoid stance after crouching on all fours to fire the railgun, "but no cigar!"

She unleashed her eight SRMs against the Nugget just as he took his first step away from her line of sight. Five of the eight SRMs were scratched by the Nugget's counterfire, but three slammed home, with one destroying the Nugget's starboard capacitor bank.

The capacitor exploded, albeit with less-than-devastating

effect since it was fully depleted following the shot. Its destruction nonetheless signaled the end of the mech's chances to notch a W against Major Xi Bao.

The Nugget limped off, sending a spray of chain-gun fire her way that harmlessly plinked off her mech's robust armor. Even the few hits he managed to land against her ruined left shoulder did little more than cause minor coolant leaks and electrical shorts, and she returned the favor with her own chain guns, which dug deep rents in the Nugget's damaged flank where her SRMs had struck.

Xi mercilessly poured hundreds of rounds in thirty-centimeter-wide groupings into the Nugget's damaged flank, causing explosions to ripple across the aspirant's stern. She smiled with satisfaction as the Nugget appeared to suffer a catastrophic drive system failure mid-stride (likely due to her preprogrammed variables rather than her relatively minor chain-gun fire) and that falter allowed her to cycle a fresh batch of eight SRMs.

And this time all eight missiles slammed home on the Nugget's hull, blowing the mech apart in a shower of molten metal and composite shards. When the virtual mech's death was final, all that remained standing was a single squat leg amid a pile of smoking debris.

The simulation cut out, prompting Xi to immediately disconnect her neural linkage and throw open the door to her simulator's pod. Even a year ago, such a quick disconnect from a link would have made her empty her guts onto the floor, and she would have been lucky to keep her feet as she did so. But today, after constant practice and acclimation, the narrowed vision and wave of queasiness were so customary that they were almost welcome sensations as she stormed over to the Nugget's pod and threw open the door.

"Explain yourself!" she demanded while the aspirant (a

bearded, large-framed man appearing to be in his late twenties) unleashed a string of curses and epithets before belatedly realizing who had opened the pod door.

His eyes wavered rapidly moving side-to-side in classic post-link nystagmus, but to his credit, he kept his lunch as he replied, "I lost...ma'am."

"Well, thank you for that, Nugget." Xi sneered. "Because despite cratering more hostiles and launching more ordnance than you've even *seen* in those holo-vids lining the walls of your neckbeard-cave, I was still uncertain of which one of us got his ass split by a snowplow just now. So thank you for that astute tactical assessment," she snapped. "I *know* you lost. What I want to know is how you hacked my system before you did!"

The Nugget seemed about ready to lose stomach containment, having turned a decidedly bright shade of green following the link break. Fortunately for him, a woman's voice piped in from Xi's back, "That was my doing, ma'am."

Xi whirled around to see a slender, reasonably attractive woman standing at something approaching attention in front of the rest of the seated applicants. "Let me guess." Xi snorted. "You two are fucking?"

The woman hesitated before nodding sharply. "Yes, Major."

"And you thought you'd upload some kind of virus into *my* VR suite," Xi took a menacing step toward the youthful woman, "in order to make your boy toy over there look good so he'd continue to squeeze you in all the right places. You brainiacs probably thought this stunt might earn you a little special attention from your evaluator, which is me. Have I got the long and the short of it, Nugget?"

"Yes, ma'am," the woman acknowledged curtly, going red from her collar to her ears as the woozy man slowly stood from the VR pod.

Xi glared at the woman, then the man, both of whom looked

resigned to whatever punishment she saw fit to give them. "Do you twitter-pated morons understand that tampering with my data core is a Tier Two felony and that you both just admitted to it?"

The woman's already round eyes went wide, while the man's shoulders slumped in resignation. "Yes, Major," the man acknowledged.

"Yes, Major," echoed the woman.

Xi shook her head, sweeping the other fifteen onlookers with a withering look. Some of them had promise, and would probably even make Jocks in the coming months, but none of the seated applicants had yet demonstrated they could handle sitting Jock in the Metal Legion.

"I'm done with you lot," she declared, gesturing to the door. "Report to Captain Winters at HQ. He'll figure out what to do with you." When the group failed to collectively bolt for the door, she bared her teeth and turned up the volume. "Dismissed!"

The fifteen seated applicants bolted upright and launched themselves toward the door, quickly filing out of the training room, leaving Xi and the two lawbreakers. The three remained in total silence for a full minute before the major pointed an accusatory finger.

"I can't tell," Xi glared back and forth between the two of them, "whether the two of you hormonal jackasses are more than just troublemakers, but fortunately for you—or *unfortunately,* if you turn out to be walking wastes of human flesh who only know how to cause your superiors trouble instead of the enemy—this outfit is almost *entirely* made up of troublemakers."

The two shared a nervous, hopeful look but Xi held up a halting hand.

"The problem I've got," Xi continued, "is that while the

Terran Armor Corps plays by a few different rules than other branches, *some* of our rules are exactly the same as theirs."

"Meaning...ma'am?" the woman belatedly asked.

"Meaning," Xi scowled, "that fraternization, specifically sexual relationships, are prohibited between officers and crews deployed together. Now, I'm not telling you two what to do with your personal lives," Xi said, finding herself increasingly upset at having to relay this particular bit of bad news, "but if you both want to ride Jock under the Legion banner someday, and if you want to do it on the same field, you're going to have to cut this relationship off. Now. Otherwise, I can only take one of you."

The two looked at each other uncertainly before the man said, "I...I guess we'd hoped that particular rule might get overlooked?"

"I'm sorry. There's nothing I can do on this point." Xi shook her head firmly, knowing that the increased scrutiny the Metal Legion was under following Operation Antivenom did not permit them to flout any more rules and regulations than were absolutely necessary.

These Nuggets had potential, but neither of them was worth upsetting the political apple cart. She had nominally battle-ready crews who could take their places, but she quietly hoped they would choose to put the Legion above their personal relationships.

She knew the Legion could use men and women like them. Ingenuity. Do what they had to do to win.

"I'll give you a minute to talk it over," Xi offered, turning toward the door. She was glad to hear the woman interrupt her before she reached it.

"That's not necessary, Major," the woman said with conviction. "We knew the regs when we applied. We're ready to commit to the Armor Corps."

"That's right," the man agreed. "We're here to do our part

for Terra. Everything else...even love," he shared an emotional look with the woman, "comes second right now."

Xi saw the same passionate fire burning in each of their eyes, and while she suspected these two would present a source of ongoing trouble in the coming days and weeks, she was glad to have them aboard. She crossed her arms and continued a silent examination, looking at each of them from head to toe.

She moved toward them, flicking her gaze back and forth between them before nodding sharply. "Welcome to the Terran Armor Corps. If you two live long enough, you might even earn the right to be called Metalheads." She produced a pair of data slates and punched in their official transfer orders before handing those orders to the Nuggets. "Report to the *Vercingetorix* immediately and find Chief Rimmer. You'll each pilot heavy haulers and serve as relief to Captain Koch's field repair crews in the upcoming op." She flashed a predatory grin when their disappointment at being assigned to haulers and maintenance crews became evident. "What, you didn't think I'd give you the keys to a battle mech right off the blocks, did you?"

"Think? No." The man shook his head.

"But hope?" the woman interjected with a sigh.

Xi snickered and gestured to the door. "If you can't do a good job at a bad job, who's going to give you a good job? Haulers are critical to success. You cannot and will not fuck up my support crews. Now, move your bony asses!"

"Lieutenant Podsednik, good of you to join us," Colonel Moon greeted Podsy from the command chair as soon as he arrived on the *Vercingetorix's* bridge. Unlike the vast majority of Terran military ships, the *Vercingetorix* had an old-fashioned bridge with portals capable of three-hundred-and-sixty-degree views on a parallel plane angled to ninety degrees high through heavily-armored transparent alloy windows. Anything from foot level and below could be seen on viewscreens using images captured by external cameras.

Newer ships had their command and control centers in the interiors of the ships, protected by multiple layers of armor and dead space to vastly improve the survivability. That had been a hard design lesson, learned at a heavy cost in precious Fleet blood.

"My apologies, Colonel," Podsy said, still shouldering the lightly-packed duffel containing his meager belongings. "The shuttles fell behind schedule, and I got stuck in limbo back at HQ."

"I'm aware of the logistical hang-ups," Moon said coolly as Podsednik approached with his transfer orders in hand. The colonel accepted the slate and affixed his signature to it before turning to the hawk-nosed young woman wearing a Fleet uniform at his side. "Lieutenant Commander Stravinsky will be serving as my XO on the *Vercingetorix*. Enter Lieutenant Podsednik's arrival into the log, Commander."

"Yes, sir." Stravinsky nodded crisply, taking the slate and tapping a series of inputs into a nearby console. "Transfer recorded, Colonel," the sharp-eyed commander reported before handing the slate back to Moon.

"Thank you, Commander," Moon replied, handing the slate back to Podsy. "Review the current chain of command, Lieutenant, and familiarize yourself with your new duties as time allows. Right now, we've got supplies coming in, and the logistics have, as you noted, have become a nightmare."

Podsednik nodded as he looked down at the slate. "Yes, sir..." His voice trailed off when he saw that the *Vercingetorix's* chain of command put him, Lieutenant Andy Podsednik, as

Ground Control Officer and also the current third in command of the newly-refitted dropship.

"Something wrong, Lieutenant?" Stravinsky challenged with an arched brow.

"No, Commander." Podsy shook his head slowly as he came to grips with the reality of his new posting.

Never in his wildest dreams had Podsy believed he would be stationed on the bridge of a warship (even one as pathetically-armed as the *Vercingetorix*), but now not only was he at such a post, he was also the third in command of the entire ship. This was different from his short-lived service aboard the *Dietrich Bonhoeffer* as its GCO in that he had an official place in the ship's chain of command to go along with an active role in ship operations.

Pushing such thoughts from his mind, Podsy snapped his best salute and said, "I'll work on the material transfers, Commander, Colonel. You can count on me."

"One other thing, Lieutenant," Commander Stravinsky said coolly, looking down at the duffel slung under Podsy's arm. "The bridge of this ship is its nerve center, and access is restricted to Terran Armed Forces personnel only. Do I make myself clear?"

Podsy cocked his head before looking down at the duffel, which held the alien gestalt intelligence core named Jem. "Yes, ma'am," Podsy said hesitantly before deciding to rise to the challenge. "It was my understanding that Jem is considered a mission-critical asset to this operation."

"The entity you refer to as 'Jem,'" Stravinsky said flatly while Colonel Moon watched the exchange with muted interest, "has, by order of the Republic's highest courts, been deemed a sentient intelligence for the purposes of determining autonomy and the application of fundamental sentient rights recognized under Terran law. That ruling effectively states that Jem is a civilian, not an Armed Forces serviceman, so until my orders include a provision excepting it from restrictions generally applied to civilians aboard TAF warships, it is not to be brought onto my bridge without authorization. Is that clear, Lieutenant?"

"Yes, ma'am," Podsednik replied through gritted teeth, fighting the urge to chew the words as he spoke them.

"On that front," Colonel Moon interjected after the exchange had ended, "it is my opinion that Jem is not only a vital asset to the Terran Armor Corps, but has also demonstrated to my satisfaction that it is a willing ally of humanity. That said, I think I'd feel more comfortable with it remaining in Lieutenant Podsednik's direct custody at all times during our upcoming deployment."

Lieutenant Commander Stravinsky nodded smartly as she produced a data slate. "Understood, Colonel. I'll make a note in the log, and I've already prepared an official order to that effect for your review and approval."

Colonel Moon accepted the order, read it thoroughly in about twenty seconds, and affixed his signature. "Very good, Commander. Carry on."

"Sir," she acknowledged, turning to tend her duties.

For the very first time since coming aboard a Terran Armor Corps warship, Podsy had the distinct impression that there might be wolves in the fold. A quick look at Colonel Moon's stoic expression suggested that his impression wasn't far from the mark.

"Colonel Jenkins," greeted Alice at the foot of Jenkins' mech as he approached. "It's good to see you again."

He drew a full breath and spoke as directly as possible. "I'm not sure what this 'observation' is supposed to accomplish, but my superiors think it's a good idea, and I'm not about to second-guess their order. Still..." His voice trailed off as a bemused smile played across Alice's lips. "How should I address you during this deployment?"

"'Alice' is fine," she replied simply, her smile broadening to display a row of picture-perfect upper teeth. "Sol is understand-ably curious about you, Colonel Jenkins. It isn't every day that an entire star system is saved by a few dozen of its far-flung cousins."

"Must be the aboriginal in us," Jenkins quipped dryly. "More balls than brains."

Alice laughed, and Jenkins was both charmed by and wary of his own reaction to the sound of her merriment. She was attractive, that much was certain, but not in the way super-models or actresses strove to be. This woman was confident, comfortable in her own skin, and content to simply be as she was.

As all people should strive to be.

She reminded him of his late wife in that regard, and that particular thought thankfully galvanized him as she spoke. "I must apologize for that, Colonel Jenkins. We thought you would react worse to that particular jab than you did, and we chose to employ it purely as a test of your character. Your composure during your interview was a key factor in deter-mining Sol's sentiment toward your mission and those who carried it out."

"Colonel Jenkins," came a gruff voice from Jenkins' back, and he turned to see a prosthetic-legged, burly-looking, forty-something man standing behind him holding a salute at atten-tion. "Corporal Krauthammer reporting for duty, sir."

"At ease, Corporal." Jenkins returned the salute, prompting the other man to relax. "So you're my new Jock?"

"If you'll have me, sir," Krauthammer nodded firmly, his bushy strawberry-blond beard jutting from his prominent chin.

"You were a Marine dropship pilot who turned to Razorbacks during the New Ghana Uprising and earned a hefty string of commendations for your work there," Jenkins stated. "But that was over fifteen years ago. Your records show you've been piloting slow-drive freighters in New Africa since then. Can you shake off the rust, Flake?" he asked, employing a decades-old epithet solely directed at middle-aged inter-branch transfers newly-arrived to the Metal Legion.

Krauthammer produced a data slate, which Jenkins accepted and found to contain the records of over three hundred hours in Razorback Mark 2-V simulations. Those records, while not top-of-the-line performance-wise, were still well above average across the board.

"That's what I can do, Colonel," Krauthammer said matter-of-factly. "If it's not good enough, I'm sorry to have wasted your time."

Jenkins gave the other man a lopsided grin. "You'll fit in just fine around here, Hammer. Your bunk's to port, mine's at the stern, and our guest here," he gestured to Alice, whose Solarian One Mind implants, while subtle, were impossible to miss, "will be berthed to starboard. Our Monkey and Wrench will arrive in a few hours, so if you've got bunk preference, now's the time to stake your claim. Any questions?"

Krauthammer's gaze flitted to Alice's One Mind implants before he shook his head. "No, sir."

"As you were." Jenkins handed the other man back the data slate, prompting the metal-legged Jock to make his way up the mech's boarding ramp.

"I was under the impression," Alice said interestedly, "that the Terran Republic Marine Corps represents the pinnacle of prestige in the Republic's armed forces?"

"It does," Jenkins allowed.

"Then why would a dropship pilot," she pressed curiously, "transfer to ground mechs rather than continue on his previous career path?"

"You might not have noticed his legs," Jenkins deadpanned. "The TFMC is notoriously rigid in terms of physical readiness standards. His dropship crashed after getting hit by capital-grade fire when his covering warship was temporarily knocked out of the fight. It's a miracle he survived at all, let alone that he put all eight of his Marines into the DZ's bullseye before ditching. He earned the highest commendations a TFMC pilot can... right before they showed him the door with a compulsory medical transfer to a Fleet Command corner desk. He transferred from Fleet to the New Africa Colonial Guard as a mech Jock, but let's just say the politics got to him and he eventually retired to a cushy and well-paid life of solitude driving freight from one side of the system to the other."

"A man with such a history seems an ill fit for deployment aboard a command vehicle," Alice said dubiously, prompting Jenkins to snort derisively.

"Your role as observer is not to question our decisions or personnel. It seems you've got a lot to learn about the Metal Legion, Alice." He gestured to *Warcrafter*'s boarding ramp. "Maybe this little exchange program isn't such a bad idea after all."

Leeroy Jenkins put on a brave face, but he wasn't amused with the situation in the least. He had a terrible feeling that she was going to get in the way at the most inopportune times, casting doubt over all his decisions.

2

THE PEARL

"All hands, this is the captain," Captain Guan declared over the *Red Hare*'s intercom, piped into every grav-couch aboard the warship, where its crew awaited the inevitable high-gee burn toward their destination once they arrived on the other side of the wormhole. "Nexus wormhole event horizon in five...four...three...two...one. Contact."

The *Red Hare* slipped through the rift in space-time, instantaneously passing from the New America 2 star system into the Nexus. The ship's sensors slowly populated with signals, which included a host of Vorr warships engaged with a pair of Jemmin formations ten light seconds from the destination gate. Jenkins could see it all on the HUD inside his helmet.

The colonel looked at the tactical plotter with keen interest to try to get his head wrapped around the total number of engaged warships in the Vorr-Jemmin battle. It took the computer to tell him it was just over a hundred. They were spread out, pecking at each other from ranges far beyond those human-built warships could effectively match. It seemed for the most part as if the Vorr were determined to prevent the Jemmin force from breaking through and interdicting the Metal Legion's ships before they reached the gate leading to the Pearl.

"No hostiles detected in local space, Captain," Sensors reported.

"Initiate burn," Captain Guan ordered, and the *Red Hare* surged forward, driving Jenkins deep into his gel-filled grav-couch. "All hands, maintain Condition One. ETA to target gate: twenty-one hours."

As Jenkins settled in for what he hoped would be an uneventful trip, he scrolled through the sensor feeds and discovered some startling revelations.

In the three weeks since Jenkins and his people had returned to Terran space from Operation Antivenom, the Vorr had destroyed three Jemmin gatecrashers in the Nexus system. Counting the one in the Pearl's system, Vorr forces had already scratched *four* of the Jemmin dreadnoughts and hundreds of other warships. The battle for control of the Nexus seemed to be proceeding precisely as the Vorr and Zeen had planned, which somehow failed to put Jenkins at ease.

Fire was exchanged between Vorr and Jemmin warships, but due to the proximity of Zeen *Home Two*, which stood sentinel over the local wormhole gates, none of the Jemmin vessels drew close enough to threaten the *Red Hare* or *Vercinge-torix* at this early stage. The duo of Metal Legion ships needed to travel to the far side of the gas giant that anchored the local gates, which would require nearly a full day for a variety of reasons.

The Zeen worldship *Home Two* sent a near-constant stream of warships from its surface, with nearly as many of their ships returning. Every minute or so, another Zeen ship would launch, and a few seconds later one of its fellows would vanish beneath the surface of the worldship. The logistics involved in repairing and rearming those warships on such a metronome-consistent schedule would have given Jenkins nightmares for life, but from the outside, the Zeen efforts seemed almost serene.

As Jenkins pored over the sensor data, he found another interesting factoid: there was not a single Vorr ship present in the Nexus that was capable of deploying and recovering terrestrial elements in force. All of the Vorr carriers and atmosphere-capable craft had been destroyed by Jemmin fire, only a few of the larger battleships remaining at the heart of Vorr formations. Those Vorr battleships were, by design, capable of independently waging planetary-scale sieges, but it seemed that Jemmin had forced them away from the wormhole gates and out into the void of interplanetary space, where they could not conduct operations like the one the Metal Legion was about to undertake.

Jemmin fears the Vorr taking possession of whatever's down on the Pearl, Jenkins suspected. He looked out across the Nexus star system, with its ongoing engagements of maneuvers, counter-maneuvers, and the occasional exchange of fire. He suspected the Pearl wasn't the only source of Jemmin's fear.

Despite the Vorr having clearly handed Jemmin a defeat in the Nexus by seizing control over local wormhole territory, Jemmin was far from panicked or frantic in its movements. To Jenkins' eye, it seemed almost as though Jemmin was settling in for a war of attrition while denying the Vorr-Zeen forces the opportunity to mount coherent counterattacks without exposing themselves to the same in reply.

There were still two thousand warships actively deployed in the Nexus System, and it seemed that nearly as many had been destroyed in recent engagements. Despite their numerical advantage, the Vorr-Zeen coalition (which had been joined by a hundred and fifty Finjou warships) was stretched as thin as graphene in covering every potential Jemmin attack vector.

The only question in Jenkins' mind was whether the Vorr and the Zeen would also prove as *durable* as graphene.

Twenty-one hours after arriving in the Nexus System, the *Red Hare* and the *Vercingetorix* were on final approach to the Pearl's wormhole gate. Jemmin forces had made a handful of half-hearted feints at the Terran ships, but none had been pursued longer than a few minutes.

During final approach, while the Terran warships slowed to a snail's pace and matched rotation in accordance with the wormhole's profile, a swarm of two hundred Zeen warships assumed protective duties and shielded them from Jemmin lasers. The Jemmin warships stabbed beams from ranges of up to twenty light seconds, but each one was relatively weak by the time its beam reached the Zeen hulls.

Jenkins had no illusions about just how much harm the Jemmin fire had done to the Zeen or how many Zeen had died shielding their Terran allies. It was yet another sobering moment for the new-minted colonel, creating turmoil within as he struggled to come to grips with whether the Vorr and the Zeen had humanity's best interests at heart. He found it difficult to grasp that they would be so selfless with the younger race.

They wanted something, and they weren't saying what.

"All hands, this is the captain," Captain Guan intoned over the ship's intercom. "We are on final approach to the event horizon. Rotation and velocities are matched; prepare for transit in five...four...three...two...one...mark."

The ship slid through the wormhole, leaving the *Vercingetorix* a full two minutes behind as the *Red Hare*'s sensors sprang to life in search of local hostiles. The tactical plotter slowly populated with signals, most of which were inert asteroids or other natural phenomena, before the Pearl itself appeared on Jenkins' display.

He focused his HUD on the handful of hostile targets orbiting the Pearl and grimly realized the Vorr intel had been spot-on.

Twelve Jemmin void fighters sprang to life, moving to a flanking posture in high orbit of the planet while a single Jemmin warship hung in low orbit. The warship seemed reluctant (or unable) to move from its spot, which was directly over the drop-zone on the planet's surface. The Jemmin forces were well over three hours away at max-burn, but that didn't mean the *Red Hare* needed to wait to engage them.

"All hands, this is the captain," Guan sharply declared. "Hostile targets identified. Prepare to engage the enemy."

The *Red Hare*, like any Terran warship, was capable of being fought from the crew's grav-couches. This was the default for a warship's crew during active engagement, although there were exceptions, such as the need to effect manual equipment repairs.

Also like other Terran warships, the *Red Hare* was equipped with a small army of remote-controlled and fully-autonomous drones. Each drone was capable of performing critical repairs in the middle of combat, and the ship's engineers could potentially remain within their couches while these robots did the heavy lifting and manual interface of ship repair.

So in theory, the *Red Hare*'s crews could conduct an entire battle from their grav-couches, and it seemed as if that was precisely what Captain Guan wanted them to do.

"Tactical," Guan said emotionlessly, "you are authorized to deploy the Starburst system at seventy-five percent. Priority targets are the enemy fighters. Helm, prepare to execute Starburst."

"Seventy-five percent, aye," acknowledged Tactical. "Locking targets."

"Ready to execute Starburst," Helm reported.

"Execute," Guan commanded, prompting the warship's hull to blossom outward as nine panels opened to reveal some of the most potent warheads in the Terran inventory.

The heavily-armored, rocket-driven platforms each contained twenty fusion-powered, single-shot laser warheads. Fusion-powered explosive energy in excess of a hundred mega-tons gently slipped from the *Red Hare*'s launch tubes, although only a small fraction of that energy could be focused on the enemy ships.

The nine rocket-driven Starburst missiles floated outward until they had cleared the *Red Hare*'s hull by several hundred meters. Then, as one, their motors ignited, and they sped off toward the enemy warships faster than any manned Terran vehicle could hope to move.

As the Starburst warheads tore through the void, the Jemmin fighters authored precise counter-fire with lasers of their own. The stationary Jemmin warship added its beams to the interceptive volley, and two of the nine Terran warheads suffered catastrophic damage before they could deploy their ordnance.

"Starburst optimal firing range in four...three..." Tactical reported steadily, "two...one. Firing."

The seven remaining missiles blew apart in a controlled disassembly fueled by micro-explosives within the missile's chassis. Each of the Starburst platforms gave birth to twenty smaller missiles, which were individually armed with a single fusion-driven laser generator. The smaller missiles issued a seemingly-chaotic series of attitude-control gas bursts, steadily gaining distance from one another as Jemmin counterfire continued to pour into the blossom of death-dealing devices.

Another twelve Terran micro-missiles were struck from the void in those ensuing seconds, but finally, the missiles had gained sufficient distance from one another to safely unleash their fury against the Jemmin targets.

A hundred and twenty-eight fusion-powered flares lit up the black of space, sending as many beams of highly-focused light into the Jemmin position. Given the range involved and the evasive maneuvers of the Jemmin fighters, most of these beams missed entirely. Some even stabbed into the dark surface of the Pearl behind the Jemmin ships. It was an extraordinarily expensive volley of fire, costing significantly more than the combined economic value of the hardware the Legion intended to put down on the planet. In pure cost-benefit terms, Starburst missiles were difficult to justify in any capacity other than last-resort defensive platforms.

But what they lacked in efficiency, they made up for in brute force. Every hit on a Jemmin fighter was lethal, and the furious volley scrapped all twelve enemy interceptors.

The battered Jemmin warship was hit by seventeen separate beams, which lanced through its damaged hull and ruptured its power core containment. The lone Jemmin warship in-system died in a miniature nova, its wreckage flying apart in a near-perfect sphere that slowly but surely began to succumb to the inexorable pull of gravity from the Pearl below.

The tactical plotter flickered green, signaling that no hostile targets remained in view. "This is Captain Guan," Guan declared with almost lazy, irritated disdain. "We have cleared the planet's orbit of hostiles. Remain in your couches until we reach orbit in two hours, forty-nine minutes."

A few seconds later, the *Vercingetorix* came through the wormhole, and the pair of Metal Legion warships continued their mission to deploy the Metalheads to the Pearl for Operation Watery Grave unhindered by Jemmin.

Lieutenant Podsednik was one of the first of *Vercingetorix*'s crew members out of his grav-couch. The *Red Hare* had already assumed overwatch of the drop-zone and was busily prepping its mechs for deployment.

Drop-deck Chief Arnold Rimmer, one of the few survivors of the *Bonhoeffer's* demise on Luna, had seamlessly transitioned to the older, smaller, and considerably-less-well-equipped *Vercingetorix* with a hand-picked team of support crew from TAC HQ.

Podsy strapped into his station at Ground Control and raised Chief Rimmer. "Drop Deck, this is Ground Control."

"Go ahead, Ground Control," acknowledged the veteran.

"Let's have a status update on the subs, Chief," Podsy urged.

"We're down to the last modifications on the cans, Lieutenant," Rimmer reported. "We should have the final weld inspections done in ten minutes, and the haulers are already prepped for hot drops. We're five-by-five down here and will be ready to drop in nineteen minutes, sir."

"Ahead of schedule, as usual, Chief," Podsy replied as Lieutenant Commander Stravisnky climbed out of her pod, tied her still-gel-streaked hair into a ponytail, and briskly made her way to Tactical, where she arrived several seconds before the Tactical Officer reached the same station. Podsy schooled his features into a neutral mask as Stravinsky's critical gaze flitted to him, prompting him to raise Major Xi. "Joker Actual, this is Ground Control."

"Go ahead, Ground Control," Xi replied promptly.

"Be advised, Commander Ulbricht's team will be ready to deploy in nineteen minutes. Our drop window is in thirty-two minutes. I'm synchronizing my clocks with yours now," Podsy reported.

"Copy that, GC," the youngest major in Terran Armed Forces history acknowledged with the calm voice of a combat professional. That would have seemed impossible back on Durgan's Folly. "Clocks are in synch; thirty-two minutes and twelve seconds to drop."

"Confirmed," Podsy agreed before piping into the company-wide comm channel dedicated to Xi's Jokers. "Joker Company, this is Ground Control. Operation Watery Grave is go. I say again: Operation Watery Grave is go. Drop window in T-minus thirty-one minutes and forty seconds. Acknowledge."

All twelve Joker icons flickered to life with green status reports as the *Red Hare* unleashed the first of its two twelve-mech companies. From low orbit, the *Red Hare* dropped its can-less Razorback Mark 2-V battlewagons into the Pearl's thick, relatively humid atmosphere. As the first of Clover Battalion's mechs fell, their disposable heat shields began to glow beneath them. The shields first burned dull red, then angry orange, followed by a furious yellow that blazed as the atmosphere served to brake the falling vehicles' descent.

Eventually, the Clover mechs slowed enough for their heat shields to go from yellow to orange and then red before going dark. Considering the likelihood of Jemmin vehicles already on the Pearl's surface, Jenkins' mechs dropped below the optimal chute-deployment altitude before popping their chutes just above the deck.

The Razorbacks splashed down on the gray surface of the world thirty kilometers from the southern edge of the mini-ocean containing the Vorr dig site. All twelve mechs moved as one to assume a covering position for both the second Clover company and the Joker company descent, at which point the second batch of mechs was released from the *Red Hare*'s drop-tubes.

The 2nd Company of Terra Han-built Razorbacks followed

the example of the first and landed forty kilometers to the west of Colonel Jenkins' position. The 2nd Company was under the command of Colonel Jenkins' XO Captain Chao, while Joker Company was under the command of Major Xi.

It was an unusual command structure, but hardly unprecedented given the dual nature of the operation. Clover Battalion's objective was to secure the dig site against Jemmin interference, while Joker Company was tasked with retrieving the packages designated by the Vorr. Given the operational security concerns, only Metalheads with multiple deployments under the TAC banner had been assigned to the Jokers.

As Chao's Razorbacks assumed a mutually-supportive position on Jenkins' flank, the *Red Hare* lifted into a higher orbit to clear the way for *Vercingetorix* to deliver the Jokers to the surface.

"Joker Company, this is Ground Control," Podsy declared as the drop clock reached one minute to go. "T-minus sixty seconds."

With the ever-watchful eye of Lieutenant Commander Stravinsky upon him, Podsy managed to conduct the drop of all twelve Joker cans without a hitch. Each can touched down within fifty meters of its designated bullseye, and Podsy allowed himself a sigh of relief when all twelve vehicles emerged from their cans and moved to form up on Major Xi's thrice-resurrected, iconic Scorpion-class mech.

3

SELF-DESTRUCTION

"This is Joker Actual," Major Xi Bao called over Joker's company channel as soon as her vehicles had cleared their cans. "Joker Company, sound off."

"*Kochtopussy*, at your back," Captain Koch reported. Koch's repair teams had been absent from the Antivenom roster, and Xi suspected the repair team leader still chafed at having been excluded from that all-important operation.

"*Sargon*, lost in thought," First Lieutenant Benjamin declared. Previously assigned to the defunct *Eclipse*, Sargon had received a specially renamed Archer-class Cruiser-grade missile mech as his command for this operation. Similar in design to the lost *Preacher*, Sargon was capable of engaging low-orbit or intercontinental targets with a variety of specialty warheads affixed to long-range missiles.

"*Murasame*, slicing and dicing," First Lieutenant Nakamura followed. *Murasame*, purpose-built as a mech-killer, was a humanoid design identical to the *Masamune*. Equipped with a quartet of all-terrain hunter-killer drones, *Murasame* would prove deadly at close range if any Jemmin vehicles snuck inside the Terran defensive arc.

"*Cyclops*, winking at *you*," Second Lieutenant Miles 'Blinky' Staubach said eagerly. *Cyclops*, a Warlock-class mech identical to the one Xi had used in the virtual interviews with the Nuggets, featured a devastating plasma cannon like those on the destroyed *Cave Troll*. Blinky was the only Jock in the entire Legion who could match her in terms of reflexes and precision. He had a lot to learn, but his career in the Metal Legion had as much blood and swash as anyone's, including Xi's.

"*Black Widow*, mourning sans tears," Second Lieutenant Quinn reported. *Black Widow*, Quinn's first official command following her outstanding work stepping in on Luna for the injured then-Lieutenant Winters, was a Fiddleback-class Tactical-grade mech weighing in at sixty tons. With robust underwater capabilities, it was slated to be part of the team that would accompany Commander Ulbricht's recovery subs to the dig site.

"*Land Shark*, picking my teeth," Corporal Cervantes continued. Cervantes was a recent transfer from the New Africa Colonial Guard, who had come with her mech. *Land Shark* was a rare two-way mech designed with equal consideration given to both surface and aquatic deployments. With both torpedo and missile launchers along with track and propeller-based propulsion, *Land Shark*'s amphibious design had been deemed vital to the operation's success. No one belabored the point that the mech was one hundred and fifty years old. At least the seals were new.

"*Gun Monkey*, where's my banana?!" Corporal Hoyt demanded. Hoyt was part of Koch's repair team, and despite its name, *Gun Monkey* was a field repair vehicle capable of delivering repair teams and then protecting those assets long enough to get a damaged mech back to minimal operational capability. He was a Flake, meaning he had come out of retirement to join the Metal Legion following Xi's wildly successful series of interviews after Ms. Sarah Samuels' inaugural DIN report had gone live.

Unlike Nuggets, who were green as grass and raw as a twitching steak, Flakes had already gone through service and likely had their best days behind them. But, Flake or Nugget, either could be forged into a serviceable Metalhead if they survived long enough.

"*Apple of Argon*, wanna bite?" Corporal Wilhelm asked playfully from another of Koch's repair vehicles, this one capable of towing or outright lifting damaged mechs and returning them to base for more extensive repairs than were possible in the field. *Apple* was a big and bulky beast of a vehicle.

"*Armored Skeptic*, open to reason," Corporal Giles, the cheating Nugget who had almost defeated Xi in the simulator, reported from one of the heavy haulers tasked with moving the sub to the deployment waters four kilometers away. The haulers were heavily-armored, but with only a pair of chain guns, they had almost no offensive capability.

"*Shoe on Head*, keeping it real," Corporal Lassiter continued from the second heavy hauler. Lassiter had uploaded the virus that had enabled Giles to get the near-kill on Xi, and the duo's creativity and aggressiveness had impressed the major enough during the interview process to include them in this operation.

"*Ifrit's Beard*, burning for you," Corporal Dela Torre reported aboard the last hauler bearing an American Navy sub.

"*Elvira III*," Major Xi finished, "clickin' my heels."

The Scorpion-class was one of the more common mech designs in the Terran Republic, but after the beating Xi had put the original *Elvira* and *Devil Crab* through, the Legion had nearly exhausted its supply of key spare parts for the design. So while there were five more Scorpions nearly combat-ready back at HQ, each lacked essential components necessary to return them to fighting order. It was entirely possible that if *Elvira III* went down on the Pearl, Xi would need to adjust to life aboard another design.

Assuming she survived *Elvira's* hypothetical death, of course.

"Joker Company," Xi broadcast over the company P2P net, "target coordinates have been uploaded designating the southern edge of the ocean four kilometers to the north as Alpha Primary. Form up in a combat V and move out."

The mechs fell into formation and burned for the three-hundred-kilometer-diameter ocean. The surface temperatures of the Pearl were sweltering, exceeding seventy degrees Celsius median temperature.

During the mission brief, Xi had learned that the world had likely once been covered by a shallow, life-rich ocean. Lacking a moon, this Earth-sized world (which had eighty-seven percent Earth gravity) was as close to a perfect sphere as any rocky world could become. With just a handful of depressions and mountains measuring more than a thousand-meter variance from the world's latitudinal median numbers, that shallow ocean had slowly sculpted the rocky surface of the planet without the aid of tidal forces.

The lack of an ongoing tidal pull like the one Luna exerted on Earth after the bi-planetary system's creation had caused this world's tectonic activity to remain impressively low. Volcanic eruptions still flared from time to time, however, resulting in the depressions that held water like the one where the Vorr archeological dig was located.

"It's hard to believe," Xi mused over the secure P2P with Podsy on the *Vercingetorix*, "that a species could destroy itself like this."

"Trace evidence on the surface," Podsy said grimly, "suggests this world's upper atmosphere was subjected to a nearly constant assault of fusion-driven explosions over five thousand years ago. The Vorr brief says they believe this world's inhabitants underwent the equivalent of an extreme Luddite movement coupled with a dangerous spike in environmental protectionism that led this species to conclude that intelligence is a blight upon the universe."

Xi snorted in disdain. "They weren't content with just handcuffing themselves and their ability to impact their environment, they wanted to erase the possibility of *any* life arising on this world that might have been able to do so."

"From an extremely narrow and patently suicidal perspective based on the priorities imposed by anti-technological and pro-environmental advocacies," Podsy agreed ominously, "it was the only logical path. You either view intelligence as a desirable product of natural environments or as an undesirable one. If you can't figure out how to extricate intelligence from the environment before that intelligence's growth destroys the natural conditions that gave rise to it, the latter perspective requires you to self-terminate."

"Which makes it fucking *wrong*. More than that, it makes them *stupid*," Xi spat. "Because not only did they destroy their own intelligence and the possibility of others following their ascent to sentience, they destroyed the very environment they were ostensibly working to protect!"

"You're preaching to the choir, Major," Podsy responded.

"What does Jem say about this?" Xi asked.

"Jem concurs with the Vorr theory," Podsy replied more guardedly than Xi had expected. "The Luddite and pro-environmental movements would be ideal mechanisms by which a species like this might be induced to self-destruction. Jemmin is almost certainly capable of surreptitiously cultivating those sentiments."

"So they intentionally cooked off their ozone, along with the rest of the upper atmosphere," Xi said, fighting the urge to growl as she spoke. "And destabilized their parent star enough to increase solar winds for thousands of years, and those winds slowly flensed away nearly all of the water that previously covered this once-beautiful world. Who the fuck could get confused enough to think this was a good idea?"

"This wasn't Jemmin's first dance, Major," Podsy replied heavily. "This planet's death was the result of thousands of years' practice in inducing self-destruction in younger, less-developed species."

"Yeah." Xi grunted. "I think Jemmin's days of grooming entire races into suicide are coming to an end."

"Hear, hear," Podsy agreed. "But my question..."

When he failed to finish the thought, Xi pressed, "Ground Control?"

"My question," Podsy reiterated in a low voice after a brief delay, "is why would Jemmin put this planet in Vorr space, knowing they would eventually find whatever is down there?"

"What does Jem say?" Xi asked, her curiosity on that matter having grown in recent days as she pored over the mission brief.

"Jem's tight-lipped on that front," Podsy replied. "But if you ask me, it's because Jemmin *wanted* the Vorr to find whatever's down there."

"That's...not exactly encouraging, Ground Control," Xi said as a chill ran down her spine. A sudden thought occurred to her. "*Gatekeeper*, the mega-ship Jemmin uses to reposition the wormhole gates...maybe it can't move *all* of the gates? Maybe Jemmin didn't have a choice except to give this star system to the Vorr?"

"It's possible, though I doubt it. The truth is that we don't know much about that ship, since the only time it's ever been seen by humans was when it brought the Sol 1-Sol 2 gate to

Earth. And even then, the only thing we know for certain is that it was *big*. Human sensor technology couldn't even get exact measurements of the thing, and it was only there for a few seconds before it disappeared, leaving the gate in stable, distant orbit of Earth. Stand by, Joker Actual," he abruptly said, filling Xi with a measure of trepidation.

The silence stretched on for nearly a minute, during which time Joker Company moved steadily toward the deployment zone at the edge of the salty waters.

Finally, his voice returned. "Joker Actual, Ground Control. Jem has a theory regarding the Vorr's role in Jemmin's plan for Nexus Space, but I don't think you're going to like it."

"Let her rip, Ground Control," Xi urged.

"Jem thinks the Vorr were never really viewed as candidates for induction into the Illumination League," Podsy explained. "Instead, the theory goes something like this: whatever the Vorr found down here was considered important enough to spur the Vorr into action against Jemmin. Jemmin would have prepared for this action and rallied all of the other League species together against the Vorr. Obviously, Jemmin would be convinced of victory in such an engagement before it began, and whichever young species survived the Vorr counterattack could be dealt with later...just like the species here was dealt with."

"So, Jem thought the Vorr were going to be the unwitting executioners of races like humanity?" Xi asked in surprise, having never considered that possibility. It was...well, it was too complex and long-lensed to be something a human mind was likely to concoct. Jem was suggesting a perspective based on centuries and millennia of carefully-planned inputs, manipulations, and subtle adjustments, all of which culminated in a single species (the Vorr) declaring war against all others and expending its vigor against targets of Jemmin's choosing.

It was the kind of plan that would send Machiavelli screaming into the night.

"For all our sakes, and for the first time I've ever felt this way," Xi said somberly, "let's hope Jem's wrong."

"Hear, hear," Podsy agreed, but she suspected *both* of them would bet the reactor that Jem was right.

"Clover 2nd Company stands ready, Colonel," Captain Chao reported shortly after assembling his mechs.

"Copy that, Captain," Jenkins acknowledged. "I'm not seeing anything on the orbital sensors, but we know Jemmin has a ground presence on the Pearl. Stay tight, and conduct a recon mission of that crevice eight klicks north of your position. If there's a Jemmin Poltergeist nearby, that'd be an ideal hidey-hole."

"Acknowledged, Colonel," Chao replied as his mechs leapt toward the indicated break in the otherwise flat, featureless terrain surrounding his position in all directions for fifty kilometers. "ETA to the crevice: five minutes."

"Impressive..." Alice mused from behind Jenkins as he sat at the comm station, where Chief Styles had spent most of his days aboard the destroyed *Roy*.

"It's all standard operating procedure, ma'am," Jenkins said dismissively. "First we secure the area, then we expand our zone of control by positioning mobile assets in a manner that limits the enemy's ability to interfere with our primary formation."

"Please," the woman said measuredly, "just 'Alice,' if you can. But it is not your procedures that impress me."

Jenkins suppressed a derisive snort before asking, "What got your attention, Alice?"

"The efficiency of Jemmin's ability to induce species like

this one...like *ours*," she amended darkly, "to self-destruction is nothing if not impressive."

Jenkins had no real choice but to agree. "Why waste ordnance and productive energy fighting someone when you can politely ask them to destroy themselves and they do?"

"Precisely." Alice nodded, her eyes seeming to make a declarative statement each time they blinked. "How many times in human history have our most influential societies nearly been consumed with movements similar to those which appear to have caused this species' downfall?"

"So you're a social scientist?" Jenkins asked, never having gotten a satisfactory answer about what Alice's role in Solarian society was.

Again Alice laughed, and again Jenkins heard echoes of his wife in her voice. "Any responsible self-aware human *must* be a social scientist, Colonel Jenkins."

Jenkins grunted. "You didn't answer my question."

"You are incorrect," Alice easily retorted. "If you wish a different answer, perhaps you should ask a different question."

"Fine," Jenkins allowed. "What is your role in Solar society?"

"In organizational terms, I was responsible for overseeing the enlightenment efforts of one-point-one million dedicated researchers whose primary duties are to construct working theories regarding this issue."

Jenkins blinked in surprise. "You're in charge of an organization consisting of over a million people?"

Alice laughed heartily. "Not as you likely envision it, but in a very narrow way, yes. I would coordinate, direct, and modify lines of thought for that many people who have undertaken a driving interest in pursuing the matter of individuality."

"How can they afford to have you away?" Jenkins asked.

"My project was deemed corrupt following the success of

Operation Antivenom," she replied simply. "It was determined that too much of our product was influenced by Jemmin manipulations. The entire product of my life's work was discarded, new overseers were selected from the body of contributors, and fresh inquiries were initiated into the field."

"I'm...sorry to hear that," Jenkins stammered.

"I appreciate the sentiment." She chuckled. "But it is unnecessary. Very few scientific inquiries produce tangible improvements in general human knowledge. Anyone who dedicates a lifetime to the pursuit of such improvements understands at the outset of such a project that it is extremely unlikely to yield much of substance. But by participating and pursuing lines of inquiry as I did, I was able to prevent others from following me down my generally unproductive lines of research. In this way, I have made tangible, if indirect, contributions to the field of study I pursued until very recently."

"That's an awfully enlightened view of—" Jenkins replied before Captain Chao's incoming transmission crackled in his earpiece.

"2nd Company has reached the crevice, Colonel," Chao reported as a flurry of updates streamed across the Clover tactical plotter, showing weapons fire from Chao's mechs. "We have engaged the Jemmin."

4

GHOSTS IN THE ROCK

"Roger, Captain," Jenkins acknowledged as he forwarded fire solutions to his 1st Company mechs. "1st Company stands ready to support."

"Hold fire, 1st Company," Chao replied tersely as a flurry of Jemmin missiles surged from the crevice. Jenkins' Razorbacks could send extended-range artillery shells across the forty-two kilometers separating 1st Company and the crevice, but neither the *Red Hare* nor the *Vercingetorix* was equipped to provide ongoing material support like the *Dietrich Bonhoeffer* had been.

Put simply, there would be no resupply drops on the Pearl.

That meant conserving ammunition was key, and as Jenkins watched, Captain Chao's miserly approach cost 2nd Company one of its mechs as a swarm of enemy missiles converged on its position with deadly accuracy. When the dust from that swarm settled, nothing larger than a subcompact car was left where the Clover mech had stood. Terran counter-missile fire scrapped most of the Jemmin ordnance from the air, with the occasional SRM landing against the heavily-armored hulls of 2nd Company's Razorbacks.

But Captain Chao had not been standing idly by while his

people died. Using the points of origin for those SRMs as targets, his eleven remaining 2nd Company Razorbacks sent a storm of railgun bolts, artillery shells, and sniper-precise missiles down into the hundred-meter-wide crevice. Some of the Terran fire was aimed at individual Jemmin vehicles, and some was directed at the crevice's vertical walls.

The effect of Captain Chao's counterattack was devastating.

A dozen Jemmin vehicles died in the furious counter-fire, while slabs of rock larger than battlewagons broke off from the crevice and crashed into a handful of Jemmin skimmers before the nimble vehicles could escape.

In a particularly notable demonstration of macabre, one hundred percent Metal Legion-approved taste, Captain Chao pumped Iron Maiden's 'Run to the Hills' across his company-wide channel as his people poured death into the Jemmin fleet of hover-vehicles desperately trying to escape the confines of the ravine. Jenkins felt goosebumps rise on his forearms as the talented son of Admiral Zhao demonstrated himself worthy of his bloodline, scoring kill after kill with railguns, artillery, missile, and even coil guns.

The crevice measured twelve kilometers from one end to the other and ran roughly east-west. Captain Chao had positioned his people near the east end, and it soon became clear that the Jemmin vehicles intended to sprint to the far end of the crevice before emerging to the surface and fleeing to safety across the flat, rocky surface of the Pearl.

"Clover Actual." Captain Chao's raised voice came over the line, with Iron Maiden's guitars shredding in the background. "This is 2nd Company, requesting artillery support at the following coordinates..."

Jenkins forwarded the targets, most of which were down-range of the fleeing Jemmin, to the rest of 1st Company. "Targets confirmed, Captain. Artillery inbound," Jenkins acknowledged as *Warcrafter's* dual fifteen-kilo guns sent ER-HE shells downrange. The rest of 1st Company's guns cleared less than two seconds later, sending a barrage of ordnance in front of the fleeing skimmers and hovertanks.

A lucky hit scrapped a mid-sized vehicle, and another pair of near misses each killed a fleeing skimmer. Ordnance exploded across the crevice's walls, sending crushing debris into the ravine. In reply, the Jemmin vehicles suddenly leapt skyward to escape the avalanche brought down by half of 1st Company's shells landing precisely where Captain Chao had requested.

Chao's people sniped the emerging Jemmin vehicles with hypervelocity railgun projectiles, but the enemy vehicles had already unleashed a second volley of missiles at the Terran mechs. Five more Jemmin vehicles died in the second before Jemmin missiles slammed into the Terran position.

Amazingly, not a single 2nd Company mech was destroyed in the volley of fire. It seemed to Jenkins that such good fortune was hardly coincidental, so he jacked into the *Red Hare's* direct sensor feeds and scoured the edge of the crevice for any anomaly that might show what the Jemmin were trying to protect with their seemingly erratic fire.

Then he saw it. For less than a tenth of a second, the unmistakable silhouette of a Jemmin Poltergeist appeared at the northern edge of the crevice.

He quickly forwarded a set of coordinates that placed the Poltergeist several kilometers to the north of the crevice to the *Red Hare's* CAC and said, "This is Clover Actual requesting deployment of Dissident Aggressor at the following coordinates. A Jemmin Poltergeist is fleeing the engagement zone in that direction."

"Coordinates confirmed," Captain Guan immediately

replied as a fresh icon detached from the *Red Hare*. "Dissident Aggressor inbound."

"Clover Company," Jenkins called over the Clover Priority channel as Dissident Aggressor's engines burned at maximum, driving the weapon toward the target coordinates at an ever-increasing velocity, "we've got a Big Boy on the way. Harden your systems against the EMP and watch for a Poltergeist if it doubles back toward 2nd Company."

"Copy that, Colonel," Captain Chao acknowledged as his people engaged and destroyed the majority of the remaining Jemmin light vehicles.

Dissident Aggressor careened toward the Pearl's surface like the fist of God Almighty, where it delivered forty megatons of fusion-powered Terran fury.

The mushroom cloud was nothing short of breathtaking, and the dome-shaped blast wave was visible with the naked eye from Jenkins' position as the Pearl's atmosphere tried desperately to contain the titanic energies released by the massive warhead.

Unfortunately, there was no sign of Poltergeist wreckage, and no anomalies appeared in the blast wave to suggest it had been enveloped in Dissident Aggressor's fury.

Several seconds passed as the blast wave slowly lost its vigor, and eventually Jenkins was forced to conclude that despite his quick reaction, he had failed to kill the enemy command vehicle.

"2nd Company reporting," Captain Chao said into the silence. "Systems unaffected by the EMP. All visible Jemmin vehicles neutralized."

"Copy that, Captain," Jenkins said sourly, disappointed that he had been unable to score a potential knockout blow in the opening exchange of the operation. "Good work. Pull back to Tango Sector and engage Aegis posture."

"Acknowledged, Colonel: Aegis posture at Tango Sector," Chao repeated as his mechs quickly drew back from the cliff's edge and made for a position a few kilometers east of their original drop-zone.

An inbound comm link request flickered on his board. Jenkins quickly accepted. "Clover Actual, go ahead."

"Clover Actual, this is *Vercingetorix* Ground Control," Lieutenant Podsednik greeted him as a data stream began to populate a nearby display. "I saw that Poltergeist up here, but be advised: there are at least two Jemmin Poltergeists on the Pearl. I say again: I have positive ID on *two* Poltergeists, including the one Dissident Aggressor missed."

Jenkins perused Podsy's data packet and, sure enough, the former Wrench had positively identified at least two of the enemy command vehicles. The first was the same one Jenkins had seen, though Podsy had collected two other glimpses of the stealthy vehicle in addition to the one Jenkins had seen. The second was located ninety kilometers to the north of Clover's position, just two kilometers from the salty ocean's shore where Xi and the American Navy team would dive to recover the archeological salvage from the dig site.

"Good work, Lieutenant," Jenkins said approvingly. "How were you able to spot the second one?"

"The EMP from the Big Boy partially illuminated it, sir," Podsy explained. "But the Jemmin adaptive camouflage systems are *quick*. I barely got that image with recon gear operating at two thousand frames per second. Jem says that without manipulating our local sensor systems, the Jemmin vehicles are still able to fool our level of technology with passive camouflage. But doing so requires enormous amounts of energy. They won't be hiding out in the open as a result, so scouring all of the crevices and depressions where they might be able to sneak out of sight is our best recommendation at this point, sir. We're still working on how to actively pierce their stealth systems, but with these latest readings, we hope to work something up in the next couple hours."

"Keep Colonel Moon and Captain Guan apprised of your progress, Lieutenant," Jenkins said, knowing it was entirely possible Podsy was stepping out of line by contacting him directly.

"Colonel Moon's in the loop, sir," Podsednik assured him. "I'll advise the colonel to include Captain Guan as well."

"Understood." Jenkins cracked a grin, wondering if Moon had actually managed to instill something approaching military discipline in the irascible Podsednik. "I want progress updates every ten minutes."

"Roger that, Colonel," Podsy acknowledged. "*V-rix* Ground Control, out."

Jenkins considered how to best approach Podsy's suggestion that the Metal Legion clear out the few potential hidey-holes surrounding the dig site. There were thirty-two surface irregularities large enough to hold a Jemmin Poltergeist within a hundred kilometers of the tiny ocean Xi's people had almost reached.

The crevice was the most obvious point of interest on the list, but a pair of volcanic depressions could also be found within thirty kilometers of 1st Company's position. Neither would be much good to Terran vehicles due to the local heat, but Jemmin technology was markedly better, so it stood to reason they might use that advantage to hide where Terrans could not.

Then again, Jemmin might choose to hide in more obvious spots in order to play against that very thought.

Scowling in annoyance at his train of thought, Jenkins shook such misleading notions from his mind. "Don't outthink yourself, Lee," he muttered.

"Wise advice." Alice nodded approvingly.

His scowl deepened for a moment before he forced it from his features. "1st Company," he declared over the company-wide while forwarding coordinates for the closer of the two volcanic depressions. "Form up on *Warcrafter*. Let's go check that hellhole."

The mechs of 1st Company formed an arrowhead that sped across the smooth, rocky surface of the Pearl, *Warcrafter* in the lead, on their way to the nearest of the volcanic depressions.

5

COMMAND AND CONTROL

On the *Vercingetorix's* bridge, Podsy worked furiously to pierce the Jemmin camouflage systems. In tandem with the Sensor operators of both the *Vercingetorix* and the *Red Hare*, he was finally ready to deploy a small flight of recon drones to test the penetrative technique he had first started theorizing after the op on the Brick.

"Colonel Moon," Podsy called after making the final adjustments to his system, "we're ready to launch the birds on your order."

"Launch the drones," Moon replied.

"Launching," Podsy acknowledged, sending five Sparrow-class recon drones from the low-orbit *Vercingetorix*. The drones spread out as they plummeted deep into the planet's atmosphere, gently adjusting their trajectories to both fan out and pull up at an altitude of three thousand meters above the surface.

The Sparrows were relatively tiny, measuring just three meters from wingtip to wingtip and less than half as long on the unmanned aircraft's main fuselage. Once the drones had reached optimal altitude and geostationary locations, Podsy remotely verified that each was ready to collect the data gleaned by his sensor ping.

Podsy initiated another secure uplink with Colonel Jenkins as 1st Company closed to five kilometers from the first volcanic depression they meant to search for concealed Jemmin. "Clover Actual, go ahead *Vercingetorix*," Colonel Jenkins replied.

"Clover Actual, be advised I'm about to perform a localized attempt to pierce the Jemmin stealth systems," Podsy replied. "Recommend you go weapons hot and eliminate targets as they appear. I'm forwarding you a live link from the drones' sensor feeds."

"Your feed is live," Jenkins acknowledged. "Proceed with your ping, GC."

"Copy that," Podsy said, making eye contact with the *Vercingetorix's* Sensor operator, beside whom the frosty Lieutenant Commander Stravinsky stood impatiently. "Ping One in five... four... three... two... one. Ping!"

Podsy's modified sensor feeds flickered as the *Vercingetorix* delivered a tightly-focused, powerful EM pulse to the surface of the Pearl surrounding the volcanic depression 1st Company had nearly reached. The Sparrow drones' scanners intently scoured the local area for meaningful feedback, but nothing appeared on his screens.

Podsy glanced over at the Sensor operator, who shook his head. "Clover Actual," Podsy said neutrally, "Ping One inconclusive. Moving to second target area."

"Copy that, GC," Jenkins replied patiently as his company of Razorbacks sprinted toward the apparently clear depression.

"Ping Two in five..." Podsy declared, "four...three...two... one. Ping!"

Again, the *Vercingetorix* sent a pulse toward the planet. The pulse was delivered with high-powered active sensor transmitters Podsy had specifically attenuated to propagate an EMP through the increasingly thick atmosphere rather than "splashing" wide on the upper atmosphere as would normally occur.

This time, as with the last, no targets were revealed by the ping, and just as Podsy began to doubt his preparations Jem's voice crackled in his earpiece. "Do not doubt this method. It is our best chance to locate Jemmin vehicles."

Bolstered by Jem's encouragement (and acutely aware of the fact that Lieutenant Commander Stravinsky appeared to have noticed the surreptitiously-placed earpiece Podsy had slipped in a few minutes earlier to facilitate clandestine conversations with Jem), Podsy redoubled his efforts and was about to target the third location on his map when a thought occurred to him.

"Unintelligent..." he mused, recalling how seemingly every non-Terran group the Metal Legion had encountered accused Terrans of possessing lower-than-average intellect. "Ok, let's see how 'unintelligent' I am. Clover Actual," he raised Jenkins.

"Go ahead, GC," Jenkins replied.

"Ping Two came back empty," Podsy explained. "I'm directing Ping Three to the same coordinates as Ping One."

"Say again, GC?"

"I'm directing Ping Three to the same coordinates as Ping One," Podsy explained.

A brief delay. "Copy that, GC. We're ready when you are."

Podsy again made eye contact with the Vercingetorix's Sensor operator, who signaled he was ready to ping the indicated area. "Ping Three in five..." Podsy called out, "four... three...two...one. Ping!"

The third EMP went down, returning to the same coordinates as the first, except this time Podsy's board lit up like a Christmas tree.

"Multiple contacts!" he declared triumphantly as a Jemmin hovertank and three skimmers were revealed in the center of the volcanic depression.

"Engaging," Colonel Jenkins intoned as 1st Company's guns cleared on-target, bracketing the fast-moving Jemmin vehicles with a hail of artillery and railgun fire. Two skimmers were destroyed outright by HE shells, the Spectre-class hovertank took a direct railgun strike that briefly knocked it to the ground, and the third skimmer vanished from the sensors before the 1st Company could neutralize it.

The company's mechs turned their unbridled fury on the damaged, exposed hovertank, unleashing coil guns and artillery shells. The Jemmin desperately launched its arsenal at its Terran adversaries, sending a flight of missiles in reply. The missiles were expertly torched by interceptor rockets almost precisely at the mid-point of their flight paths.

Terran railguns stabbed tungsten bolts into the Jemmin tank, sending it crashing to the molten rock again, where it slowly sank two full meters before its power core lost containment. A shower of lava spewed skyward, propelled by the Spectre's death throes and looking very much like a volcanic eruption.

When the last droplets of lava splashed down, the Terrans had eliminated three more Jemmin vehicles without suffering a single hit in reply. Podsy felt a thrill of satisfaction when he realized that the technique had worked. Moreover, he had played on Jemmin arrogance by circling back to a previous target that the Jemmin commander had apparently thought would be a safe hiding place for a time, at least.

"Good work, GC," Colonel Moon said neutrally. "Forward your readings to the *Red Hare* and to Comm. Let's put every brain we've got on fine-tuning your method and maximizing its area of effect."

"Yes, sir," Podsy replied with relish, drawing an openly disapproving look from the *Vercingetorix's* Fleet-uniformed XO. But Podsy didn't care. She could look down her nose at him all she wanted. He had just struck a major blow for the Legion, and he wasn't about to act as if he hadn't.

A muted look of disapproval from Colonel Moon was somehow enough to dash most of his exuberance, and as Podsy coordinated with the rest of the emissions specialists aboard the two Metal Legion warships, he wondered just how much his time in the military had changed him.

"Contacts!" Podsy declared after the nineteenth ping. A Spectre and two more skimmers were revealed by the increasingly-fine-tuned EMP, and Clover Battalion wasted no time in engaging the vulnerable targets.

Railgun bolts skewered the Spectre while artillery shells fell around the tightly-packed vehicles. The enemy sent a small volley of missile fire back in reply and somehow managed to slip three SRMs through 2nd Company's defensive shell. One of Captain Chao's mechs suffered an unfortunate hit to a previously-damaged segment of its forward armor, causing the Razorback's capacitors to discharge their collected energies directly into the mech's cabin. The mech collapsed to the ground, its hull mostly intact, and the furious Terran fire scratched the Spectre and skimmers from the board even before the dead Razorback ceased its motion.

"Clover Actual," Podsy said, pushing past the loss of a second mech from Clover Battalion, "I'm forwarding the next package of coordinates."

"Copy that, GC," Jenkins acknowledged. "Coordinates received. Fire when ready."

"Be advised," Podsy continued, "Joker Company is within engagement range of the next targets and will provide fire support."

"Confirmed, GC," Jenkins replied with unvarnished amusement. "I never thought I'd be taking orders from you, Lieutenant."

Podsy blushed at Jenkins' jab, and his embarrassment deepened when Lieutenant Commander Stravinsky shot a withering glance his way. "Confirmed, Clover Actual," Podsy declared in kind. "I doubt it will become a pattern." He switched over to the direct line with Xi. "Joker Actual, this is Ground Control."

"Go ahead, Ground Control," Xi acknowledged as her mechs finished establishing base camp at the edge of the salty waters where the American Navy salvage team would soon deploy.

"I'm forwarding target coordinates within your effective engagement zone," Podsy explained.

"I was wondering when you'd get around to *my* needs, Ground Control," Xi said in a mock pout. "So far it's been 'no girls allowed' out there."

"Blame the Jemmin, Major." Podsy cracked a grin.

"Oh, I *do*," Xi assured him, Her words carried a savage undertone that reminded Podsy to *never* get on her bad side.

Sensors gave him the thumbs-up, and Podsy piped into both Clover and Joker channels, "EMP inbound in five...four...three...two...one. Ping!"

Again the *Vercingetorix* sent a pulse of electromagnetic energy down to the planet's surface. Ionizing gas as it went, the pulse splashed down on an area nearly half a kilometer in diameter, fully five times the diameter of the first successful pulse.

Yet another trio of Jemmin vehicles, consisting of a Spectre hovertank and two skimmers, were revealed by the pulse. Xi's mechs were slightly closer to this particular formation and sent their first wave of ordnance tearing through the air at the fast-fleeing Jemmin.

Her people refrained from launching missiles to conserve

their limited supply of the valuable munitions, but despite lacking railguns, the Jokers managed to land a direct hit on the Spectre with AP artillery shells.

Momentarily crippled, the Spectre was surrounded by a storm of HE shells delivered by Clover's guns. Near-misses splashed all around the wounded hovertank, but this particular tank would not fall to fifteen-kilo shells.

Lieutenant Miles 'Blinky' Staubach, commanding the Warlock-class *Cyclops*, charged his main weapon and unleashed a raging inferno of plasma upon the flagging Jemmin hovertank. Sailing through the air and trailing a massive, billowing cloud of smoke, *Cyclops'* heavy plasma cannon dropped a five-kiloton portal to hell less than fifty meters from the Spectre.

The Spectre was vaporized by the conflagration, which rapidly filled the crater where the Jemmin trio had taken refuge prior to Podsy's exposing them.

"Target neutralized," Blinky declared with relish over the Joker company channel.

"Put your pants back on, *Cyclops*," Xi chastised the exuberant young officer. "There's nothing worse than a thumb-dick who can't hold back."

"Yes, ma'am. Just give me another chance. It won't happen again," Blinky replied with patently false contrition.

"Ground Control," Xi called up, ignoring the obviously sexual double entendre, "we're ready to engage the next target on your signal."

"Copy that, Joker Actual," Podsy acknowledged as Sensors forwarded some concerns about the pings' wear and tear on the Vercingetorix's active sensor systems. He piped Jenkins in on the line, "We've got a few kinks to work out up here before the next ping. Hold position and await updates."

"Roger, GC," Jenkins acknowledged.

"Standing by," Xi said a second later.

Podsy removed his headset and made his way over to Sensors. "What's the problem?"

"Focusing these pulses is causing some damage to the emitter, Lieutenant," Sensors explained. "We can get another twenty pulses for certain, but after that, I'm not sure we can focus them like this. The system was designed for sixty-degree pings of void space, not pinpoint strikes through heavy atmosphere against ground targets."

Lieutenant Commander Stravinsky came over from Tactical wearing a well-masked look of concern. "If we can't funnel the energy as we have, the method will be useless. The pulse will dissipate in the atmosphere."

"Options?" Colonel Moon asked, appearing at Podsy's shoulder.

Sensors cocked his head dubiously. "The *Red Hare*'s system isn't much different from ours. I suppose we could have them remove their emitter and start making significant modifications to it. We might be able to get...I don't know...a hundred pulses out of their system with the proper mods. With the wear and tear we've put ours through, we won't get more than fifty before we brick the system entirely."

Moon shook his head irritably. "If we had just one squadron of Vipers, we could scrape the surface clear of these things. Viper active sensors are purpose-built for high-altitude pings like this."

"Agreed." Stravinsky nodded gravely. "The enmity between Fleet and Armor Corps is unfortunate; a short-range fighter carrier would have proven invaluable on this op."

"I think we need to play the hand we've been dealt and will always be dealt," Podsy replied.

"Fleet could have handled this op entirely on its own." Stravinsky scoffed.

"Table this," Moon commanded before Podsy could

respond. The colonel turned to Sensors as the Lieutenant Commander shot daggers Podsy's way. "Get with the *Red Hare*'s Sensor team and see if they can implement or improve on your proposed modifications. The Jemmin have already started to scatter following our pings, and they're unlikely to make this any easier on us." He turned to Podsy. "Limit your pings to ten more clear-outs of the immediate area surrounding the dig site. Save the rest of the *Vercingetorix's* emitter for later."

"Yes, Colonel," Podsy acknowledged, drawing a heated look from Stravinsky as he made his way back to the Ground Control station.

Podsy couldn't care less about the Lieutenant Commander's irritation or disdain. He had a job to do, and Metalheads on the Pearl were counting on him to do it. He turned his back on her and focused on his job.

6

IN THE NAVY

The southern shore of the ocean was a relatively gentle slope of limestone. The rippling surface of the saltwater had washed the stone smooth, and for at least five thousand years, the solar winds above had scorched the once-beautiful ocean world into a blasted, desolate hellscape where few living creatures outside the Arh'Kel could hope to survive.

The mirage effect was profound, with warbles of light playing tricks on the naked eye all across the flat, salty sea. To Xi, it seemed even less hospitable than the hellish Durgan's Folly.

"Water, water, everywhere..." Lieutenant Carl "Sargon" Benjamin sighed. "If you tried to drink this stuff, you'd only survive if your stomach managed to expel it. There's so much potassium in this ocean that it might be fatal if you just took a mouthful and didn't even *try* to swallow."

"Don't let the water's placid appearance fool you," chided Blinky. "It's so hot you'd scald your mouth on contact."

"The major must feel right at home, then," Nakamura noted playfully.

"Don't make me come over there, *Murasame*." Xi grinned as

the heavy haulers slowly reversed down the slope into the water, where they would soon deploy their submarines.

"As threats go, that one falls a little flat, ma'am," Nakamura quipped.

"No flatter than that dangly flap of lard you call an ass, Lieutenant," Xi retorted.

"Major," called Corporal Giles, the Nugget who had tried (and failed) to cheat his way to victory in the simulator, "the water's playing havoc with my hydraulics. I don't think the system will remain stable after more than a couple minutes of this."

"Then get in there and drop your load ASAP, *Skeptic*," Xi urged, prompting Giles to speed his descent into the water, where the sub soon became buoyant enough to lift its stern off the cradle.

"Not often you hear a girl say that..." Sargon mused.

"First you have to get one interested enough to do the deed, *Sargon*," Quinn quipped, "and then you've got to be so boring she'd rather just get it over with and move on to something more fun. Like a high colonic or electro-shock therapy, for instance."

"What she said." Xi cackled as Giles delivered the first sub into the scalding water. The other two haulers deployed their vehicles in the same manner—a mad dash and drop with a quick exit from the hot and caustic ocean.

"Major Xi, this is Lieutenant Commander Ulbricht," came the American Navy officer's voice over the Dive Channel. "We're green across the board. The sooner we get down there, the better. These ships' environmental systems are near the redline, compensating for the heat."

"Copy that, Commander," Xi acknowledged. "You're up first, *Black Widow*."

Black Widow, the spider-shaped mech under Lieutenant Quinn's command, moved into the water a hundred meters from the floating trio of subs just as the heavy haulers emerged from the water and made their way to the relative safety of the dry shoreline. *Black Widow*'s expansive central hull was one of the most naturally buoyant in Joker Company and actually required water ballast to be taken on in order to dive.

Outfitted with a pair of torpedo launchers and six remote-controlled short-range aquatic interceptor drones, *Black Widow* was one of the three most valuable submarine mechs in the company and proved worthy of its inclusion as Quinn filled the ballast compartments. The spider mech slowly sank into the water until just the top meter of its back was visible above the surface. Once there, the modular propeller system affixed to the *Black Widow*'s undercarriage moved the mech with surprising speed, driving it to a position several hundred meters ahead of the American subs.

"*Black Widow* is five-by-five, Major," Quinn reported after taking point.

"Roger, Lieutenant," Xi acknowledged. "*Land Shark*, you're next."

The bullet-shaped *Land Shark*, a purpose-built amphibious mech, rolled on its tracks down the slope and into the water. Despite its dual nature as both a land and seagoing vehicle, *Land Shark* was primarily designed to 'crawl' along a seafloor rather than float through the water. Equipped with inflatable buoys, the vehicle could use those buoys for rapid ascent or for maneuvering through tricky or soft bottom terrain.

But what *Land Shark* gave up in maneuverability, it more than made up for in raw firepower. Equipped with six torpedo launchers in addition to a pair of hybrid SRM-torpedo systems, the *Land Shark* packed enough underwater firepower to stand sentinel over an entire high-traffic port.

"*Land Shark* is wet, Major," Corporal Cervantes reported. "Ready to roll."

"Roger, Corporal," Xi replied before moving *Elvira III* to the edge of the water. She sucked on her teeth as she drove the Scorpion-class mech into the salty sea. "How we doing back there?" she asked her Wrench and Monkey after they had fully submerged

"All systems green, Major," reported Chief Lu, her mech's former Wrench-turned-Monkey who had just been released from the Legion burn unit prior to the *Vercingetorix's* deployment. She was glad to have him back following his rehab for injuries suffered on Shiva's Wrath, and from the gleam in his eye when he stepped aboard the newest rebuild of *Elvira*, he was as glad to return to her command as she was to have him. "Caulk sensors are looking good, ma'am. Sealant is expanding as expected."

"How are you doing, Penny?" Xi asked her new Monkey, a young woman with a checkered past who had immediately caught Xi's eye on the recruitment rolls.

"SRM one is offline and stowed, ma'am, with no detected breach in the water seals," the diminutive woman replied promptly. "SRM two's torpedoes are showing green across the board and ready to deploy on your order."

"Good," Xi replied, silently cursing the stupidity of purposely driving a mech underwater as the vehicle moved deeper and deeper into the increasingly dark water.

The specs looked good, and she had been assured by the Legion's senior-most technicians that *Elvira III* would be an excellent submersible. In fact, only a handful of mechs were "out-of-the-box" capable of diving to the depths required for this mission, and the Scorpion was among them. The Fiddleback and Bulette designs were also out-of-the-box submersible to those depths, which was why *Black Widow* and *Land Shark* had been selected for Operation Watery Grave.

But there was still something discomfiting about the notion

of walking a mobile artillery platform into the water, and Xi found her pucker factor growing with each passing second. Eventually *Elvira* was fully submerged, at which point (and to Xi's amazement) the Scorpion-class mech's bow gently floated up ten centimeters or so before bobbing back down to the rocky bottom.

"You've got to be kidding me..." she muttered into a muted mic. "It floats."

"Sorry, Major?" her Wrench called from the cabin's rear.

"Nothing, Chief," Xi said dismissively, reactivating her cabin mic as she walked the mech farther below the surface, where its vertical bobbing became more pronounced until it floated completely off the bottom. "Let's test the auxiliary propulsion system," she ordered.

"Propellers online," Lu acknowledged.

"Ballast compartments ready to fill," Penny added.

Xi gently guided the mech ahead with the small propellers and was rewarded with a sluggish shot of forward motion. "Propellers online," she confirmed. "Flooding ballast tanks."

A handful of air-filled compartments within *Elvira's* armored hull were quickly filled with salt water, causing the mech to slowly sink to the flat, rocky surface below. Unlike *Black Widow*, *Elvira's* design did not permit nimble submarine maneuvers, which meant the Scorpion-class mech would be half-walking, half-propelling itself down the slope to the dig site.

"Deep Dive, this is Major Xi," Xi declared over the team channel. "Begin descent to the dig site." She switched over to the Joker command channel. "Captain Koch, Joker is yours."

"Acknowledged, Major," Koch replied. "Good hunting."

With command of Joker Company transferred, the Deep Divers in formation with *Black Widow* on point, and *Elvira* and *Land Shark* crawling on the ocean floor a hundred meters to either side of the formation, the archaeological recovery team headed into the dark, a place they had found themselves far too often.

Demons & Wizards' *Beneath These Waves* was playing on *Elvira's* cabin speakers at low volume when Xi's neural-link HUD flickered with a wave of fresh contacts at a depth of four hundred meters.

"Vorr auto-defenses located," Lieutenant Commander Ulbricht reported as Xi turned her focus to the new signatures. Using *Elvira's* underwater sensors was so disorienting that Xi had opted to employ a purely visual HUD similar to the one she would use if she had a broken neural link. The HUD, transmitting directly to her optic nerve rather than displaying to her eye, showed seven scattered icons representing Vorr defensive assets.

But the Vorr brief had shown that there should have been nearly three times as many defensive platforms as she was seeing, which suggested the rest had already been sanctioned by Jemmin efforts to penetrate the dig site's perimeter.

"Establishing handshake protocols with the Vorr system," Xi declared, transmitting a set of digital authentications over a secure Vorr frequency. It seemed the Vorr, perhaps in accordance with their species' history as prey rather than predators, had not deigned to place any Vorr personnel in the dig site. That left the entire operation to be conducted via automation managed remotely.

Some of their reluctance to deploy Vorr operators might have been due to the Vorr's thermal tolerances, which required their environments to be kept within five or ten degrees of freezing for long-term survival. The saltwater of the Pearl was over forty degrees too hot for Vorr to survive, and while Xi had always enjoyed scalded octopus with a hefty side of wasabi, she didn't exactly blame the Vorr for wanting to stay out of the nearly boiling sea.

The handshake protocols came back as confirmed, and the Vorr auto-defenses piped limited status reports and data logs into Xi's system. Scanning through the logs, which were filtered by a program Chief Styles had worked up to quickly translate Vorr data of this type, Xi came upon a number of inconsistencies and apparent errors.

Xi raised the battalion's intelligence officer and chief technical asset, currently embarked on one of the American Navy subs. "Chief Styles, I need a second set of eyes to look over this data. Either it's corrupted or there's some weird shit going on."

"Copy that, Major," Styles acknowledged. "Send it over, and I'll see what I can do with it." A moment later, while the formation continued to make its way down the increasingly steep ocean floor, she sent the information for Styles' review. A few minutes later he sent modified files back. "A lot of the data was too corrupted, but I was able to clear some of it up."

Xi scanned the revisions and nodded approvingly. "Good work, Chief. According to the Vorr logs, Jemmin last attacked this facility an hour before we dropped. They made a hard push to penetrate the shield, but it looks like they failed. Vorr sensors are a *lot* better than ours." She frowned and rubbed her eyes as if that would help clear her mind. "Even they weren't able to spot the skimmers before they unloaded their torpedoes. *Black Widow*," Xi commanded, "deploy your drones to maximum safe operating distance. I want an active sensor net thrown over the dig site ASAP."

"On it, ma'am," Quinn acknowledged, sending a handful of drones speeding outward in a fan-shaped pattern. "Drones away. Sensor net should be up in three minutes."

"*Land Shark*," Xi continued, "I need you to go down and secure the tunnel mouth. Stay dark until you're within fifty meters of the opening, then go hot on your torpedoes. Let's not give potential hostiles any more help spotting us than they already have."

"Copy that, Major," Corporal Cervantes replied before driving her mech down the slope at speeds seemingly impossible underwater. Using a combination of propellers and tracks, *Land Shark* was able to drive at nearly fifty kilometers per hour down the steep ocean floor.

The dig site was, according to the Vorr brief, located approximately twelve kilometers up an artificial tunnel dug into the ocean floor. Running parallel to the surface, the tunnel was supposed to intersect a vast, labyrinthine network of similar passages, the purpose of which was unknown.

TAC technicians and other mission specialists had debated the tunnels' purpose but had failed to establish a compelling theory prior to the Legion's deployment. It was left to Legion personnel to determine the purpose.

Given that the long-dead intelligent species that had called the Pearl home were relatively shallow swimmers, it was unlikely these deep tunnels represented a working piece of vital infrastructure. Some had posited that the network might have been the equivalent of a fallout bunker, built to protect against an unexpected catastrophe that might render the surface oceans uninhabitable.

Others, including Styles, had argued that the depth of the facility suggested it was instead a military installation. Inaccessible to the aquatic species without the use of special vehicles, these tunnels would serve as the perfect site for a secret military base or research facility.

Still others, chief among them Lieutenant Commander Ulbricht, believed the tunnels supported some sort of scientific research effort. Xi was torn between the second and third theories, but thankfully she would soon have the chance to determine once and for all why the suicidal species had gone to such great effort.

It seemed the Vorr had intentionally collapsed all tunnels leading to the underwater labyrinth except this one. They had then fortified the underwater position against intrusions while standing overwatch with a flotilla of warships.

Unfortunately for them, Jemmin had overcome their orbital assets with a devastating assault. The Vorr had managed to prevent Jemmin from destroying the dig site, albeit at extreme cost. They had been unable to prevent Jemmin from landing at least two Poltergeists and upward of a hundred vehicles on the Pearl.

As *Land Shark* drew within a kilometer of the tunnel network's lone entry point, the Vorr-augmented sensor feeds were filled with inbound tactical icons.

Torpedoes. *Thirty* of them.

"Deep Dive, we've got inbound. Launch interceptors," Xi commanded, loosing a quartet of interceptor torpedoes from SRM two. All eight of that launcher's tubes had been loaded with specially-designed interceptors that fit the launcher as snugly as any SRM and were capable of launching from the platform while submerged.

Black Widow sent a pair of her own interceptor torpedoes up to meet the inbound weapons. *Land Shark*, meanwhile, never broke stride as Cervantes' mech burned for the tunnel's mouth.

The Vorr auto-defenses remained ominously silent as the torpedoes descended toward the tunnel. The six Terran interceptor torpedoes seemed woefully outnumbered by their larger, more numerous counterparts, but the interceptors soon proved their worth as they each split into six separate warheads.

Each of those was equipped with flotation buoys, which immediately inflated and held their charges in place while the onrushing torpedoes converged on the tunnel mouth *Land Shark* had nearly reached. Normally, this type of interceptor would be deployed in a fleeing sub's wake, where they would form a wall of explosives that could deny a horizontally-oriented torpedo. But under Xi's guidance, these interceptors had been slightly modified to make them equally effective at intercepting vertically-driven ordnance.

Xi's visual HUD showed the Jemmin torpedoes adjust course to avoid her shield of interceptors, but it was too little too late. The Terran interceptors activated as soon as their proximity sensors tripped, causing a ripple of underwater explosions to create a short-lived dome of light that illuminated the ocean floor below.

Twenty-three Jemmin torpedoes were destroyed by the powerful explosions that went off a hundred meters above the ocean floor. Xi's neural link relayed the shockwaves from those explosions as a sharp pain in her sinuses, causing her to reflexively snort in annoyance as seven of the Jemmin weapons slipped through the interceptor shield and drove for the tunnel mouth. But even as they did so, her sensors managed to locate four Jemmin vehicles two hundred fifty meters above the dig site.

"Hostiles located," Xi declared, locking her torpedoes on the enemy subs. "Deep Dive is weapons-free. Engage targets."

Xi instantly transmitted positioning data via the P2P.

"Engaging," Lieutenant Commander Ulbricht acknowledged, and the trio of American Navy subs each sent four torpedoes upward at the enemy vehicles while *Land Shark* sent another six from the edge of the dig site tunnel. Xi added another two to the volley, making twenty counter-torpedoes on the way to their Jemmin targets.

But seven Jemmin torpedoes were still en route to the dig

site opening, and just as they were about to hit, the Vorr countermeasures sprang to life with deadly precision.

Vorr laser beams swept above the tunnel mouth, scraping one torpedo. Then another. Another, then another, and another. Finally, the last two torpedoes were eliminated by Vorr counterfire less than thirty meters from *Land Shark*'s position. The concussive wave slammed into the mech, shaking it from stem to stern. The damage was reflected in the warning lights that filled Xi's virtual HUD.

But *Elvira* had problems of her own as red lights flashed throughout the mech's cabin.

"We've blown welds in ballast tanks two and five," Lu reported.

"Get to the port junction, Penny," Xi snapped, knowing that if they lost those tanks, they might be forced to slow-walk their way back up to the surface.

"I've got the compound in hand, Major," *Elvira's* newest Monkey replied shortly as the nimble, small-statured woman removed the access panel. Penny quickly inserted the tube of expanding compound into Tank Two's emergency access valve. The material shot into the tank, where it expanded on contact with the water there and quickly filled the compartment, forcing most of the water out in the process. "Tank Two sealed," Penny reported before moving on to Tank Five.

Meanwhile, the Jemmin vehicles above them broke for safety far more sluggishly than their sleek frames suggested they would. They managed to reach speeds approaching eighty kph as they tried to evade the wave of torpedoes.

Xi watched with satisfaction as Jemmin countermeasures failed to protect the first two vehicles, both skimmers scratched by near-miss torpedo explosions.

The other two managed to drag their trailing torpedoes for several hundred meters, during which they employed evasive rolls and corkscrews. The maneuvers almost saved the third Jemmin, which slipped past three of its four pursuing torpedoes before the fourth managed to go off close enough to scrap the thin-hulled skimmer-turned-submarine.

The fourth Jemmin vehicle drove straight for the surface, nearly outpacing the Terran torpedoes that glacially slowly closed the distance to their quarry. For several seconds, it seemed as though the Jemmin skimmer would break the surface and flee to safety. Four of the pursuing torpedoes were from the American subs, while the fifth came from a significantly different angle, having been launched by *Land Shark*.

Suddenly, the American torpedoes went off in rapid succession, sending shockwaves bubbling up beneath the Jemmin skimmer and causing it to briefly falter in its ascent as its drive system was compromised and failed.

That brief break in its surface-bound sprint was all it took for *Land Shark*'s torpedo to close and scrap it. A shower of slowly-falling ceramic debris filled the water above the dig site, and Xi returned her attention to her mech's status to find that Lu and Penny had successfully sealed off the second damaged tank.

"Good work, people," Xi congratulated them, her voice less steady than she would have liked as unwanted visions of being crushed under four hundred meters of water filled her mind's eye. "Quick thinking on the micro-foam, Penny. We'll need to watch our buoyancy figures, but we should be able to maneuver just fine down here with that patch job."

"Thank you, Major," Penny replied between panting breaths. "But I...couldn't have done it...without the Chief's help."

"All I did was hold the door open for you," Lu quipped.

"Like any true gentleman," Xi said approvingly as she

scanned *Land Shark*'s worrisome status reports. "*Land Shark*, are you mobile?"

"Stand by, Major," Cervantes replied tersely. Her crew's background chatter suggested the amphibious mech's status was still far from stable. "Give us a few minutes to plug the leaks. We're running out of fingers over here."

"Roger," Xi acknowledged grimly, knowing there was nothing anyone could do for *Land Shark*. It was up to Cervantes and her crew to save the vehicle and, by extension, themselves. She set her jaw and switched over to the main Deep Dive channel. "Deep Dive, proceed to the tunnel at best speed."

A stream of acknowledgments came from every vehicle except *Land Shark*, whose crew continued working furiously to save their mech from being filled with near-boiling water or crushed by the four hundred meters of water pressing down from above.

Fortunately, before *Elvira* moved into the tunnel behind the American subs and *Black Widow*, *Land Shark*'s Jock signaled that the damage had been contained and it was ready to resume its position in the formation.

Moving together, the six Terran vehicles entered the millennia-old mysterious tunnel and were soon under the relative safety of the planet's natural rock.

7

ROCK OF AEGIS

"Poltergeist on the scope," Jenkins declared just before a Jemmin laser beam stabbed into *Warcrafter's* bow. "Range: eighty-five-point-two kilometers," Jenkins called tersely.

"I see it," Krauthammer growled while spinning and ducking *Warcrafter* in an intense effort to evade the Poltergeist's laser beam. *Warcrafter's* railgun spat a tungsten bolt at the enemy command vehicle, but despite its speed, the sliver of tungsten missed its target by two full meters as the Poltergeist more than matched *Warcrafter's* evasive maneuvers.

At eighty-plus kilometers from a mobile target, *Warcrafter's* artillery was worthless. The farthest even the extended-range shells could engage in the Pearl's gravity and atmospheric conditions was about sixty kilometers, and even that was stretching it for any target smaller than a house, let alone one as mobile as a Poltergeist.

Jenkins' tactical display showed that fourteen Jemmin vehicles, four Spectres and ten skimmers, had appeared just beyond artillery range. They seemed to be begging him to send missiles their way, which he was reluctant to do.

Those missiles would be invaluable against exposed Poltergeists should Jenkins' people manage to damage one of the command vehicles' stealth skin sufficiently to maintain weapons lock on the fleet-footed hovercraft.

He considered calling in an orbital nuke from the *Red Hare* against the Poltergeist, but he had already tried that move with the highest-yield device the Legion brought to the Pearl. The *Red Hare* was now down to four one-megaton missiles and twenty tactical nukes in the ten-to-hundred kiloton range. It also had a single Starburst multi-laser missile remaining, but he would not call it into play unless he had a kill-shot lined up on an enemy command vehicle.

If they could kill the Jemmin command vehicles, the rest of the Jemmin remotely operated vehicles would be rendered useless. They had learned that the wild combat on Shiva's Wrath had been against a single Jemmin who had almost wiped out an entire company.

"No!" Jenkins grimaced as the Jemmin Spectres and skimmers sent a flight of missiles into the mechs of 2nd Company. "We've got to hold fast until we crack their stealth systems. We need confirmed kills."

Seeming to read his mind, the Poltergeist vanished from the scopes while the smaller Jemmin craft scattered from 2nd Company's extended range artillery counterfire.

A second Poltergeist appeared, this one just over a hundred kilometers to the north on the western shore of the sea. The Jemmin command vehicle fired a capital-grade laser at a stationary mech in Captain Chao's 2nd Company. It had suffered serious damage from the preceding Spectre-launched missiles and was a sitting duck. The laser shredded the mech's systems, knocking it out of the fight, but the crew had escaped and survived to fight another day.

Jenkins angrily clenched his jaw. 2nd Company's missile shield was more porous than it should have been. Even after suffering a trio of losses thus far, including the latest, the Clover Razorbacks should have had ample intercept capability to repel the early Jemmin missile flights.

Something was wrong with Chao's company, and Jenkins intended to get to the bottom of it at the next break in the action.

Captain Chao's mechs sent a storm of counterfire at the enemy skimmers and Spectres, stabbing tungsten bolts into the enemy vehicles. Three skimmers and a Spectre were scrapped by 2nd Company's focused barrage, paying back the Jemmin for 2nd Company's early losses.

Jenkins' 1st Company mechs were less successful, managing to scratch only a single skimmer with scattered ER-HE shells sent several kilometers beyond their rated range.

Fortunately, despite his unit's issues with sustaining an intact missile shield, Captain Chao's mechs remained in tight formation while observing strict fire discipline. Volleys went out with expert coordination, and 2nd Company executed textbook evasive maneuvers across the Pearl's butter-smooth surface. Zigging and zagging at variable speeds, the mechs of Clover Battalion looked from the outside like a smooth-running unit.

But to Jenkins' eye, there seemed to be a division between 5th Platoon and the rest of Captain Chao's 2nd Company. 4th and 6th Platoons correctly provided mutually-supportive fire even at the expense of maneuverability, but 5th Platoon seemed more focused on executing optimal evasive maneuvers than maintaining missile shield integrity. As a result, none of the 2nd Company losses thus far had been to 5th Platoon, but had instead been suffered by 4th and 6th when 5th's evasive maneuvers put them in poor position to intercept inbound ordnance.

Jenkins called up 5th Platoon's roster and saw its CO was a lieutenant named Hao Yong. A seventeen-year veteran of the Terra Han Colonial Guard, Lieutenant Hao had served with distinction under Major Brighton until her transfer to the

Terran Armor Corps. Brighton's official entries to Hao's jacket painted the picture of an ambitious, capable officer with impeccable tactical acumen and a mean streak that ran as deep as her desire to move up the ranks.

"2nd Company," Jenkins called Chao over the secure P2P command link, "this is Clover Actual."

"Go ahead, Colonel," Chao replied as his platoon sent a perfectly-coordinated volley of artillery down on an isolated Jemmin skimmer, scratching it with two near-misses that destroyed its drive system with explosive shrapnel.

"Your missile shield needs tightening, Captain," Jenkins said bluntly. "2nd Company is advised to withdraw three klicks to the south, where we can provide greater mutual support."

"Our position is good, Colonel," Chao replied firmly but without so much as a whiff of insubordination. "Request permission to advance two klicks to the west to increase effective intercept of northern hostiles."

Jenkins was glad to hear Chao stand up for himself, but he wasn't quite sure if it was merely pride or warranted confidence that drove the captain. Whatever it was, Jenkins knew that advancing and broadening the missile shield was the only way Captain Koch's basecamp would be protected. Somewhat counterintuitively, a move several klicks to the west (placing 2nd Company even farther from the dig site) would increase Chao's ability to intercept low-flying ordnance.

"Permission granted," Jenkins grudgingly allowed, "but tighten your formation, Captain, or I'll pull you back and do it myself."

"Understood, Colonel," Chao acknowledged. "The Terra Han Colonial Guard transfers won't let you down—and we have five thousand years' experience addressing discord in the ranks."

Jenkins wasn't entirely certain what Chao meant by that last bit, except to say that Terra Han culture prided itself on its Chinese roots. With a philosophical anchor set in the Han period of Chinese history, which had spanned five hundred years in some form or another, Terra Han's connection to its cultural roots was deeper and richer than any of the other Terran colonies.

So, when Captain Chao invoked five thousand years' of experience addressing martial discord, Jenkins suspected that Admiral Zhao's estranged son was alluding to methods of redress he probably considered barbaric.

But Jenkins reminded himself that the Terra Han Colonial Guard was probably as powerful as the rest of the Colonial Guards combined. Militaries weren't built on guns and ships, they were built on discipline, structure, and tradition. Terra Han hadn't gotten as powerful as it was by preserving regressive military traditions, so despite Jenkins reluctance, he decided to wait and see how Captain Chao would deal with the rebellious Lieutenant Hao.

Jemmin vehicles darted in and out for the next two hours, with the Poltergeists making occasional appearances at seemingly random points just beyond the Legion's effective engagement zone. None of Jenkins' tactical projections lined up with the Jemmin tactics, but as he incorporated the enemy's movements into his simulators, he began to see patterns that were later contradicted in the ongoing series of feints and fast strikes.

Lieutenant Podsednik's detection method had become decreasingly useful the farther the Jemmin vehicles fell back since it could not reliably locate enemy vehicles more than five hundred meters from each ping's center.

Jem's theory that the Jemmin active stealth systems were extremely energy-intensive seemed plausible, but thus far the Jemmin stealth limits had not been found. Jemmin Spectres and skimmers slid in and out of view at random intervals before slipping back into the safety of their sensor fog. It only took relatively minor damage to render a Jemmin vehicle visible long enough to neutralize it, but even landing near-misses on the fleet-footed hovervehicles was a tall order.

Over the next hour of this latest exchange, Clover's kills climbed to twelve Jemmin hovervehicles, while a fourth Razorback was knocked out of the fight by Jemmin missiles. But of the four Razorbacks to fall, only one was destroyed outright, while the others were salvageable. Even before the Poltergeists had withdrawn from the field, Captain Koch's trio of repair vehicles sped out from basecamp. The newest members of the Legion, a pair of Corporals named Giles and Lassiter, drove their heavy haulers *Armored Skeptic* and *Shoe on Head* out in support of the field repair mechs *Kochtopussy, Gun Monkey,* and *Apple of Argon.*

Jenkins found himself nodding in approval as the Nuggets kept formation with Koch's people. Xi still had a lot to learn about her new place in the chain of command since the elevation to major entailed the most significant step up in organizational responsibility this side of making the colonel-general transition, but when it came to recognizing talent, it seemed her eye was keen.

The Metal Legion's ranks were dangerously thin, which made the rapid promotions of essentially everyone with combat experience extremely problematic. Jenkins had no doubt that some of his recent promotions would flame out, possibly with lethal consequences, but Admiral Zhao had been right.

It was time for the Metalheads to step into General Akinouye's shoes...or get out of the way so someone else could.

With that thought in his mind, Jenkins watched with interest as Captain Chao's Razorback sped across the terrain toward an in-person rendezvous with 5th Platoon's CO, Lieutenant Hao.

Jenkins would have liked to listen in on that particular conversation, but he had other matters to attend to at present.

"Clover Battalion," Jenkins called as Chao's mech rolled to a stop alongside Lieutenant Hao's Razorback, the *Warning of Wuchao.* "Status report."

As indicators flashed across his terminal, Jenkins' video feed showed Lieutenant Hao disembark her mech and board Chao's recently-renamed *Fourth Leaf.*

Jenkins hoped his faith in the young man proved well-founded. If Captain Chao couldn't maintain control over a single platoon of Terra Han Colonial Guardsmen, Jenkins' prospects of controlling a full *brigade* of the transfers were grim...at best.

Sighing in frustration, Jenkins was assured, now more than ever, that the responsibilities of upper command were both more tedious and even more dangerous than those of fighting a mech on the battlefield. On the field, you knew who your enemies were. The only question was if you could kill him before he killed you.

From his current chair, it was his own people he needed to defeat before sending them out to sow chaos and destruction among the enemy.

Jenkins snorted as a sudden thought came to him. "You're not the bullet anymore, Lee," he muttered. "Now you're the barrel."

"Excuse me?" Alice asked, snapping Jenkins' attention from his station. She had been so quiet and unobtrusive that he had forgotten she was present.

"Duties change." Jenkins shook his head dismissively. "We either change with them or we fall to the wayside, leaving ruined bodies in our wake."

"You fear yourself incapable of proving worthy of the position you now hold?" Alice clarified. "That hardly seems an ideal psychological state from which to command a military force."

"I already told you." Jenkins made brief but pointed eye contact with her. "Fear drives *everything* I do, Alice. It's who I am, and even if I could change it, I wouldn't. It's up to the universe to decide if I'm unworthy, but until then, I'm going to do the best I can."

"Fascinating..." Alice mused.

A few minutes later, when Lieutenant Hao emerged from Captain Chao's *Fourth Leaf*, Jenkins thought he saw a hitch in the rebellious young woman's stride. But his vantage, provided by a low-altitude visual drone, was far from detailed.

Even before Lieutenant Hao regained her vehicle, Chao's *Fourth Leaf* was already tearing across the gray limestone that covered the Pearl's surface. Chao was apparently satisfied with the surprisingly brief exchange, so, for now, Jenkins would wait and see if 2nd Company's CO had done an adequate job of restoring order to his ranks.

8

A DISTURBING THEORY

Podsy splashed ice-cold water into his eyes, savoring the stinging sensation as he shook the droplets from his face. He was beginning a two-hour break ordered by Colonel Moon and knew he would need to get some shuteye if he was to be at his best when he returned to the *Vercingetorix's* bridge

He unwrapped a protein bar and popped the top off an electrolyte-rich bottle of water. He had nearly wolfed the whole thing down when Jem unexpectedly said, "I can remember what it was like to eat. I can even recall the specific sensations of various foods moving through my alimentary canal, but my frame of reference is disjointed. Unauthentic. I lack the biological structures necessary to frame the memories, so they are not as *real* as the other memories my forebears gave me."

As Jem spoke, Podsy finished off the protein bar and washed it down with the water. "That seems odd," he admitted. "I'd have thought that one memory would be just like another."

"Imagine having a dream where you had wings or a tail," Jem suggested. "Have you ever experienced such a vivid fantasy?"

"Of course." Podsy shrugged as he flopped down on his bunk, ensuring that his earpiece was properly set to continue the conversation as he closed his eyes.

"And during the dream," Jem pressed, "you are able to feel your wings and tail, and you remember these feelings when you awaken, but you know they are false because you do not have those things. Your realization is due less to your *direct* observation that you do not have these appendages than to your *indirect* observation that you do not *feel* their presence."

Podsy cocked his head contemplatively. "I guess you're right about that, though I'd never thought about it before. That must be...confusing for you."

"It is," Jem agreed, "but I rarely devote conscious thought to such matters. Prior to your retrieving me from the final resting place of the Jem'un, little of my existence was what you might consider 'conscious.' I was part of a complex probability-calculation system, and in a sense, I actively directed some of those calculations. But my only socialization came from my interactions with the Vorr, and later, with you. It was the opinion of the most celebrated Jem'un scholars and philosophers dedicated to the subject of sentience that consciousness is reflective. Reactive, if you will. The Jem'un believed that the only way a being can be truly conscious is by interacting with other conscious beings. A rare point of absolute consensus among the Jem'un was on the matter of what you call an 'information singularity.' They believed, as I therefore believe, that such a singularity represents the certain end of consciousness as a phenomenon."

"Even if that's true," Podsy argued, "isn't 'consciousness' just another way to think of flawed or limited perspective?"

"Partly," Jem allowed, "but it is also purposeful in that consciousness serves a logical purpose. In organic lifeforms, that purpose is primarily biological. In synthetic lifeforms, the purpose is less narrowly-defined but no less integral to its ongoing existence. Even, or perhaps most especially, automatons exist to fill specific roles within a system. Without this 'logic,' what purpose does their individuality serve? One can think of an artificial intelligence as moving further from individuated purpose and, by extension, further from consciousness. The more perfect an intelligence becomes, the less conscious it becomes."

Podsy snickered as he threw an arm over his eyes to shield them from the soft light in his quarters. "Human philosophers have often suggested that attaining total enlightenment results in something like oblivion for the one who reaches that vaunted state."

"These philosophers are wise," Jem observed approvingly. "Their suppositions seem to be in line with my forebears' clearest thoughts on the matter."

Podsy cocked his head and sat up fractionally. "This conversation had a purpose. What was it?"

"I...have a growing concern," Jem said hesitantly.

"Regarding?" Podsy asked steadily, although he could feel his heart rate accelerate at Jem's ominous tone.

"This operation," Jem explained heavily, "does not appear consistent with the Vorr's stated goal of removing Jemmin's influence from what you call Nexus Space."

Podsy's full attention was on Jem as he sat all the way up and swung his legs over the edge of his bunk. "What do you mean?"

"When the Vorr first approached me, there were minor discrepancies in their stated purpose and their methods of pursuing that purpose, but these discrepancies were not significant enough to prevent my supporting their efforts as my forebears directed."

"What kind of discrepancies are you talking about?"

"The Vorr's stated timelines were incongruous with indirect observations I had made during my time on the world you called 'Brick,'" Jem explained. "Again, these were minor and unworthy of detailing at that time, but they were significant enough for me to conduct clandestine information-gathering operations prior to your arrival. My methods were limited, and so were my results, but the calculations produced a possible scenario that was too probable and distressing to ignore."

Podsy waited for several long, tense seconds for Jem to expand on that thought. When Jem failed to do so, Podsy finally bit. "What scenario did you calculate, Jem?"

"Using data gathered since my first interaction with the Vorr," Jem replied, enunciating clearly and slowly, "I predict with a growing confidence—which, following incorporation of data gleaned from the ongoing battle for the Nexus, now stands at twenty-nine percent—that the Vorr wish to supplant Jemmin as the controlling species in Nexus Space. The possibility that they will simply remove Jemmin and the structures that grant it supremacy has fallen from ninety-two percent at my earliest calculations to forty-one percent following my latest revisions."

"Those revisions include ship movements and battle strategies?"

"They do," Jem confirmed. "Although the most important change in variables is the one regarding this world and the resources the Vorr seek to reclaim from it. Jemmin sent one of its gatecrashers, as you call them, to this star system, which means Jemmin views this world's spoils as important enough to divert critical resources from other operations in Nexus Space. That gatecrasher could have crushed half the disorganized Finjou, who lack the necessary firepower to prevent a Jemmin invasion once a ship of that caliber was introduced, but instead of functionally removing an entire species from the tactical picture, Jemmin sent that gatecrasher here."

Podsy nodded grimly. "And the Vorr sent enough ships here to destroy it."

"Data suggests the Zeen were the most influential force in this particular gatecrasher's destruction," Jem corrected, "although Vorr warships were certainly present."

"And Jemmin hasn't let Vorr warships near this system since then, although Zeen patrols were considerably closer to this gate than any Vorr patrols," Podsy mused, rubbing his chin thoughtfully. "Which suggests Jemmin doesn't think the Vorr have told the Zeen about what's down there."

"Most astute, Lieutenant Podsednik," Jem agreed. "I concur with your assessment: the Vorr are keeping the Zeen in the dark about the true nature of this operation, and the Vorr think that whatever salvage is down there is worth losing dozens of warships to preserve."

"And Jemmin thinks it's important enough to have at least *two* Poltergeists come down and crack the Vorr's defensive shell." Podsy grimaced. "Preventing Terran-Vorr cooperation on Shiva's Wrath was only worth *one* Poltergeist's attention. But that brings another question," he said irritably. "Why would Jemmin put this planet and its secrets in Vorr territory? Jemmin knew about this species' presence long before the Vorr were invited to join the Illumination League, right?"

"Jem'un scientists were aware of this world's budding intelligence prior to the Jemmin Holocaust," Jem concurred. "The only theoretical conclusions that fit available data are as follows: first, that Jemmin wanted, and *still* wants, the Vorr to discover whatever is buried here. Following this theory should lead us to conclude that the gatecrasher was sent to instill a sense of urgency into the Vorr, thus manipulating their timetables to

Jemmin's advantage. This theory requires the sacrifice of a gate-crasher in order to sell the falsehood to the Vorr. It is certainly not impossible that this is the case, given Jemmin's deviousness and exceptionally long perspective on such matters, but this theory's probability diminishes with every update to my calculations' fundamental variables."

"And the second theory?"

"The second theory, which has increased in likelihood with every variable update since I first met the Vorr," Jem said heavily, "is that whatever is buried here is of greater use to the Vorr than Jemmin initially believed, and that this increased utility represents a potentially existential threat to Jemmin."

"What could represent an existential threat to the most powerful...*faction*," Podsy struggled to find the right word, given Jemmin's peculiar nature, "in known space?"

"It is almost certainly information of some kind," Jem replied matter-of-factly. "If we assume the Vorr are seeking to usurp Jemmin's primacy in Nexus Space, that information will likely be related to the precursor technology collectively referred to by humanity as 'Nexus tech.'"

"Another backdoor like the one we used on Sol?" Podsy asked hopefully.

"Certainly not," Jem rejected. "At least, nothing so broad in its utility. Jem'un scholars devised multiple methods by which Nexus technology backdoors could be functionally blocked, and some of those methods were implemented prior to the Jemmin Holocaust. But in the past several thousand years, Jemmin has almost certainly reverse-engineered many of the fundamental components of Nexus tech, and is therefore insulated against such coarse subversion methods."

Podsy considered what Jem was telling him...and it didn't give him warm fuzzies. It was a disturbing theory that cast all of humanity's future into even greater question than it would have otherwise been. The Vorr had made significant gestures in support of humanity in recent months, but military history would suggest that a trusted ally could present the gravest threat. That very trust could be used as a weapon at the worst possible moment.

But that wasn't the only thing that gave Podsy pause. Jem, despite its ongoing support, was little better than the Vorr in his eyes. Yes, Jem had undertaken Operation Antivenom at personal risk, if such a term even applied to a gestalt intelligence like Jem, but even that assistance might have been given as part of some Machiavellian plot that eventually called for Jem to betray humanity for some as-yet-unknown set of motives.

"I'm going to be honest, Jem." Podsy sighed. "I can't trust you on this, or at least not enough to act on it, even if I was in a position to do so."

"That is an understandable and, if I may be so bold, *correct* response, Lieutenant Podsednik," Jem replied approvingly. "I present to you, and to your parent organizations, many of the same threats I suggest the Vorr are capable of. Threats Jemmin has already demonstrated itself willing to act on. There is nothing objectionable in your wariness. In fact, I will anticipate another of your concerns and say that if Colonel Moon is listening in on this conversation, he will likely keep that surveillance secret since there is nothing he can presently do about it. And if Colonel Moon is not eavesdropping on this conversation, I suggest that you not reveal the content of this exchange to him until after the operation has concluded."

"You're suggesting I keep key information from my CO until after it is no longer useful," Podsy clarified skeptically.

"No, Lieutenant," Jem replied confidently. "I am suggesting you share this with your ship's CO as soon as there is something practical that can be done with it. The Terran-Sol alliance, even if acting with unity, is at the bottom of the power structure in

Nexus Space. Humanity cannot afford to anger the Vorr, who are fast becoming the most powerful species in Nexus Space, so refusing to hand over the salvage you agreed to retrieve for the Vorr would be tactically inadvisable from any logical perspective."

Podsy scoffed. "You're saying that even if we're being treated like tools by the Vorr, we should just grin and bear it?"

"I am unfamiliar with that particular colloquialism," Jem allowed. "If I understand its meaning, however, then yes, your only viable course of action is to continue with the operation as planned and behave as though you are unaware of the Vorr's ulterior motives."

Podsy was unconvinced by Jem's argument. He felt it was prudent, even essential, that he inform Colonel Moon about this latest revelation as soon as possible. But the more he thought about it, the more he was convinced that Jem might actually be right.

But Podsy wasn't about to make such an important decision on two hours' sleep in the last thirty-six, so he dimmed the lights and did his best to get an hour of shuteye before his next shift on the *Vercingetorix's* bridge began.

"While you rest," Jem added casually, "I will continue to refine my calculations, specifically pertaining to exploiting possible gaps in Jemmin's stealth systems. I will share the results of those calculations once they have reached a minimal threshold of confidence."

"Sounds good, Jem," Podsy replied before slowing his breathing and forcing his mind to relax. "Do you know the difference between information and intelligence?"

"Not in the human definition," Jem allowed.

"Information is nothing until it's been analyzed and refined and an actionable conclusion drawn. Then it becomes intelligence."

"I understand. I have given you information, not intelligence."

Podsy didn't confirm Jem's deduction. Had he been conscious, he would have been surprised by how quickly he had fallen asleep.

9

THE DEEP SIX

Xi focused *Elvira's* lights on the rocky walls as they passed the fourth ring of strange, quasi-organic material set into the perfectly cylindrical tunnel. "What the hell is that stuff?" she asked, peering intently at the gross, mucousy-looking matter where it clung to the tunnel walls.

"Probably some kind of defunct pressure-regulation system," Lu suggested. "We use similar technology in deep-submersion aqua-mining facilities on Terra Han."

"We have them on New America, too," Penny agreed, "but nothing this big. Most of our pressure membranes are just a few centimeters across and serve to help separate heavier minerals from lighter ones. They use salt as catalyzers to drive water through reactive nanofilaments that regulate water pressure to ultra-fine tolerances."

"Some combination of increased heat, rising salinity, and thousands of years' general deterioration," Lu observed, "led these pressure-locks to fail. The four we've passed would be more than enough to provide the chamber beyond with precisely-regulated water pressure anywhere between surface pressure and the natural pressures at this depth. Judging by the thickness of those rings, and assuming their tech was a stone's throw from ours," he added as *Elvira* stepped over the meter-thick, semi-gelatinous residue, "they could probably cycle the pressure two or three times an hour."

"That would explain *how* these fish-people survived down here," Xi quipped as they passed the twelve-kilometer mark of their journey down the dark aquatic passage. "Now the question is *why* they would come down here when their entire planet was once covered in an ideal low-pressure habitable zone a kilometer above our heads? Why go to the trouble?"

"My best guess," Penny mused, "is that this was some kind of research facility. With nearly a kilometer of stone above, the cavern would be well-protected from ambient radiation and spikes in solar output. This system's primary is less stable than a typical star of its size, so controlling for that variability would be essential for performing sensitive experiments."

"You think they dug a particle collider down here, Monkey?" Lu chuckled.

"Maybe." Penny shrugged, doing a good job of hiding the irritation in her voice at Lu's jab. "Or maybe they were measuring some kind of interstellar phenomena, like how we used subterranean arrays a few hundred years ago for cataloging supernovas."

"*Elvira*, this is *Triton's Horn*." Lieutenant Commander Ulbricht came over the main Deep Dive channel. "We've got active EM signatures in the cavern ahead."

"Copy that, Commander," Xi acknowledged as the *Triton's Horn*, Ulbricht's submarine, forwarded relevant sensor data gleaned by its specialized underwater arrays. "*Black Widow*, you're up. Investigate the cavern and get visual ID on the six EM signatures. Deep Dive, hold position while Black Widow sweeps the cavern."

A chorus of acknowledgments streamed over her HUD as

Quinn drove *Black Widow* into the expansive chamber at the end of the twelve-kilometer tunnel. *Elvira* and the other four vehicles remained stationary half a kilometer from the cavern's mouth as the Fiddleback-class mech forged ahead.

"*Elvira, Black Widow*," Quinn reported after a few seconds, forwarding her data over their closed net. "We've got what look like defunct automated Vorr salvage vehicles. Some appear to have sustained damage, while others look like they're just offline. All power plants are cold, but capacitors and comm transceivers look to be operating on backup. Please advise."

"Stand by, *Black Widow*," Xi replied. "Commander Ulbricht?" she pressed, knowing that the American Navy officer was better-equipped to appraise Quinn's findings than Xi was.

"I concur with *Black Widow*'s assessment," Ulbricht replied after a brief delay. "Something interrupted Vorr remote control of these recovery drones or possibly even interfered with the vehicles' local automation protocols. These vehicles all self-destructed to various degrees, but it looks like they did so in a span of just a few seconds. Some of them are still attached to their containers, and those containers were sealed and prepped for retrieval."

"Are there any automated defenses inside the cavern?" Xi asked, prompting *Black Widow* to send out active sensor pings.

"Nothing on scanners, Major," Quinn replied promptly.

"Mr. Styles." Xi raised the newly-elevated Chief Warrant 5th Class. "Double-check our sensor readings. Make sure we're not missing anything through these rose-colored glasses."

"Stand by, Major," Styles replied, and silence followed for nearly a full minute. "I've got some anomalous readings on the far side of the cavern, ma'am, but it looks like this place is clean of any counter-intrusion systems. We're clear, *Elvira*."

"Roger," Xi confirmed with satisfaction, knowing that if

Styles couldn't see it, no human in the Pearl's star system could. "*Triton's Horn*, proceed with retrieval operation."

"Copy that, Major," Ulbricht acknowledged as *Elvira* led the rest of the Deep Dive team into the cavern. "Extricating those parcels from the Vorr drones could take a few hours. We'll get to work."

Xi thumbed open to the direct line to Styles. "Chief, I want you collecting our own parcels while the rest of us take recordings of the area. Exercise your best judgment on which items to bring back to the surface. We won't get a do-over on this, and I want to know what the Vorr stuffed inside those cargo pods before Jemmin showed up and crashed the party."

"Understood," Styles replied. "I've already got a dozen priority targets lined up."

"Quality over quantity, Chief," Xi chided as *Elvira* emerged into the immense chamber, which was filled with rubble and traces of what must have been an impressive—probably even *beautiful*—arrangement of structures inside the three-kilometer-diameter cavern.

"Acknowledged," Styles replied promptly as Xi's eyebrows rose in surprise at the sheer scale of the watery ruins. Every twenty meters or so, on the flat roof sixty meters above *Elvira's* roof, were the 'roots' of unnatural stalactites a uniform three meters in diameter. Beneath those bases on the cavern floor before *Elvira*, were the crumbling bones of what must have been breathtaking ivory-white constructions that likely stretched more than three-quarters of the way from the ceiling to the floor.

Like great, hollow fangs, the stalactites looked to have had interior spaces large enough to comfortably house hundreds of humans, but now, after thousands of years of degradation, not a single one remained intact. Only a handful of rubble piles on the cavern floor featured pieces large enough to suggest the original size and shape of the stalactites. For most of the rubble piles, just chips and shards of white bony-looking material rested beneath each of the fixture points on the cavern's roof.

Without tidal forces to tug at them or current drawing water over the rubble piles, they had rested untouched for thousands of years before Vorr diving drones had come down to extract their all-important secrets.

Xi had the distinct impression she was walking through a graveyard and took care not to disturb the piles any more than absolutely necessary. For all she knew, this cavern represented the final tomb of a species that had been killed by Jemmin's machinations thousands of years ago. It was sobering to think that humanity might have shared their fate if not for the keen foresight of General Akinouye and the unyielding determination of his Metalheads.

Despite her care, Xi was unable to avoid disturbing one such pile. She was dismayed to see her mechs' prop-wash had cast most of that pile outward in a billowing chalky cloud that left just a tiny fraction of larger, more intact bony shards in their original resting place.

Silently cursing herself for her clumsiness, she was glad to see that Commander Ulbricht's subs had already risen high enough above the cavern floor to avoid disturbing the debris piles.

"I've got something over here, Major," Quinn called after navigating *Black Widow* to the far side of the cavern to an area that was completely devoid of the white stalactites' unnerving remains. Xi focused *Elvira's* sensors on the patch of cavern floor Quinn had indicated and began to nod her head in agreement.

Xi raised Styles. "Chief, I think Quinn just found your first dig site."

"Agreed, Major," Styles concurred as his submarine adjusted course to investigate the debris on the far side of the cavern. Elvira's computer examined the rubble and virtually reconstructed its original appearance in a matter of seconds, revealing it to have been a hemispherical arrangement of hexagons and pentagons, like the surface of a soccer ball. "It looks like some kind of collection array...I'm not familiar with the materials used, but the configuration seems consistent with the receiver array of a sonar system."

"What do you think they were looking for, Chief?" Xi asked.

"Probably high-energy particles of some kind," Styles said uncertainly. "But without a computer core as powerful as the *Bonhoeffer's*, we're going to need days or possibly even weeks to come up with a reasonable idea of this thing's purpose."

"We don't have *weeks*, Chief," Xi said sourly, knowing that both Colonel Moon and Colonel Jenkins had ordered her to clandestinely gather as much information on the Vorr objective as possible without compromising the integrity of the operation. No matter what she found, she was to bring the Vorr pods back to the surface and prepare them for transfer, but she intended to dig up as much information as possible while Deep Dive was down there.

"I'm sorry, Major," Styles said grimly. "We're dealing with too many variables. Some of the materials used here are nonstandard for any tech familiar to Republic scientists, and despite this thing's similarity to rudimentary high-energy particle sensors, we aren't even sure that's what it was built for. It's like putting together a jigsaw from the reverse side. We can do it, but it's going to take a lot more time than usual."

"Understood, Chief," she said stiffly. "You're on the clock. I want as much as possible brought back to the surface, and we don't delay one second after the last Vorr pod is secured."

"Copy that," he acknowledged as his sub slowly moved over to the ruined device. "I'm guessing that the Vorr already took this thing's data storage systems. I'll focus on retrieving a few of the better-preserved collector panel fragments."

"You're the egghead," Xi quipped with a lopsided grin, knowing that just a few years earlier she, too, had been a self-described 'egghead.' She briefly wondered just how much further from that imprisoned young girl she would move as she continued to grow within the Metal Legion. *"Black Widow, Land Shark,* spread out and investigate the cavern. Let's see if we can help narrow down the points of interest."

"Yes, ma'am," replied both Jocks in tandem.

"I still don't understand," Penny muttered over *Elvira's* cabin comm channel, "how a species could just self-destruct like this."

"Jemmin wielded significant influence," Xi offered. "But just because a theory fits the facts doesn't make it right. There are always more facts out there than the ones we can see, and some of them might crush our precious theories as surely as this depth would crush your skull if you went outside for a swim, Squeaker."

"I understand that, but I don't," Penny said, sounding deflated. "Thank you, ma'am." Penny breathed a sigh of relief, drawing a laugh from Lu farther back in the cabin. Since General Akinouye's death, Xi Bao had dug deep for every bit of tradition she could find in the Metal Legion's annals. Apparently, 'Squeaker' was meant to invoke inadequate lubrication between a fresh Metalhead and her surroundings, and the term was one which the old man had employed extensively during his youth.

Xi Bao had come to admire, respect, and even idolize two men in her life. The first was Colonel Lee Jenkins, who had plucked her from a life of imprisonment and given her a chance to not only be free but to be *herself* while contributing to the betterment of humanity. In a very narrow way, he was an uncle-father she suspected she would never fully deserve.

The second idol in her young life was General Benjamin Akinouye. The old man epitomized everything that was the Metal Legion: honor, integrity, savagery, shrewdness, and above all, independence. He had never compromised himself or the Legion, and had only ever employed either in service to humanity...and he had done so with *style*.

"All right, Deep Dive," Xi echoed over the local channel. "Let's get what we came for and head back to the surface. Be careful not to disturb the ruins. This cavern might hold the last traces of a long-dead species. Treat it like your mother's grave," she added, hoping her words of caution hit the mark. Having no mother of her own, Xi Bao was uncertain if the expressed sentiment was the correct one.

For the next two-and-a-half hours, Deep Dive worked to extricate Vorr cargo pods from their retrieval drones' death clutches. Styles managed to recover two more handfuls of artifacts, some of which appeared to have once featured some kind of data storage capability.

With the deed done and their salvage in tow, Deep Dive came about and marched back down the twelve-kilometer tunnel that had provided access. Two other tunnels adjoined the chamber, but both of them had collapsed (probably by Vorr efforts, in Xi's estimation), which left the Terrans no choice but to return to the ocean, where Jemmin and Terran forces continued to battle for control of the shoreline.

10

AN INCISIVE STROKE

"*Vercingetorix* Ground Control to Clover Actual," Podsy called down to Colonel Jenkins after completing his latest round of modifications to the sensor ping system. He'd come up with a plan that just might tilt the field in the Legion's favor, and every second that ticked by decreased that plan's effectiveness.

"Go ahead, GC," Jenkins promptly replied.

"I've been refining the ping system up here and going over our available ordnance," Podsy explained eagerly. "I think I can give you a fifty-fifty shot at scratching one of those Poltergeists, but it'll be costly. I'm forwarding the brief now under the heading 'Birdshot.'"

"Packet received," Jenkins acknowledged, and silent seconds stretched into two minutes without reply.

As Podsy waited, the hawk-like gaze of Lieutenant Commander Stravinsky seemed to find him every three or four seconds. He had already gone over some of his plan's details with Colonel Moon who, despite Stravinsky's objections, had authorized the latest batch of modifications to the *Vercingetorix's* sensor grid. It seemed like every passing hour on the *Vercingetorix's* bridge increased the tension in what seemed to be a contest of wills between the ship's XO and its Ground Control Officer.

It was a fight Podsy had no desire to lose, but he was more interested in executing the mission than winning the office politics war.

"GC, this is Clover Actual," Jenkins finally replied.

"Go ahead, Colonel," Podsy acknowledged.

"Looks good to me," Jenkins said, causing Podsy to silently pump his fist. "Give us three minutes, and we'll be in position to execute Birdshot."

"Birdshot in three," Podsy declared, holding up a trio of fingers for Colonel Moon and Commander Stravinsky to see. They each acknowledged with a silent nod before moving to prepare the Metal Legion's various sections for what was to come. Colonel Moon, in particular, got on the line with Captain Guan of the *Red Hare* and quickly secured his support for the upcoming maneuver.

The rest of the bridge crew scurried about at a brisk pace to prep for Birdshot, and this particular operation was Podsy's brainchild. Hundreds of Metalheads, representatives of all seven Terran Colonies, were now moving in unison on what were essentially his orders.

It was a humbling moment for the lifelong ne'er-do-well who knew that they were about to fire an extremely expensive shot at the enemy. If that shot hit, the Metalheads might cut the Jemmin force on the Pearl in half.

If they missed, they'd be open to counterattack from any lurking Jemmin warships in the area.

"Leave it all on the deck," Podsy muttered. He firmly believed that the best defense was a good offense, which was why he had not been shy about emptying the *Red Hare*'s surface-capable arsenal for this particular maneuver.

To Podsy, the most shocking part was that both Captain

Guan and Colonel Moon agreed it was a good idea.

"Birdshot in thirty seconds," Podsy called as the *Red Hare*'s weapon ports opened and a flight of heavily-armored rocket-driven missiles slipped their moorings and drifted away from the warship. "Sensors, prime the transceivers."

"Transceivers priming," Sensors replied as Colonel Jenkins' mechs suddenly broke formation at a sprint, moving to assume optimal position for Birdshot.

"*Red Hare*'s missiles are hot," Podsy confirmed after a brief check of telemetry. The *Red Hare*'s thirty-six missiles suddenly surged forward, leaping toward the surface of the planet as their warheads went active. Two of those missiles were one-megaton deep-penetration devices capable of destroying subterranean infrastructure as far down as ten kilometers. The other thirty-four were smaller nukes ranging from twenty to fifty kilotons.

All of the missiles were heavily-armored, and each would take a concerted interceptor effort to bring down before they delivered their payloads.

The key to this maneuver was to ensure that the megaton-yield missiles survived long enough to issue low-altitude EMPs rather than deliver their destructive energies deep into the planet's crust, where they could potentially cause a fatal cave-in of the tunnels Deep Dive currently navigated.

"Missile impact in twelve seconds," Podsy called as the *Red Hare*'s missiles drove steadily toward the planet's surface. He had isolated ten likely hiding holes, and targeted each one with a small nuke while spreading the rest of the *Red Hare*'s missiles over an area of nearly five hundred square kilometers. "Pings to follow three seconds after impact," Podsy said, making eye contact with Sensors and receiving a confirmatory nod in reply. The missiles picked up speed once they penetrated the upper atmosphere. "Impact in five...four...three...two...one...flash!"

To Lee Jenkins, for the briefest of moments, it seemed as though the maw of hell had opened to consume the entirety of Pearl and everyone on it.

Thirty-six nuclear warheads went off in near-perfect unison, the two largest bursting a full kilometer above the Pearl's surface while the rest touched off on the dead gray surface of the inhospitable planet.

The Clover Razorbacks were heavily hardened against EMPs, but given the nature of these particular EMPs, even *Warcrafter's* systems were temporarily affected.

He lost a precious half-second to sensor failure, but when their feeds resumed, he saw that Captain Chao had already sent a storm of missiles at the suddenly-exposed fleet of thirty-two enemy vehicles.

Vehicles that included one incredibly juicy-looking Poltergeist.

"Engage target," Jenkins barked as the Poltergeist's location was highlighted for his new Jock.

"Firing," Hammer replied, sending a tungsten bolt streaking through the Pearl's sweltering atmosphere. The railgun strike landed a second after three of Captain Chao's mechs slammed into the mighty Jemmin command vehicle's starboard flank. Missiles tore through the air, seeking to finish the Poltergeist off, but the Jemmin commander would not go down so easily.

The Poltergeist sent a wave of counterfire skyward, scratching all but four Terran SRMs. Two of those SRMs missed the Poltergeist entirely, and another managed a near-miss that sprayed rocky debris across the Jemmin command vehicle's port flank. Just a single SRM struck the Poltergeist squarely, but luckily for Jenkins and his people, it hit the Jemmin right up the proverbial tailpipe.

The Poltergeist, which had been accelerating toward four hundred kilometers per hour, faltered and skidded along the rocky surface of the Pearl. As it struggled to recover, every single Clover mech unleashed high-speed weapons and artillery on its position.

The weight of fire on the briefly-hobbled hovertank was precise, intense, and thoroughly devastating.

The first four shells slammed down on the Poltergeist's roof in rapid succession, knocking it off-course and causing the fifth shell to near-miss, while the sixth hammered into the Poltergeist's bow.

Nine more high-explosive shells rained down on the Poltergeist in the ensuing four seconds, with eleven others missing off the Jemmin bow as the hovertank's slowed movement slowed to a snail's pace.

Jenkins' mechs cratered the ground before the Poltergeist in a beautiful textbook line that had correctly anticipated the Jemmin vehicle's course. Had the Poltergeist continued its run, it would have suffered more than just thirteen direct hits and a handful of near-misses.

As it was, thirteen was *not* the Poltergeist's lucky number.

The hovertank's motive systems failed spectacularly, causing it to collapse to the ground mere seconds before another volley of Clover artillery screamed through the air. When the explosive shells descended upon the hapless Poltergeist, Jenkins almost felt sorry for the beleaguered vehicle and its Jemmin operator.

"Almost." Jenkins smirked as the first shell tore into the battered hovertank. "But not quite."

The wave of ordnance annihilated the Poltergeist, only four shells near-missing and the rest splashing down into the growing crater of debris that less than a minute earlier had been one of the most fearsome vehicles ever fielded in Nexus Space.

"Poltergeist neutralized," Jenkins declared with relish as Clover's mechs, supported by missile fire from Joker Company at base camp, moved to engage thirty smaller Jemmin vehicles. Nine Spectres and twenty-one skimmers, suddenly faltering and thrown into disarray just as Lieutenant Podsednik had anticipated, lay visible following the high-risk, high-reward exposure method employed by the *Vercingetorix's* Ground Control Officer. "This is Clover Actual. All vehicles are weapons-free. Engage targets," Jenkins called as the first Joker missiles erased a pair of skimmers from the board.

Railguns stabbed and artillery rained on the fragmented Jemmin vehicles, which slowly resumed something approaching disciplined coordination and started to scatter in the face of the Terran barrage.

"Good work, Podsy," Jenkins muttered under his breath as he worked to forward fire packages to Clover's Jocks. "One Poltergeist down, one to go," he added, watching a Spectre fall to Captain Chao's railgun.

Podsy raised Joker Company's Trebuchet-class mech. "*Sargon*, I need a Purgatory at the following coordinates."

"Purgatory on the way," *Sargon* replied as one of the specialty missiles tore loose from its moorings and flew toward the indicated target zone.

"*Cyclops*," Podsy continued, switching over to the individual mech's comm line as he identified a likely flight point for a Jemmin Spectre, "send a plasma bolt to this location."

"Slow and steady...on the way," Blinky acknowledged as his mech belched a bolt of superheated plasma toward the target zone. Podsy had no illusions about the slow-moving projectile actually hitting the Spectre, but he didn't need it to hit. He just needed it to splash down on that point at that moment.

"Captain Chao," Podsy raised Clover's 2nd Company CO while transmitting a likely path for the Spectre to take as it sought to evade *Cyclops'* inbound plasma fire, "hold your Company's railgun fire for twelve more seconds and put eyes on this corridor while splashing artillery at the indicated coordinates."

A brief but meaningful delay preceded Chao's reply. "Copy that, GC."

For a glorious moment, Podsy watched as the perfectly-coordinated storm of fire he had just orchestrated herded six Jemmin vehicles into the kill-zone. Sargon's Purgatory-class missile ignited an inferno that was visible to the naked eye from the *Vercingetorix's* position, spreading a ring of smoke and fire out from the northern edge of the kill-zone. He couldn't stop himself from jumping up in elation as the plasma fire splashed down, driving the Jemmin vehicles into a surprisingly straight line stretching five kilometers from front to back.

"I've got 'em lined up like Rockettes!" Podsy declared as Captain Chao's railguns stabbed into the Jemmin hovercraft one after another.

Two skimmers fell to the first wave of fire, along with a Spectre. Two more skimmers managed to avoid instant death under Clover's guns, but Colonel Jenkins' mechs finished them off before they could scatter. The last vehicle in the short-lived line, a Spectre, returned fire and got a lucky strike on one of Chao's Razorbacks.

Podsy's exhilaration was dashed by the Clover casualty and further diminished by the dual silent rebukes from Colonel Moon and Commander Stravinsky. The latter he couldn't have cared less about, but the former stung. Moon's disapproving look was precisely the same as Podsy's father had given him growing up. At that moment, Andy Podsednik was six years old again and in trouble for one of his countless ill-conceived misadventures.

Thankfully the moment passed, and he was able to resume focus on the task at hand. "*Sargon*," he called down as the Jemmin vehicles sent a hail of missiles at the Clover mechs, which replied with anti-missile rockets while filling the sky with coil-gun fire. "I need another Purgatory at the following coordinates."

"Purgatory on the way," *Sargon* replied, loosing the second of his mechs' prized Purgatory-class missiles.

"*Cyclops*," Podsy continued, eyeing the plasma-cannon-armed mech's slower-than-expected recharge data, "what's the status of your HPC?"

"Capacitor Two isn't taking a full charge," Blinky replied tersely. "I'll need an additional eighteen seconds per cycle until I get it under control."

"Discharge the entire capacitor, Blinky," Podsy immediately commanded, knowing that Cyclops would be useless for this coming volley if it needed eighteen more seconds to fire. Better to get the system back on spec ASAP than the limp along at such a deficit. "After you've got it down to less than three percent charge, reverse polarity in the shunt's control system. The contacts must have gotten thrown out of alignment from the cannon's recoil; you'll buy yourself a few more shots at optimum if you clear the system. If you don't clear it, you run the risk of welding the contacts and overloading the feeds."

A pregnant pause preceded the data feeds showing that Blinky had done precisely as Podsy had directed. "Capacitor discharged, and the shunt's been cleared. Two's now accepting a full charge. Thanks for the tip, Ground Control," Staubach said gratefully. "We'll keep that one on file."

"Any time, *Cyclops*," Podsy replied, glad to find that literally hundreds of hours poring over technical specifications and Metalhead maintenance logs had finally paid off. "Have Captain Koch take a look at the system ASAP. If the contacts are out of alignment, that's a sign of significant structural damage. They'll need to be manually repaired or the whole system will fail in another eight or ten shots."

"Copy that, GC," Blinky agreed as the Joker and Clover mechs took full advantage of the coordinated efforts Podsy had overseen, engaging and scrubbing another trio of enemy hardware while suffering not a single loss in the exchange.

For Podsy, what came next was a moment of realization he knew would change his life forever...

He was conducting a major battle, and despite Commander Stravinsky's persistent disapproval, he was doing a damned fine job of it!

"Clover Battalion," Jenkins called after all thirty-one of the exposed vehicles including the first Poltergeist, had been scratched from the irradiated battlefield that had been lit up with nuclear fire mere minutes earlier, "pull back to previous positions and resume missile defense posture."

All of Clover's Razorbacks signaled acknowledgment of the orders as they returned to their previous positions. When the battalion was back in order, Jenkins initiated a P2P with Captain Chao.

"Go ahead, Clover Actual," Chao promptly replied.

"I need a report on your unit's status, Captain," Jenkins said firmly, referring to 2nd Company's previous failure to maintain an airtight missile shield. It was a failure that had already cost them as many as two mechs, and possibly a third since the lone loss suffered in Podsy's wildly successful Birdshot maneuver might not have been hit if the previous two had not fallen.

"The situation is under control, Colonel," Chao reported. "Shield integrity will be at or above optimum from this point on, sir. You have my word."

"Not good enough, Captain," Jenkins snapped. "We've lost people because of 2nd Company's hiccups. Rendezvous at these coordinates in two minutes," he ordered, forwarding a location to Captain Chao and to *Warcrafter's* new Jock. "I expect a detailed report immediately upon your arrival at *Warcrafter*."

"Understood, sir," Chao replied stiffly as both mechs sprinted toward the indicated meeting area.

Jenkins had carefully considered the issue since it had first presented itself, and had deduced that the only viable response was to have a face to face with Captain Chao. Chao had done the same with the officer at fault for compromising 2nd Company's missile shield, so despite Jenkins generally disapproval of face-to-face meetings on the battlefield, he suspected that doing so would pay dividends in this particular instance.

There was too much at stake and too many variables in play to let the Terra Han Colonial Guard transfers be given free rein. That included the undeniably talented and seemingly loyal Captain Chao, at least until Jenkins was satisfied that the group could be counted on for the remainder of Operation Watery Grave.

The identical Razorback Mark II-Vs converged, and Captain Chao disembarked his mech before making his way to *Warcrafter's* airlock. A few seconds after Jenkins opened the outer door for his Battalion XO, the inner door cycled and Captain Chao entered *Warcrafter's* cabin wearing a self-contained enviro-helmet over his field uniform.

Chao removed the helmet and tucked it under his arm before saluting. "Captain Chao, reporting as ordered, Colonel."

"At ease, Captain." Jenkins grunted. "Let's cut through it: why did 2nd Company previously fail to maintain its missile shield?"

"Sir," Chao said, standing at ease and making brief eye contact before turning his gaze to the bulkhead behind Jenkins, "I take full responsibility for—"

"Stop right there, Captain," Jenkins snapped. "I don't have time for political word-mincing. I'm too old to spend my time parsing meaning from people's duplicitous words. I'll ask again, and I expect a forthright and blunt reply to my question if you can manage it. Why did 2nd Company fail to maintain its missile shield?"

Chao briefly faltered, his eyes moving uncertainly to meet Jenkins' for several seconds before his brow lowered. "Sir, it was my fault. I hadn't properly prepared my officers for the mission. I take full responsibility for Lieutenant Hao's...misaligned priorities."

"Now we're getting somewhere." Jenkins glowered. "Details, Captain."

"Sir..." Chao hesitated before stiffening his spine. "Permission to speak frankly?"

"I'm pretty sure I just *ordered* you to speak frankly, Captain," Jenkins said in a warning tone.

"Colonel, I'm not convinced that everyone who transferred over from the Terra Han Colonial Guard is trustworthy," Chao said, surprising Jenkins with both his frankness and the implications of his words.

"Go on, Captain," Jenkins said, failing to mask his interest.

"I don't think we have any active problems, sir," Chao explained, meeting and holding Jenkins' gaze unflinchingly as he spoke, "but I do think that THCG High Command sent us some of their best and, unfortunately, some of their worst. Lieutenant Hao is one or the other, and if I'm being forthright, I'm not yet sure which she is."

"You have my attention, Captain Chao," Jenkins stated.

"Lieutenant Hao is clearly aware of THCG High Command's desire to transfer as many ranking officers to TAC as possible in an effort to seize some measure of control over the Metal Legion," Chao explained. "She's an ambitious officer, sir, but her loyalties have been divided...until *very* recently," he added with a knowing look.

"Details, Captain," Jenkins growled, rolling his finger to encourage his XO to be more forthcoming.

Chao hesitated before producing a small cryonics cylinder from his jacket's left side pocket. It was the kind of canister used to retrieve wounded soldiers' lost fingers, eyes, or the like from the field for later reattachment.

Jenkins' brow lowered thunderously. He did *not* like where this was heading.

"Lieutenant Hao has a lucrative athletic career awaiting her after her service is concluded, Colonel," Chao explained, holding the thirty-centimeter-long cylinder before himself. "But she was insubordinate, and that insubordination likely cost the lives of at least three of her fellow servicemen. In accordance with Terra Han Colonial Guard military law, and as a gesture of contrition that her CO accepts as valid, she surrendered the first digits of both feet rather than be relieved of duty for her failure."

Jenkins' eyes narrowed as they came to rest on the canister. He could hardly believe what he was hearing. It was so unexpected and so barbaric that he felt compelled to clarify. "You're saying that you cut off her big toes as punishment for insubordination?"

"Yes, sir," Captain Chao affirmed. "And since these wounds were suffered as punishment for insubordination, both Terra Han and TAC regulations prohibit surgical repair or rehabilitation efforts to be provided without the express approval of at least three members above her in the chain of command."

"I'm not sure..." Jenkins seethed, "that the TAC military code aligns with your...*liberal* interpretation, Captain Chao. But regardless of what the lawyers might think," he shook his head damningly, "I assure you that I'm... I want to say disappointed, but honestly, I'm at a total loss for words to describe how thoroughly *disturbed* I am by your chosen method of redress here, Captain. This is the kind of thing that warrants immediate suspension from active duty and the instigation of a formal inquiry."

Chao winced just barely enough that Jenkins could see it. "Yes, sir," he acknowledged stiffly.

"I'd relieve you of duty, *Captain*," Jenkins continued, "but we're under fire here, and more hangs in the balance than I can afford to jeopardize at the moment. Let me assure you, Captain," Jenkins shook his head disapprovingly, "that you and I will revisit this issue at the earliest post-op convenience. Is that clear?"

"As a Solarian's conscience, sir," Chao said, drawing a soft snort from Alice who, until that moment, had seemed invisible at the back of the compartment. Chao went slightly red-faced when he realized his faux pas but kept his head high as Jenkins gestured toward the door.

"You're dismissed, Captain. But leave the evidence here," he said, gesturing for Chao to put the canister on a nearby shelf.

Chao complied, offering a salute before turning crisply, replacing his helmet, and departing *Warcrafter* through the airlock.

After he had left, Alice laughed softly. Jenkins turned to face her and saw mixed amusement and concern on the woman's face. It was a bizarre expression, and it took him so much by surprise that his initial irritation at her laughter was replaced by curiosity. "Do you have something to say, Alice?" he asked levelly.

"Captain Chao understands his people, Colonel Jenkins," she replied serenely. "We Solarians have studied the various branches of Terran humanity with great fascination these past decades.

"Like scientists observing monkeys?" Jenkins quipped, still chafing at being repeatedly referred to as 'aboriginal' during his interrogation on Luna.

Alice shook her head dismissively, ignoring the barb while continuing, "One of the things that continues to bewilder us is just how little you understand one another. So many fundamental facets of your disparate societies are identical, and so many of your greatest differences are far more superficial than you seem willing to admit."

"You think lopping a subordinate's limbs off on the battlefield is a 'superficial' difference between Terran military organizations?" Jenkins scoffed.

"I think that corporal punishment, including dismemberment, no longer carries the same significance or permanence that it once did," she replied matter-of-factly. "I also think that Terra Han culture draws heavily on historical methods of intervention, and most of those interventions are based on admittedly crude ancient practices. But, much as the people of Sol might dislike the notion, sometimes the old ways truly are best."

Alice's revelation surprised Jenkins enough to raise his eyebrows. "You're saying you approve of corporal punishments like this?" He gestured to the cryonic canister.

"Certainly." She nodded with conviction. "Especially when they are primarily superficial in their *actual* costs while retaining the balance of their perceptual significance. The removal of a person's toes was once a lifelong debilitation. But now? The cost to repair or even replace such appendages is less than one year's salary for a military serviceman. And for a woman with a five-year contract at ten times that annual earning power awaiting her upon discharge from military service, the cost to rehabilitate her feet is inconsequential from her perspective. *Especially* if it means that punishing her in this manner results in the saving of even one more life by refocusing her on the task at hand."

Jenkins had to fight to keep his jaw from falling open in shock at what he was hearing, but he managed to get his emotions under control long enough to consider the situation more carefully. As he did so, he grudgingly came to admit (if only to himself) that there was something to Chao's and Alice's perspective.

"The most sublime facet of the young captain's response," Alice continued blithely, "is that even if Lieutenant Hao chooses to pay for the surgical repairs, she cannot qualify for them under Terra Han law without the approval of her superiors within the Terran Armor Corps. She was ready to discharge in six months, Colonel, at which point she would resume her professional athletic career. If she ever wants to achieve her dream..." Her voice trailed off pointedly, drawing a scowl from Jenkins since she clearly meant for him to finish the thought.

He eventually decided to oblige her, although his scowl barely lightened as he spoke. "If she ever wants to play professional ball again, the only path to that dream is to do her utmost under Chao's command until her term of service is fulfilled."

Alice nodded approvingly. "Which means that for at *least* the next six months, she will perform to the upper limits of her ability. Either because she wishes to return to her athletic career, or because she has decided that her military service is more important and deserves her full attention."

Jenkins snorted derisively. "You think she'll re-up after losing her toes?"

"I think you are a fine commander and an even better man, Leeroy Jenkins," Alice said, her lips curling into a bemused smile he found less than amusing. "I also think you have much to learn about fundamental human nature...or, perhaps," she allowed, issuing another of her bewitching laughs as she finished, "merely about *feminine* nature."

"You make that sound like it's a bad thing." He grunted, drawing a half-snort, half-chuckle from Hammer in the pilot's chair.

"If you think that, you have more to learn than I thought."

Try as he might, Jenkins was unable to come up with a worthy retort, so he conceded the exchange to Alice and returned his attention to the tactical plotter.

Where it belonged.

11

BUBBLING UP

"Deep Dive, this is Joker Actual," Xi declared as they neared the end of the aquatic tunnel. "Anticipate hostile presence at the tunnel mouth. *Black Widow*, you're on point, with *Elvira* in support. Bubble up and identify targets for Commander Ulbricht's torpedoes."

"*Black Widow* on point," Quinn acknowledged, driving her mech toward the tunnel mouth while Xi moved *Elvira* to support the egress. What had begun as a nerve-wracking underwater excursion had somehow become almost fun to Xi. The constant threat of immediate death via crushing water pressure was far from amusing, but the tactical limitations imposed by their underwater arsenal were stimulating in the extreme. Xi found her mind leaping from one tactical manipulation to another as she considered how to exploit their strengths while limiting their weaknesses.

The trio of mechs and their three escorted submarines moved steadily down the passage, *Black Widow* pulling farther and farther ahead of the formation to reach the tunnel mouth first.

Once there, Quinn waited. *Elvira* was thirty seconds behind her, and those thirty seconds proved to be among the fiercest in Xi Bao's young career.

"Multiple contacts!" Quinn declared as *Black Widow's* neural feeds displayed twenty new enemy icons arrayed just beyond the Vorr auto-defenses' range.

"Get clear of the entry and put up interceptors, Quinn," Xi barked, pushing *Elvira* as fast as she could go as *Black Widow*'s buoyancy systems activated and the mech slowly floated up from the tunnel mouth. As it did so, a storm of forty inbound torpedoes surged toward the tunnel mouth while their authors sped close behind. Five Spectres and sixteen skimmers, which were spread out in a faint crescent, rapidly converged behind their wall of underwater ordnance.

"Interceptors away," Quinn declared after sending eight individual interceptor mines identical to those Xi had used in the previous submarine engagement. As the balloon-buoyed interceptors floated up and out from the tunnel mouth, they spread out to form a wall of explosives capable of destroying all of the enemy torpedoes if they arrived in unison.

Unfortunately, their Jemmin adversary was aware of that fact.

The wave of torpedoes, which had previously moved in a collapsing crescent identical in proportion to the one made by their firing vehicles, suddenly faltered. Some of the torpedoes surged ahead even faster, while others greatly reduced their speeds. In just eight seconds, what had been a perfect line of enemy ordnance became a scattered cloud.

With such a staggered volley inbound, it was unlikely that Quinn's wall of interceptors would neutralize more than a quarter of them. And if even one of those torpedoes carried a ten-kiloton warhead, the entire tunnel would collapse and everyone in Deep Dive would be consigned to a watery grave.

Fortunately for the Terrans, the remaining Vorr auto-defenses sprang into action. Laser beams swept across the inbound ordnance, killing torpedo after torpedo from the wave of fire. Even with the refraction issues caused by the highly saline water, the Vorr lasers were somehow able to deliver enough energy into the inbound torpedo chassis' to destroy their targets outright.

But that took several seconds of sustained beam contact per torpedo, and Xi watched helplessly as the Jemmin vehicles surged forward with their own beams stabbing into Vorr positions. For that moment, Xi saw the conflict in which Terra had become embroiled as functionally the same as Deep Dive's: the Terrans fought to retrieve critically important intelligence while the Vorr and Jemmin battled for control of the sky over their heads.

She wondered at that moment if Terra was destined to be nothing more than a pawn in this high-stakes game between the opposed superpowers of Nexus Space.

That particular thought sharpened her mind, snapping her focus to the task at hand.

"I'm *nobody's* pawn," she growled as *Elvira* neared the tunnel mouth.

Before she could emerge from the passage, *Black Widow*'s wall of intercepting mines went off one by one. Eleven torpedoes were scratched by the minefield, while twice as many more were destroyed by Vorr counterfire.

Which left seven torpedoes streaking through the falling debris of their predecessors.

"Ulbricht, you have your targets," Xi snapped, knowing she couldn't afford to wait. "Fire all torpedoes now. Fire! Fire! Fire!" *Elvira* was still in the tunnel and could potentially be hit by friendly fire as the American torpedoes shot past her, but she would rather risk getting hit by the American Navy torpedoes than to allow the enemy fire to rain down on her without reply.

"Firing," Commander Ulbricht acknowledged, and a dozen torpedoes sped up the tunnel at Xi's back. Xi would have been ashamed to admit that she bit her lip bloody in those tense seconds before the American ordnance mercifully drove past *Elvira* and leapt out of the tunnel mouth. "Torpedoes away," Ulbricht declared.

As the American torpedoes swam upward, they latched onto their targets and moved to intercept at top speed. Xi knew it would be close, but she had no choice. The enemy had gotten the drop on them with a picture-perfect underwater ambush. Merely surviving would be both a major success and a minor miracle.

Ulbricht's torpedoes intercepted their Jemmin counterparts, with all twelve detonating in rapid succession near their targets. Of the seven remaining Jemmin torpedoes, five were scratched, one was knocked off-course and took a new trajectory toward the surface, and the last torpedo streaked through the water and struck *Black Widow* in the stern.

It exploded violently, rending metal and freeing a cloud of atmosphere to bubble through the explosion on its way to the surface.

Xi snarled in frustration at having lost the mech and its crew. The direct hit had destroyed the mech's entire rear compartment, the place that contained ammo and capacitors, but strangely the capacitors did not fail as energetically as she would have guessed.

"*Elvira, Black Widow,*" Quinn's beautiful, defiant voice came over the comm. "We're at critical here. All personnel are in the cockpit behind the pressure wall, but it's not rated for these depths."

"Dump your torps and deploy your floats, Quinn," Xi urged. "You've done your part down here."

"Copy that, Major," Quinn replied, sending eight fresh torpedoes out at the diminished line of enemy vehicles. "Deploying emergency buoys," she added, sending eight inflatable balloons up from compartments. The balloons rapidly expanded, lifting *Black Widow* up from the ocean floor. They took the battered mech back up to the surface while the rest of Deep Dive continued the battle.

As *Black Widow*'s torpedoes accelerated toward the heart of the scattered enemy formation, *Elvira* prepped six of her own. Beams continued to lance back and forth between the Vorr placements and the Jemmin vehicles, which now numbered four Spectres and ten skimmers.

By firing her torpedoes, Xi was gambling that the Jemmin had already fired all of their underwater ordnance and were now down to beams. Her mechs were designed to soak up damage from beams and other varied weapons, but dealing with the crushing force of deep water that followed every torpedo strike was something they were decidedly *not* designed for.

She was banking on the Jemmin lasers being less dangerous to her mechs than their torpedoes, but torpedoes were her sole offensive weapons in the aquatic environment. To hold them in reserve as defensive systems was to act like prey.

Xi Bao was many things, some of which were objectionable or even shameful, but prey was not one of them.

"Torpedoes away," she declared when *Elvira* finally breached the tunnel mouth and moved to the left, firing her six prepped torpedoes as the Jemmin skimmers intercepted all but two of *Black Widow*'s inbound eight . One of those two torpedoes landed a direct hit against a skimmer, while another near-missed a Spectre with enough delivered force to briefly stun the large Jemmin vehicle.

That momentary break in its maneuvering proved lethal as three Vorr beams stabbed into its hull before it could resume its locomotion. The Spectre exploded violently, sending a cloud of expanding gas bubbling up to the surface as the vehicle's ceramic-composite hull fragments floated to the ocean floor.

"*Land Shark*," Xi called to the last of her three mechs as Commander Ulbricht's subs began to emerge from the tunnel. "Empty your tubes as soon as you reach the tunnel mouth."

"Copy that, Major," Cervantes acknowledged as *Elvira's* six torpedoes closed with the enemy.

"Commander Ulbricht," Xi continued, snarling as five of her torpedoes were intercepted by Jemmin beams, while the sixth maintained course long enough to near-miss a skimmer to little effect. "You are weapons free."

"Incoming!" declared Ulbricht as a fresh wave of twelve Jemmin torpedoes appeared on the sensor grid.

Xi set her jaw. Even if the dwindling Vorr defenses, down to four permanent placements, intercepted ten of the enemy weapons, this was going to hurt.

A lot.

"All hands, brace for impact," Xi ordered as Vorr beams stabbed into the Jemmin torpedoes, slowly scratching them one by one while Jemmin beams carved into the fixed Vorr weapons. Two Vorr platforms went down in the exchange, but Commander Ulbricht's torpedoes surprisingly scratched a pair of Jemmin skimmers and one of the Spectres.

Try as they might, the Vorr defenses were unable to intercept all of the inbound torpedoes. Four of the Jemmin weapons sped toward the tunnel mouth.

Xi gritted her teeth, knowing it was unlikely her mech would survive a direct hit, let alone *four* of them.

But at the last instant, the torpedoes slightly adjusted course and drove down into the tunnel itself, where *Land Shark* had nearly emerged.

"Hold on!" Xi yelled helplessly as the torpedoes streaked into the tunnel one after another, with the fourth and final aquatic missile exploding against *Land Shark*'s already battered hull. The shockwave propelled it through the water, slamming into Xi's mech with sufficient force to cause several of her mech's pressure seals to fail.

The cabin was immediately filled with the hiss of spraying water, but Xi knew where her attention needed to remain. It was up to Lu and Penny to keep *Elvira* alive while she fought the enemy. It was up to Xi to deliver *Elvira's* deadly sting.

Xi didn't even need to see *Land Shark*'s data feed to know it had been destroyed with all hands. The tunnel mouth collapsed in on the mech, burying it in hundreds of tons of rubble and cutting the passage off from further exploration.

Strangely, as the crushing water threatened to violate *Elvira's* hull and deliver a lethal dose to her crew, what Xi focused on was the fact that the enemy had deemed *Elvira* unworthy of attention. They had instead sent three of their torpedoes streaking down the tunnel, where they would probably drive as far as their fuel stores permitted before detonating. That meant Jemmin thought there might still be something of value to be had down that hole.

It also suggested that Jemmin was confident it could destroy Deep Dive before its precious cargo could be returned to the Vorr.

Xi refocused on the battle, which had proceeded without her attention for several seconds as she processed *Land Shark*'s death and the circumstances surrounding it.

She was alarmed to find that the American subs had come under beam fire from the Jemmin vehicles, and one of the three subs was faltering. Xi briefly feared it was the sub bearing

Styles, but that fear was allayed when she saw that neither Styles' nor Ulbricht's vessel had taken damage.

Ulbricht's people sent a fresh storm of torpedoes at the remaining six enemy vehicles, which had scratched all but one of the Vorr auto-defensive placements. Even the damaged sub in the Deep Dive squadron managed to add two of its own aquatic missiles to the salvo, making an even ten torpedoes surging up to their suddenly fleeing Jemmin targets.

The Vorr auto-defenses delivered a critical hit on one of the fleeing skimmers, but for a moment it seemed as though the remaining vessels, one Spectre and four skimmers, would elude Ulbricht's fire.

Unfortunately for Jemmin, the American Navy proved worthy of its proud, storied legacy.

The American torpedoes suddenly sprinted as gas-powered thrusters augmented the propeller-driven platforms in pursuit of the automated vehicles. It was immediately clear that the American ordnance would intercept the Jemmin craft, and with single-minded unity, the five Jemmin vehicles came about to face their would-be killers.

Beams stabbed into torpedo hulls, four of which quickly failed, while the remaining six streaked toward their targets. A skimmer died from a direct hit and was joined by another that suffered a pair of near-misses. A third skimmer evaded its targeting torpedo entirely, while the fourth was unable to do the same and died after a direct strike.

The Spectre, largest of the Jemmin vehicles, poured its beams into the lone torpedo burning toward it. It seemed like it would keep its beams on the torpedo's nose long enough to destroy it, but the American weapon proved equal to the task and drove straight into the Spectre's flank, exploding on impact.

The Spectre's hull outgassed violently as crushing water assaulted it from all sides. The vehicle's robust armor shattered into thousands of tiny splinter-like fragments, each of which slowly drifted to the ocean floor below, while the parent vehicle split into three roughly-equal segments that slowly drifted to their final resting places.

The last Jemmin skimmer sped upward, intent on evading Terran fire and likely aiming to bring data records of the battle to the Jemmin operators on the surface.

Xi had no intention of allowing Jemmin to realize success with either objective.

Loading the last of her torpedoes, Xi loosed the twin devices and sent them in pursuit of the fast-fleeing vehicle. The Vorr beam stabbed upward, but it was operating at the upper limit of its range. The skimmer darted hither and thither, twisting and rolling as it increased the distance between itself and the last Vorr weapon platform. But each of its evasive maneuvers cost it valuable time, and Xi's torpedoes devoured the distance between them and their quarry. The pursuit persisted for a full minute, with the torpedoes slowly but surely closing the gap. Then, in a last-ditch evasive maneuver, the skimmer came about and tried to split the two weapons before they could arm and detonate.

It proved unequal to the daunting task and suffered a devastating near-miss explosion that rendered the vehicle inert.

Xi breathed a sigh of relief before realizing the hiss of water had not yet stopped in the cabin behind her. "How are we doing back there?" Xi asked tightly.

"Almost done with the last hole now, Major," Lu reported in a raised voice as he and Penny worked to inject the fast-hardening sealant into an access panel through which water continued to pour. "But we need to get surface-side ASAP. These patches are weak as shit."

Xi snorted approvingly. "Understood, Lu. Commander—" She was cut off when *Wolfsbane*, the flagging sub of Ulbricht's squadron, suffered a sudden and catastrophic hull failure. Like a tin can in a vice, the American Navy submarine was flattened by the enormous pressure, and Xi closed her eyes in silent acknowledgment of what had just happened.

During the pre-op briefing, Xi had come to learn that submariners were a special breed. Metalheads could usually, if not always, egress their vehicles if they sustained too much damage. Warship crews had escape pods to flee in if their ship fell to enemy fire. Even void pilots could eject and survive aboard their detached cockpits for hours or possibly days following the destruction of their craft in combat.

But submariners? The only time they would be in danger of losing their vehicle was when they were under so much pressure that there was nowhere they could escape *to*. When they went to exchange fire with the enemy, they knew precisely how hard their backs were up against the wall, and those crazy fuckers did it anyway, month after month, year after year.

"Ulbricht to Joker Actual," the Navy officer's unshaken voice came over the line as the destroyed sub fell gently to the ocean floor. "We're going to need a few minutes to retrieve the packages strapped to *Wolfsbane's* hull."

"Roger, Commander," Xi acknowledged. "My buoyancy systems are non-functional; I've got to slow-walk back to shore ASAP."

"Understood," Ulbricht replied smartly. "We'll stay down here to collect the packages."

"Acknowledged," Xi said before offering a silent prayer for both *Land Shark's* and *Wolfsbane's* crews. She wasn't generally prone to prayer of any kind, but the longer she served in the Metal Legion, the more relevant the practice became to her for reasons she could not rationally express.

Twenty minutes later, Commander Ulbricht's two remaining subs drove up from the ocean floor with all of the collected salvage strapped to their hulls. Xi knew the American Navy vessels would reach the surface an hour before she did, and she also knew she needed to tread carefully for these next few minutes to avoid re-opening *Elvira's* wounds.

With a slow and steady gait, the iconic Scorpion-class mech walked its way up the increasingly gentle slope leading to base camp at the salty water's edge.

12

POWER STRUGGLES

"Colonel Moon?" Podsy called as soon as he had finished running some calculations. "I've got an idea I'd like to run by you."

"XO," Moon said, gesturing for Lieutenant Commander Stravinsky to join him as he made his way to Podsy's Ground Control station. Stravinsky complied, slicing a frosty look Podsy's way before schooling her features into a professional mask. "What have you got?" Colonel Moon asked after arriving a few strides later.

"We know there's one more Poltergeist down there," Podsy explained, "and while it's possible there's more than that, I have to assume there's just the one."

"Based on what, Lieutenant?" Stravinsky challenged, adding the faintest emphasis on his rank.

"Based on the fact that even back at Shiva's Wrath," Podsy explained evenly, "there was only one Poltergeist on the entire planet. That operation, from Jemmin's perspective, included at least two priorities: first, preventing the Vorr from retrieving archeological salvage similar to what we're here to collect, and second, preventing the Legion from making diplomatic contact with the Vorr."

"You seem to have forgotten that the Zeen were also on Shiva's Wrath, Lieutenant Podsednik," Stravinsky said coolly.

"No, Commander." Podsy shook his head firmly. "I haven't forgotten that. But at the time, and based on what we've come to learn about Jemmin behavioral priorities," he turned a brief but pointed look at Colonel Moon, who made no gesture of acknowledgment before Podsednik continued, "we have every reason to believe that the Zeen's presence on Shiva's Wrath was a surprise to Jemmin.

"Bringing it back to the Poltergeists," he said, hoping to stifle another argument with the ship's XO, "if preventing archeo-tech from being retrieved *and* preventing the Terran Republic from conducting clandestine diplomacy with the Vorr was only worth a single Poltergeist, I doubt more than two were sent here."

"You might not have forgotten about the Zeen," Stravinsky smirked, "but you seem to have forgotten that the Jemmin sent a gatecrasher here."

"Again, no, ma'am," Podsy countered. "That gatecrasher was probably already en route to this system before Jemmin learned about the dig on the Pearl. Moving those things is no small task, and one of Jemmin's primary reasons for shutting down the wormholes was almost certainly so that it could send those gatecrashers to their various targets. Based on what we've learned of gatecrasher maneuverability, it would take *days* to send one from a Jemmin gate to this Vorr gate while matching velocity and rotation to the wormhole's event horizon."

Stravinsky made to object, but Moon grudgingly interrupted, "Fleet High Command concurs with your appraisal, Lieutenant."

"My theory," Podsy continued eagerly, "is that the Jemmin Poltergeists were sent here *after* Jemmin faltered at New

America 2, where the gatecrasher was destroyed by Admiral Wallace and the Zeen. Jemmin's all about efficiency, Commander," he added, fighting to keep the smugness he felt from creeping into his voice. "It wouldn't have sent two Poltergeists and their commanders to this world without good reason."

"Even assuming, for the sake of argument, that your theory checks out," Stravinsky allowed irritably, "what's your point, Lieutenant?"

"My point," Podsy replied, "is that we should consider removing that last Poltergeist as the top priority for this task force. We should devote every available resource toward that effort, and we should do so without delay."

Stravinsky's eyes narrowed direly. "What are you proposing?"

"I've run through the latest sensor diagnostics," Podsy explained, gesturing to a pair of nearby monitors that displayed the results of those tests. "At best, the *Vercingetorix* can make another five or six sensor pulses before our emitter array is fried. I'm proposing we remove the mods, return the system to a broad transmission, and use it to find that Poltergeist."

Stravinsky scoffed. "Narrowing the emissions is necessary if we want to cut through the Pearl's atmospheric and EM interference, Lieutenant Podsednik."

"From low orbit? Yes, ma'am." Podsy nodded with conviction. "You're absolutely right about that."

Stravinsky's eyes widened while the hint of a smile played at the edges of Moon's mouth. "You cannot be suggesting..." the Fleet officer scowled darkly "...that we take the *Vercingetorix* down to the Pearl's surface?"

"I'm not proposing any direct contact with the planet, Commander," Podsy retorted with a grin. "But on standard settings, our ship's sensors will work just fine to locate that

Poltergeist with up to a kilometer of atmosphere between them and the target."

Stravinsky shook her head adamantly. "Taking a warship, even one designed for limited atmospheric deployment like the *Vercingetorix*, that close to a planetary surface violates at least seven major regulations governing Terran military vessels. We'd be placing the ship and its crew in unnecessary jeopardy, which would threaten operational integrity in more ways than I'd care to describe."

"You're right, Commander," Podsy retorted. "The *Vercingetorix* is, in fact, designed for atmospheric maneuvers like the ones I'm proposing. We'll lose a few comm towers and probably weld a few airlocks shut along the way, but this is the only way I can see to locate that last Poltergeist. Deep Dive is ready to emerge from the surface and begin transferring the salvage from the subs to Joker's haulers." He gestured to the main Ground Control, where the pair of American Navy submarine icons rested just over a hundred meters below the surface. "The longer we wait, the better that Poltergeist's position will be to destroy that salvage and prevent us from returning it to the Vorr as planned."

Podsy turned to Moon. "This is the only way I can see to complete the mission, Colonel."

"Your priorities are out of alignment, Lieutenant Podsednik." Commander Stravinsky shook her head. "If you were planet-side in a mech, your plan would at least make some sense, but you're placing this ship's crew in unnecessary jeopardy. We still haven't located any Jemmin orbit-capable fixed weaponry. Do you honestly think there are none down there?" Her lips tightened into flat lines. "They'd love for us to make some kind of suicide run like you propose, which is precisely why Fleet regulations prohibit maneuvers like those you propose." Her visage softened fractionally as Podsy felt his ears begin to burn. "Ground Control of a dropship is a difficult post, Lieutenant, especially when its occupant has a personal relationship with the men and women on the ground. GC requires an extraordinary amount of priority-balancing that most sane humans are incapable of consistently demonstrating. The dropout rate is over ninety percent, with most returning to their previous posts with ground forces."

"Is that your longwinded way of saying I belong in a mech rather than on the bridge, Commander?" Podsy snapped.

"Your words, Lieutenant," she replied with a thinly-veiled smirk, "not mine."

Podsy was just about to agree with her. The constant bickering and divisiveness while Metalheads were planet-side and *dying* were proving to be something he wanted little part of. But before the words could pass his lips, Colonel Moon surprisingly put his oar into the conversation.

"Lieutenant Commander Stravinsky is right," Moon said heavily. "The relevant Fleet regulations apply here as surely as they do to any Terran military exercise. Those regulations are intended to safeguard not just the ships and crews, but also to maintain the Terran Armed Forces' ongoing ability to field an effective fighting force."

"Thank you, Colonel." Stravinsky nodded, and a triumphant twinkle entered her eye.

"However..." Moon continued, making sympathetic eye contact with the ship's blond-haired XO, "as a recent transfer from Fleet, you could be forgiven for not knowing that the Metal Legion sets its own operational priorities. A TAC dropship like the *Vercingetorix* is not a mech taxi, nor is it a warship tasked with maintaining overwatch," he explained in what sounded like a sincere tone that seemed to catch Stravinsky off-guard. Colonel Moon smiled as though at some private joke only he was aware of before explaining, "General Akinouye once said that Fleet's biggest systematic error in judgment when it came to arrangement of assets and priorities was in thinking that Marines and other ground forces were extensions of the warships that carried them. I believe his exact words were that it was 'the most ass-backward, patently absurd idea since the Bradley Fighting Vehicle.'"

"Sir?" Stravinsky asked in genuine surprise, which Podsy shared.

Moon inclined his chin to Podsy's workstation. "Ground Control is indeed a difficult station aboard a Fleet warship, Commander. And it is made doubly so because, to a lifelong Fleeter, Marines and Terran Fleet Ground Forces are assets to be controlled, deployed, and directed. But to a Metalhead?" He shook his head firmly. "They're the reason we put on the uniform, Commander, and their Jocks form the spirit of the Terran Armor Corps. On a TAC ship, Ground Control isn't a liaison to facilitate commands from the ship to the ground forces. In fact, you'd be more correct in saying it's the exact opposite."

Realization seemed to dawn in Stravinsky's eyes as Podsednik came to understand Moon's rebuke was aimed at both of them in equal measure. Podsy's earlier jubilant outburst at coordinating the Metalheads' efforts on the Pearl had been self-serving. He had misunderstood his role, even if only briefly, but judging by the set of Stravinsky's jaw, her misunderstanding was deeper-rooted than Podsy's would ever be.

"TAC orbital assets, including the interceptors I exclusively commanded during my earlier career," Moon continued pointedly, "are extensions of the ground forces they cover. We exist to *support* ground forces, not the other way around. Our mechs are the reason we have dropships and interceptors, Commander. As such, we consider some 'risks' that would blanch most Fleeters to be no risk at all. We also consider some regulations to be...

well," he grinned, "more like guidelines than laws carved in stone."

Stravinsky's spine went rigid as she nodded. "Understood, sir."

"You're doing good work, Commander," Moon assured her with unvarnished sincerity. "The Legion has a steeper learning curve for transferees than most branches. But one thing I can assure you we value greater than Fleet is individual perspective. So keep it coming whenever possible, is that clear?"

"As a Solarian's conscience, sir." The XO nodded, slightly relaxing at Moon's last words.

"Good." The colonel nodded before turning to Podsy. "I assume you've come up with an imaginative name for this proposed maneuver of yours, Lieutenant?"

Podsy was momentarily dumbfounded and could not immediately recall his original title, so instead he blurted the first thing that came to mind. "Operation Flyby, Colonel."

Moon pursed his lips in annoyance. "Not exactly a creative masterpiece, but it does the job. All right." The colonel nodded in approval. "Operation Flyby is approved. Coordinate with Colonel Jenkins and Captain Guan, then get back to me with your earliest timetable and flight plan no later than six minutes from now."

"Yes, sir," Podsy acknowledged.

"As you were, Lieutenant." Moon nodded before gesturing for the XO to join him at the command chair. Stravinsky shot Podsednik a final look, but the animosity in her eyes was significantly diminished from only a few minutes earlier. After she had turned her attention to the command chair, Moon shot a final mildly approving look Podsednik's way before he turned his back and quietly conferred with the *Vercingetorix*'s XO.

For a long moment, Podsy was awestruck. He realized that Colonel Moon had just accomplished multiple key objectives with his little speech, not least of which was to smooth out the kinks between the ship's XO and its Ground Control Officer. But even more importantly, he had provided a valuable lesson on the Metal Legion's posture to a pair of officers who *needed* it.

It was the kind of thing Podsy knew could only come from a lifetime of watching better men do their jobs higher up the chain of command. Podsy had never really striven to be a military commander or officer of any kind. He had originally viewed his enrollment in Colonel Jenkins' test program as a way to game a system that had little love for him or appreciation of his sense of duty. His time aboard a mech was supposed to have been some grand attempt at turning the system against itself. The kind of thing he could laugh about for decades to come after he'd left military life well behind him.

But now? After watching men like General Akinouye and Colonel Moon in action, he found himself increasingly fascinated by and, surprising no one more than himself, drawn toward the path those men had walked since before he was born.

"You're definitely slipping, Podsy," he muttered as he initiated secure comm links with the *Red Hare* and *Warcrafter*.

Warcrafter was first to accept the link, and Colonel Jenkins' voice crackled in Podsy's earpiece. "This is Clover Actual, go ahead."

"Clover Actual, this is Ground Control," Podsy greeted him as the *Red Hare* also accepted his call. "Stand by while I bring in the *Red Hare*. I've got something I need to fly by you..."

13

THE PUSH

"Confirmed, GC," Jenkins declared after the three-minute meeting had concluded. "Operation Flyby in T-minus eighteen minutes, on your mark."

"Copy that, Colonel," Podsy replied. "Set your clock at eighteen minutes...now."

"Good work, Lieutenant," Jenkins offered. Deep Dive was already primed for extraction, having retrieved the salvage from the ocean floor, but even on the most optimistic timetable, that process would take at least three hours from the time they crested the surface to being returned to the *Vercingetorix's* drop deck.

He had been unable to secure the surface on schedule, and that failure had placed the entire operation in jeopardy. Their Jemmin adversary (Jenkins believed there was but a single Jemmin operator left alive on the Pearl) had proven difficult to locate following its companion's destruction. Not only that, but it had also done an outstanding job of keeping not only the Poltergeist command vehicle but also the vast majority of its Spectres and skimmers from view.

The benefit to Clover Battalion was that they retained most of their ordnance. Had the battles continued unabated, the mechs would have been running on empty. Jemmin had misjudged. Jemmin would pay.

Jenkins' best estimates put the total number of Jemmin vehicles still on the Pearl at just under forty—one Poltergeist, fifteen Spectres, and the balance in skimmers. By any measure, destroying them would be a daunting task for anything less than a full brigade of armor.

Thankfully, Lieutenant Podsednik had once again proven his worth by crafting an ingenious if risky plan to even the odds.

"Clover Battalion, new orders," Jenkins declared, forwarding details for the first leg of the operation via P2P. "Joker Company," he continued, transmitting a similar packet to Captain Koch, who was in command of Joker Company until *Elvira* breached the surface. "I need *Sargon*, *Cyclops*, and *Murasame* on the line for this push."

"Roger," Captain Koch acknowledged as the quartet of Jokers moved out from the water's edge at flank speed. "Units transferred to your command, sir."

"Keep working on those checks, Captain," Jenkins urged, knowing that three of Clover's mechs were still down-checked at base camp. He thought that two of them might be able to contribute with long-range artillery in the coming engagement if Koch's people stayed on-task.

And where Jenkins was going, he could use as much fire support as possible.

"*Xiliang Pride* will be weapons hot and mobile in eight minutes, sir," Koch said confidently. "*Tragedy of Taiwan* will follow twelve minutes after that, but she'll be stationary for another twenty minutes. Her drive train was hit harder than we thought."

"Understood," Jenkins acknowledged. Two more Razorbacks offering fire support at extreme range might not seem like a lot in the grand scheme of things, but Jenkins had learned the hard way that sometimes a single well-placed shell could turn a fight. "All right, Metalheads," he piped into the Flyby main channel, which included every element assigned to the critical maneuver. "It's time to earn our pay. Form up as indicated and proceed to your assigned zones. Hold those positions at all costs until you receive new orders."

A chorus of rapid acknowledgments flickered over his plotter, and *Warcrafter* surged beneath him toward its assigned post in the formation. Hammer had a rougher hand at the helm than Chaps had displayed, but Jenkins felt surprisingly invigorated by the lurching, bumpy ride across the Pearl's surface.

The mechs of Clover Company broke out into trios and quartets, with broken platoons merging wherever necessary to ensure that at least three mechs moved to a given position. Five remade platoons drove out across the blasted rock of the Pearl's surface, including the Jokers that took up the eastern-most slot, and soon the Metal Legion's V-shaped formation was revealed.

On the inverse of that V, which would eventually measure two hundred kilometers from tip to tip when the formation was complete, was the likely target zone for the remaining Poltergeist. The Jemmin's accompanying vehicles were probably within fifty kilometers of its position, but in order for the Poltergeist to keep its guns on the base camp, it would need to remain no farther out than the span of the V-tips.

The formation was wholly the work of Lieutenant Podsednik, who had scoured all available intel on Jemmin technical specifications before determining the Poltergeist's most likely location. Apparently even Jem had concurred that there was a ninety-two percent probability that the Poltergeist would be somewhere within the triangular target area.

That was good enough for Jenkins to push his whole stack to the middle of the table.

Clover mechs sped toward the western edge of the formation, while Jenkins' *Warcrafter* took up the central slot with just a pair of Razorbacks flanking him.

Three minutes before Podsy's countdown reached zero, Jemmin made its presence known.

Captain Chao's platoon, working the westernmost edge of the V, was suddenly targeted by a storm of missiles. At a glance, Jenkins could see that the fire was not sent by Spectres, skimmers, or even a Poltergeist. The rate of fire and speed of the projectiles were consistent with pop-up placements, which sent micro-rockets streaking into Chao's platoon as the Clover Razorbacks sent up clouds of chaff and interceptive coil-gun fire.

Chao's people were sharp, sniping eighty percent of the tiny rockets from the air while scratching over half of the placements that fired them in the opening four seconds of the exchange. Rockets slammed into the Razorback Mark 2-Vs, which featured upgraded armor specifically designed to protect against Jemmin weaponry. The vast majority of the hits were soaked up by the Razorbacks' formidable shells, though one of Chao's four mechs suffered a bad hit to one of its legs and had to slow to half the speed of its fellows.

Not a word was spoken by any Metalhead, but the big-toe-less Lieutenant Hao (whose platoon was between Chao's and Jenkins' in the western edge of the V) sent a hail of ultra-precise coil-gun fire sweeping across the cluster of revealed Jemmin pop-ups. Most of the pop-ups were little more than camo-blanketed launchers lag-bolted to the rocky surface and were sanctioned by relatively minor damage. But six of them were armored and capable of withstanding coil-gun fire while continuing to pour out micro-rockets in a near-constant stream.

Lieutenant Hao sent an SRM at each of these, along with

railgun bolts from her two still-functioning railguns. Three of the placements were scrapped by her precise fire before Chao's unit destroyed the fourth, and just as quickly as it had started, the exchange ended, and the Metalheads resumed erecting their formation.

The damaged mech of Captain Chao's platoon fell steadily farther behind its platoon-mates, but given the accuracy of its guns during the short-lived exchange, Jenkins was confident it would make significant contributions in Operation Flyby.

Finally, the clock wound down to zero, at which point the *Vercingetorix's* engines burned in low orbit and the dropship moved off its previous overwatch position. It came about, moving south and descending at a dangerous rate that quickly saw its hull enveloped in raging fire.

Rather than gently descending through the Pearl's atmosphere, the *Vercingetorix* burned its engines at precisely their atmospheric-rated maximum and accelerated *toward* the planet's surface in a seemingly suicidal maneuver.

Of the Metalheads on the Pearl, only Jenkins knew the *Vercingetorix's* flight plan. Podsy had painstakingly crafted it with Colonel Moon's assistance in order to limit the Poltergeist's ability to counter by displacing either to the east or north.

The Jemmin commander almost certainly knew what the *Vercingetorix* was about to do, but Podsy had left the Poltergeist no choice: it could either flee south, straight into the teeth of the 'Flying V' of Metalheads, or it could flee west, which would eventually drive it out of firing range on the base camp. If it moved north, Jenkins' Flying V would chase it down, eventually driving it out of firing range. And if it moved east toward the base camp as might seem the obvious choice, it narrowed down its potential hiding holes in the event the *Red Hare* authored another series of revelatory EMPs.

Podsy had left the Jemmin commander no easy out, which

meant that things were about to get ugly—just the way the Metal Legion liked them.

"I won't ask for details," Alice said casually, once again surprising Jenkins with her uncanny ability to blend into the background whenever she was silent. "But I admit to being impressed by your unit's cohesion."

"You mean without the One Mind link?" Jenkins shot back as the *Vercingetorix* sped off toward the horizon, where it would soon disappear from his sensors.

"Precisely," Alice agreed. "I assume there are tactically-relevant updates being fed to each vehicle's commander, but the coordination on display here," she gestured to the tactical plotter, which showed the quintet of mech platoons moving with unified purpose as they stretched the Flying V's arms ever-longer, "is impressive."

"For aboriginals?" Jenkins quipped, wondering why his sarcasm meter was pegged, but it drew another laugh from Alice.

"For *any* human force," she replied. "Something that came into question immediately following Antivenom was Sol's collective certainty in our superiority. It took less than two hours of debate to determine that our previous sense of supremacy in human affairs was not reflective of our individual or even collective opinions."

"Jemmin got its fingers deep into Sol," Jenkins said with grudging sympathy.

"We were foolish to permit it to do so," Alice agreed, a rare note of hostility suddenly threading her words.

"Your study of individuality..." Jenkins mused. "It's why you were assigned as an ambassador to the Republic, isn't it? It's Sol's way of trying to correct an error in judgment based on Jemmin influence."

"Partially, yes," she allowed. "Though I was forthright when I said that my life's work was effectively rendered useless after Jemmin's corruption was discovered to have affected it."

Jenkins' brow furrowed in confusion at her words as the *Vercingetorix* finally disappeared from the tactical plotter. "You're saying you were entrusted with being an envoy to reestablish formal contact with the Terran Republic, but that you can't be trusted to restart your life's work?"

"Trust has nothing to do with it, Lee," she said matter-of-factly. "I am forty-one years old, and while I am expected to live to one-hundred-forty-six, my area of research can be better explored by someone younger. It may sound strange to you, but long before you arrived on Luna, I had already approved the young man who has succeeded me in my research post should my participation no longer be valued by Sol."

"That sounds awfully cold." Jenkins shook his head in disgust. "You spend your entire life leading your field of study, but because someone was actively manipulating you and everyone else in the Solar One Mind, they cast you aside and start over with someone else simply because they're younger?"

"My successor will accomplish more than I could have in the same time." She shrugged indifferently. "It was only natural that I be reassigned. Besides," she added as the Flying V finally reached its optimal dimensions, "my assignment here may prove to be even more important than my research might have been."

Jenkins made a halting gesture with his left hand, silencing Alice as he connected with the *Red Hare* on a secure line. "*Red Hare*, Clover Actual."

"Go ahead, Clover Actual," Captain Guan personally replied.

"We're ready for your pings, Captain," Jenkins declared, prompting Alice to sit back and tighten her harness's straps.

"Pings primed," Guan declared. "Ping One in three... two...one."

Warcrafter's tactical plotter lit up as the *Red Hare*'s targeted pulse splashed down on a point just north of the imaginary line connecting the inverted Flying V's western and eastern tips. A trio of targets was outlined, two skimmers and a Spectre soon coming under a vicious crossfire from the eastern Joker platoon and Captain Chao's western platoon.

The trio of Jemmin hovercraft sent a storm of missiles in reply, exclusively targeting the Jokers even as the first of Chao's artillery slammed into the Spectre's stern.

Murasame's anti-missile rockets leapt out to intercept the wave of Jemmin fire, and *Cyclops'* plasma cannon belched a slow-moving ball of fiery death as the Jokers' sudden ferocity gave the lie to their misleading unit name. *Murasame's* interceptor rockets tore all but two of the Jemmin missiles from the sky, but the remaining Jemmin missiles slammed into *Cyclops'* torso. Plates and shards of ablative armor fell away from the Warlock-class mech's chest, but Blinky drove his vehicle forward and calmly re-charged his plasma cannon even as the first projectile neared the end of its flight less than halfway to the highlighted Spectre.

Chao's artillery rained down, scratching a skimmer with a direct hit while badly damaging the Spectre with two hits to its stern. The second skimmer slipped from view, its cloaking system resuming just before *Cyclops'* plasma projectile fell almost precisely halfway between the eastern Jokers and the central Spectre, which soon fell to a direct hit by Chao's artillery.

And when *Cyclops'* ordnance impacted, erupting into a hellish mushroom cloud spawned by Blinky's 'miss,' another skimmer was outlined by the blast wave as it spread across the Pearl's surface.

Artillery flew out from the Flying V's 'elbow' platoons, situated between the tips and Jenkins' anchor platoon at the V's base. But the Jemmin skimmer outlined by *Cyclops'* well-placed 'miss' had already escaped the strike zone when the shells finally impacted.

Precisely on schedule, Captain Guan called down, "Ping Two in three...two...one. Pinging."

The second of the *Red Hare's* pings struck twenty kilometers to the west of Captain Chao's formation. It was one of just two hiding holes available in that area, and just as Podsy had suspected, the ping revealed Jemmin targets.

Unfortunately for the Metalheads, it revealed more than they expected.

"Twelve enemy contacts at Ping Two," Jenkins declared over the main comm line. "Six Spectres, six skimmers," he called as the vehicles scattered from view. It seemed his Jemmin adversary had prepared its own surprise for the Metalheads.

Judging from the collection of assets revealed by the *Red Hare's* ping, Jemmin meant to outflank Jenkins' formation after drawing it into a counter-trap.

"New ping targets," Jenkins commanded, sending a fresh batch of pings up to the *Red Hare*.

"Replotting pings," Captain Guan intoned as the Jemmin vehicles fell silent. Jenkins' people knew better than to waste ordnance at that range, but he quickly worked to reorient his formation while piping into the *Red Hare's* tactical simulators and running tens of thousands of projections per second on where the Jemmin vehicles would most likely appear next.

Silent tension filled *Warcrafter's* cabin for the ensuing three minutes as ping after ping splashed down where Jenkins had requested them, but none of the pings revealed Jemmin activity, which slowly narrowed down the potential posture of the Jemmin forces. As the pings lashed the planet, the Metal

Legion's mechs pivoted their formation counterclockwise, dropping Captain Chao's platoon to the south while pushing the Jokers north and sending Jenkins' platoon east.

And with each failed ping, the picture became increasingly grim for the Metalheads.

"Metalheads, we've got at least twenty Jemmin vehicles to the west and the remainder to the north," Jenkins called over the main channel. "Maintain formation and prepare to receive an enemy charge," he commanded, knowing there was a very real chance that he was turning his ass toward the Poltergeist.

If he were the Jemmin commander, he would have hunkered down as close to the eastern base camp as possible. On its own, a Poltergeist had enough firepower to overwhelm a full platoon of Razorbacks, or possibly even two if it gained the element of surprise. That much firepower, combined with a full-frontal assault from the west and flanking fire from the north, would be absolutely devastating.

Then again, Jemmin was supposedly more intelligent than humanity...and Lee Jenkins hadn't earned his callsign by consistently opting for the smartest play.

Still, even Jenkins was loathe to expose his ass to the enemy. The *Red Hare* splashed down a trio of pings to the east on the very spots Jenkins would have hidden his command vehicle if he'd been in charge of the Jemmin forces. None of those pings yielded anything, which allowed Jenkins to focus more intently on the western front mere seconds before Jemmin opened fire.

And when that fire came, it was utterly devastating.

Thirty-two Jemmin vehicles positioned thirty-five kilometers from Captain Chao's platoon revealed themselves by unleashing a hundred and sixty-two missiles in perfect unison. Arranged in an east-north crescent, the Jemmin hovercraft moved at a sprint toward the Terrans Captain Chao had positioned to receive the worst of the enemy fire.

Chao's Razorbacks, including the straggler (which, as fate would have it, was only three kilometers from its fellows after the Flying V's reorientation hastened its reunion) unleashed their remaining anti-missile rockets. Lieutenant Hao's western elbow platoon did likewise, but Jenkins' mechs were too far away to lend support.

But the anti-missiles rockets were only a tiny fraction of the barrage sent out by the Metalheads, who emptied their launchers and cleared their mains on the charging enemy formation. The Jemmin hovercraft scattered to avoid the artillery, but their evasive maneuvers only served to help the Terran missiles home in on their respective targets.

Missiles crisscrossed mid-flight, the Terran ordnance heading north and west while Jemmin rockets flew south and east. Dozens of missiles from each side were scrapped by counter-fire, and for a brief moment, there was a rare symmetry on the field. Each side had put enough ordnance into the air to completely destroy the other three times over, which meant the opening exchange was now down to whose countermeasures proved superior.

Fortunately, the Metalheads emerged the victors in that respect. Over seventy percent of the inbound ordnance was blown out of the sky, but despite the missile shield's relatively strong performance, the exchange was still costly

In the extreme.

Two of Chao's mechs were destroyed outright, while Chao's *Fourth Leaf* was struck three times by SRMs, suffering severe systems damage.

Three of Hao's Razorbacks died when each suffered five direct hits, and Hao's mech suffered two direct hits and three near-misses that crippled her drive system and slowed her to a crawl.

Even Jenkins' formation took fire, one of his mechs cratering and *Warcrafter* taking a pair of direct hits that rocked the cabin so violently he chipped his left canine tooth despite preemptively clenching his jaw.

But when the Terran fury fell upon the Jemmin in reply, the damage was three-fold what the Metalheads had suffered.

"Eight Spectres down," Jenkins declared, shaking off the surprisingly severe pain in his tooth. "Ten skimmers scratched. All mechs, engage targets at will. Fire! Fire! Fire!" he roared, prompting *Warcrafter's* guns to thunder with authority as they sent ER-HE shells down-range into the beleaguered hovercraft, specifically the ones damaged by near-misses.

As the Jemmin forces split up to maintain a combat spread, the remaining enemy vehicles were well-positioned to roll up the Legion's flank, starting with Captain Chao's lone mech on the V's westernmost point.

As the Jemmin hovercraft surged forward, authoring a second wave of fire, an alarming thought occurred to Jenkins, which he instantly gave voice to. "Hammer, come about and face south. Now!"

A quarter-second after adjusting posture as Jenkins ordered, *Warcrafter* lurched violently to starboard and a handful of alarms sounded. Hammer's quick thinking, following Jenkins' well-timed order for a southern reorientation, slid the command vehicle out of the path of the Poltergeist's devastating backstab attack before the focused laser beam could overcome the Razorback's formidable forward armor.

If that armor had been standard Mark 1, or even Mark 2 without the Vorr modifications, *Warcrafter* would have certainly died from the fire it sustained prior to evading. As it was, the forward armor was down to just under fifty percent effectiveness.

"*Sargon*, fire package 'Fearsome Foursome,'" Jenkins barked as the Jemmin command vehicle slid from view as quickly as it had appeared. "Engage that target!"

"Fearsome Foursome on the way," *Sargon* acknowledged, sending a quartet of LRMs toward the Poltergeist's position fifty klicks to the south.

The Poltergeist had already disappeared from view, likely thinking itself safe as it slid back into the figurative shadows provided by its stealth suite. With its speed and ability to climb to high altitudes as nimbly as any Terran aircraft, the Poltergeist would egress *Sargon's* strike zone in mere seconds.

Jenkins watched breathlessly as *Sargon's* quartet of high-powered missiles tore through the sky, splitting apart and blossoming in a perfect square of impacts that unleashed hundred-kiloton warheads. A direct hit was too much to hope for, so Jenkins had opted to blanket the area with the warheads' blast waves in the hope of revealing the Jemmin command vehicle.

The four nukes' mushroom clouds rose to the heavens above, while blast waves surged out and eventually collided with each other. But despite their frame-perfect deployment, they failed to outline the Poltergeist.

"All right, asshole," Jenkins growled as an icon reappeared in the sky to the south, "let's gamble."

Tearing through the Pearl's atmosphere and moving faster than a ship of its class had any business going through such a thick blanket of gases, the *Vercingetorix* barreled north less than a hundred meters from the planet's surface.

The Metal Legion dropship screamed toward the engagement zone with a simple, binary decision ahead of it, billowing smoke from a dozen breaches in its hull and throwing an impressive rooster tail of dust five hundred meters skyward in its wake. If they guessed wrong, the enemy commander would slip from view and return to harass the Terrans in the hope of preventing them from leaving the planet with their aquatic spoils.

But if they guessed right, they just might be able to bracket that sneaky sonofabitch long enough to eliminate the Jemmin from contention for the Pearl's archaeological prize.

"Heads, I win." Jenkins sneered as the *Vercingetorix* banked to the west of Sargon's nuclear strikes. "Tails, you lose. Call it."

14

A CAESAR SALAD

"Hold course. Steady," Colonel Moon affirmed as the *Vercinge-torix* hurtled through the Pearl's atmosphere. "Sensors, be ready. You'll only get one chance at this."

"Sensors ready, sir," acknowledged the operator, and Podsy felt his heart beat faster with each passing second.

"We've got multiple breaches in the forward hull, Colonel," Damage Control reported tightly as alarm after alarm appeared on her board. They had suffered significant damage during descent, and there was concern that the ship might not be able to resume orbit following the maneuver. The ship's engineers had worked frantically (and not without losses) to close the breaches in the aged ship's relatively thin hull as soon as they opened, but the longer they fought the atmosphere, the more it would become a losing battle.

"Confirm inner seal integrity on those sections," Moon stated as they drew steadily nearer to their target. "We can't afford to stay down here any longer than necessary. We're not slowing down."

"Contacts!" Sensors reported as a cluster of icons appeared

forty kilometers to the north of the enemy position. "Twenty-seven inbound missiles."

"PD." Moon swiveled his command chair to face the Tactical section, where Lieutenant Commander Stravinsky had strapped into the ship's point-defense station. "Intercept with forward systems only."

"Forward systems, aye," Stravinsky acknowledged, deftly manipulating her station's controls in anticipation of the coming exchange.

"Flyby in five...four..." Sensors called as the *Vercingetorix* pulled up sharply on approach to the western edge of the four mushroom clouds, "three...two...one. Flyby online!"

The ship's sensors burst to life, sending active sweeps along the ground and nearby skies, using the systems more in line with how their designers intended. The air around the *Vercingetorix* crackled and arced as the transceivers pumped maximum wattage into the surrounding environment. Each burst swept dozens of degrees of view as the dropship's formidable sensor array sought to locate the fleeing Poltergeist.

As the sensors swept the ground and sky in search of the predator-turned-prey, Commander Stravinsky opened fire on the inbound missiles with the dropship's forward point defense grid. Eight coil guns in four batteries sent streams of slugs into the air in search of Jemmin rockets, sniping one after another after another from the sky.

To Podsy's amazement, just four Jemmin missiles snuck through the shield. Those missiles struck the *Vercingetorix*'s forward hull in rapid succession with jarring force, setting off a whole new chorus of alarms that prompted Damage Control to urgently direct repair teams to the affected areas.

For three full seconds of flight, the *Vercingetorix*'s sensors revealed nothing. The flyby would last only eight seconds before the ship's sensors would overload. Podsy held his breath as the fourth second ticked by without result, followed by the fifth. When the sixth second had passed, he felt a crushing sense of despair. Flyby had been his idea, and already four of the *Vercingetorix's* engineers had died while working to repair damage suffered in-flight. Three sons and one daughter of Terra would never return home because of what looked like a bad plan, and as the seventh second lapsed without contact, he wondered if he could face his colleagues in the teeth of such failure.

The eighth second came, and he felt a brief glimmer of irrational hope as it hung for what seemed like an eternity on the timer displayed beside the bridge's main plotter.

Then it passed, and he exhaled in resignation as the ninth second ticked by...followed by the tenth.

Somehow, the sensor grid had not yet collapsed. The ship climbed skyward as it sought to escape the Pearl's clutch of gravity, and as the eleventh second ticked over, a new icon appeared on the western edge of the enemy formation.

As luck would have it, the Poltergeist was just twelve kilometers from the *Vercingetorix* at the moment it was revealed.

"Poltergeist located!" Sensors declared as the ship's sensor transceivers finally failed.

"Engaging," Lieutenant Commander Stravinsky declared, showing all the poise of a brain surgeon as she targeted the freshly-revealed command vehicle with the entirety of the *Vercingetorix's* PD grid.

Two hundred micro-rockets, normally used as missile interceptors, sped off toward the Poltergeist while thousands upon thousands of rounds were spat by the ship's coil guns. Moving as the ship was through patches of turbulent atmosphere and with dozens of other variables Podsy couldn't even hope to itemize, it would have taken a miracle for any of those coil gun rounds to strike the fleeing Poltergeist as the Jemmin vehicle moved at six hundred kph to the northwest.

But the *Vercingetorix* was used to shooting at fast-moving targets.

The coil guns, in Podsy's opinion, were nothing but desperation on Stravinsky's part. The micro-rockets were what would make or break the maneuver, and he watched with rekindled anxiety as they streaked through the atmosphere at the flickering icon of the Poltergeist. The Jemmin was juking and weaving on its way back to the planet's surface while working to reestablish its stealth suite, which the *Red Hare* managed to hit with a well-placed sensor ping that kept it on the board as the *Vercingetorix's* interceptor rockets sped toward their quarry.

The swarm of micro-rockets descended on the fast-fleeing Poltergeist, which abruptly came about and swept its powerful beam across the sky. The beam persisted for two full seconds and cleared ninety percent of the PD rockets from the sky as it wove back and forth while the Jemmin command vehicle continued to sprint toward safety.

Five of the twenty remaining rockets missed entirely. Twelve near-missed, sending shrapnel up into the Poltergeist's underside, where damage to the hovertank's stealth system would be the least helpful to the Metalheads.

And of the three micro-rockets that struck the Poltergeist's hull, only one hit the target center-mass. The others barely nicked the edges of its sleek, curved armor.

Strangely, even these three minor hits seemed to do enough damage to cause the Poltergeist's six-hundred-kph sprint to falter, and its speed plummeted to just forty kilometers per hour as it careened off the planet's surface.

And when it did so, the first of Stravinsky's 'desperation' coil gun slugs fell to the ground behind it. The next handful struck the stone fifty meters off the Poltergeist's stern, just as the Jemmin vehicle resumed its acceleration and vaulted forward to two hundred kph.

The coil-gun fire, which fell in a breathtakingly-precise fan-shaped pattern, seemed to chase the Poltergeist farther and farther down-range. For a moment, it seemed as though the Poltergeist would evade the nearly-harmless depleted-uranium slugs as it accelerated to three hundred kph while pellets fell mere meters from its stern.

Then the first heavy projectile hammered into the Jemmin's stern. Followed by a second, and a third. A fourth. A dozen slugs plinked into the hovertank's roof in the span of two seconds before Stravinsky's expert fire fell silent, and while none of those pellets did structural damage to the tank, they did cause seemingly catastrophic damage to the Poltergeist's camouflage system.

The tank's hull warbled and rippled with bent, distorted images as the craft's stealth systems tried and failed to compensate for the damage caused by the *Vercingetorix's* PD systems. After five seconds of attempting to compensate, the Jemmin commander seemed to abandon the effort as the warbles of light ceased. The tank banked hard to the north before slewing around to face the nearest mechs of Clover Battalion.

"Target painted," Sensors declared after confirming that the *Red Hare's* systems had locked onto the enemy vehicle.

"Helm, make orbit," Colonel Moon commanded. "Damage Control, confirm interior seal integrity before we pass the void threshold. If we're going to decompress the ship's interior, I want to control how it happens."

"I can plug the holes in time, Colonel," Damage Control declared with confidence, issuing rapid-fire orders to the engineers, technicians, and automated repair systems working to make the ship spaceworthy.

"Divert whoever you need," Moon urged, drawing a silent nod of acknowledgment while DC continued issuing orders to the ship's repair crews. The colonel turned to Podsy, whose eyes kept wandering back to the tactical plotter, which showed a fresh exchange of fire between the Metalheads on the Pearl and the Jemmin forces that had begun to consolidate around the Poltergeist in preparation for what seemed like a counteroffensive. "Operation Flyby was a success, Lieutenant," Moon said, forcing Podsy to reluctantly tear his gaze from the tactical plotter. "Good work."

"Thank you, sir," Podsy allowed while feeling anything but pride or triumph. He couldn't help but remember the four people who had died during the *Vercingetorix's* approach, and while he knew the casualty list would climb much higher than that before the day was out, he also knew that those four had died because of *him*. If he had done a better job of planning, perhaps...

"Commander Stravinsky," Moon continued. "That was the finest display of gunnery I've had the pleasure of witnessing firsthand. Well done."

"Thank you, Colonel," the commander replied stoically, but if Podsy's read was right, she was sweating behind that well-practiced mask of professionalism.

"We've done well," Moon declared in a raised voice. "But this fight's not over. Maintain action stations. I want to be ready to jump as soon as we get the call. Is that clear?"

With one voice, the bridge crew (including Podsy) enthusiastically replied, "Yes, sir!"

"Good." Moon nodded, sweeping the bridge with a stony gaze. "The Metal Legion doesn't rest until the last mech is wheels-up. Sensors, work to get your systems back online. We need as many eyes down there as possible."

No matter how hard Podsy tried to focus on the task at hand, he was unable to stop thinking about the four shipmates who had lost their lives because of him.

15

BREAKOUTS

"We'll be in comm range in one minute, Major," Lu reported. He was probably trying to help soothe Xi's fraying nerves at being forced to slow-walk her mech up the underwater slope for what seemed like an eternity.

Unfortunately, his attempt had the opposite effect.

"The next patronizing word I hear from *anyone* in this can," Xi snarled, "is going to lead to my kebabbing their gonads for a barbecue on the radiators. Is that understood?!"

"Yes, ma'am," her Wrench and Monkey acknowledged promptly, though there was a note of resignation to their voices that she disliked even more than the patronizing one from Lu.

She forced herself to draw a deep, steadying breath. "Look, guys, it's chapping my ass," she allowed half-heartedly, leading to a barely-audible snicker from Penny. "But I swear to fucking Christ," she continued irritably, "that if we miss so much as a single step before breaching the surface, I'm going to rip some-one's throat out—"

She was cut short when her comm link crackled to life with an incoming message. "Joker Actual, this is Captain Koch."

"Go ahead, XO," Xi acknowledged, glad for some sort of

distraction as a stream of tactical data filled her system. The HUD painted the clear picture that Colonel Jenkins had already begun the final charge against the Jemmin forces on the planet.

And he'd done it *without* her.

"We've got two Clover Razorbacks that will be mobile in six minutes," Koch reported, "but their crews are out of the fight, ma'am. Neural overloads and severe burns."

Xi hammered a fist into the metal wall beside her position at being left out of the Pearl's final charge. That quickly morphed into a shark-like grin. "We've got a pair of link-equipped Nuggets, don't we?"

"Yes, ma'am," Koch acknowledged. The pair of Nuggets who had tried to cheat their way to victory during the interview process had both rated exceptionally high on a lengthy series of tactical performance evaluations during the *Vercingetorix's* flight to the Pearl. So high, in fact, that both Xi and Koch had agreed that they would be first up to fill vacant pilot seats in the event there was a shortage.

There were a few reasons for opting to use the Nuggets over Koch's more experienced repair Jocks. The first was the Nuggets' tactical aptitudes, and the second was that switching back and forth between various mech links during deployment could lead to catastrophic deficits in both performance and neurological stability.

It usually took weeks to rate a Jock on a mech, during which time the link systems would be fine-tuned to their new pilot's unique neurophysiology. But molding that interface was a two-way street: it took the pilots as much time to adjust as it took the systems.

So, in many ways, a fresh Nugget who had only interfaced with a simulator was a better last-minute replacement than a ten-year veteran who was rated on a significantly different mech.

"Saddle them up, Captain," she commanded. "Assign Corporals Sten and Leibrancht as their Wrenches, and if you've got anyone else you can spare for their Monkeys, they could probably use the help."

"Copy that, Major," Koch replied. "They'll be live-link in two minutes."

Xi smirked in approval. It took at least six minutes to complete the initial bootup for a new Jock's link. About two-thirds of that time could be spent well in advance of performing the first live link's checklist, which meant Koch had anticipated her orders and moved to cut down as much time as possible.

"Perfect, XO," she said with genuine approval. "We'll break the surface in six minutes. Have the Nuggets ready to roll when we arrive; I'll need you to remain and oversee the transfer of the salvage while we move to support Clover's push."

"We'll be ready, ma'am," Koch acknowledged, and not for the first time since receiving her latest promotion, Xi felt surprisingly self-conscious at being called 'ma'am' by someone who was over twice her age.

Koch had served with distinction in the Terra Americana Planetary Defense Force for twelve years before a series of bad decisions (including the ingestion of some high-powered pharmaceuticals) saw him booked for a laundry list of crimes, including manslaughter when a parking lot fistfight turned deadly. He had managed to avoid a dishonorable discharge and was therefore able to transfer his rank when his sentence was commuted to service in Jenkins' pilot Combined Arms program.

Like every other Metalhead who had earned the moniker, he had no shortage of personal demons to contend with. But he was a good man, and Xi was glad to have him at her side during Watery Grave.

Xi's eyes snagged on the tactical plotter, which showed Jenkins' Razorbacks in hot pursuit of the westward-fleeing Jemmin forces. At the furthest edge of the Jemmin formation was the unmistakable icon representing a Poltergeist, and while it was moving much slower than its maximum rated speed, it was still putting plenty of distance between itself and Jenkins' mechs.

She clenched her teeth in frustration as *Elvira III* slowly crawled its way to the shore. But the Poltergeist's flight had given her an important opportunity to transfer the artifacts into the armored hulls of Koch's repair mechs.

It was an opportunity she intended to capitalize on.

"We're rolling west in support of Clover as soon as those Nuggets are jacked in," Xi snapped when *Elvira's* fifteens finally broke through the surface of the hot, salty water.

"*Fledgling Phoenix* is online," reported Giles, the Nugget who had attempted to capitalize on his girlfriend's simulator virus.

"Didn't your girlfriend ever tell you not to get ahead of yourself, Corporal?" Xi quipped, mildly impressed that he had completed his initial uplink to the Razorback so quickly.

"All the time, ma'am," both Giles and Lassiter replied in near-perfect unison, drawing an approving nod from Xi as a grin spread across her lips.

"At least you're honest," Xi deadpanned as *Elvira's* rooftop emerged from the water. "Which, from where I'm sitting, is a *big* upgrade over our first meeting."

"Yes, ma'am," Giles replied, sounding appropriately chastised.

"Lassiter," Xi called as *Elvira* slowly but surely made its way to the shoreline half a kilometer away, "what's your status?"

"I'm having trouble with the handshakes, Major," Lassiter

replied with evident frustration. "I keep getting booted out of the link in the second stage."

"You've got to relax into it, Corporal," Xi urged, recalling the first few times she had unsuccessfully attempted to link with a new mech in training. "It's not as adaptive as the simulator. This system needs you to be more flexible than a training link. Just focus on the dots," she encouraged, referring to a barely-perceptible ring of sequentially-flickering dots that served as an attention-grabbing device to facilitate initial linkage. It had been so long since she'd needed them that she barely even realized they were there, but for the first few weeks of her Jock training, they had been vital.

"Yes, ma'am," Lassiter replied after a short sigh, prompting Xi to offer another bit of sage advice to the young recruit (who was five years older than Xi).

"Just think of it like an especially clumsy-but-adorable boyfriend," she suggested. "It's awkward, inflexible, and focused on pushing past your defenses faster than you'd care to drop them. But no matter how messy it gets or how rushed parts of it feels, you both want to make it happen. Relax and try not to fight it too much. The link is only as much a part of you as you let it be."

She hardly considered herself an authority on the subject of harmonious couplings, but she felt like she had to say something to encourage Lassiter's efforts.

A moment later, the icon for the second damaged Razorback at base camp flickered green before Lassiter gushed, "Link is live! Thank you, Major!"

"Act like you've been there before, Corporal," Xi snapped, equally surprised and irritated that her advice seemed to have paid off.

"Sorry, ma'am," Lassiter apologized before reporting, "*Razor Bamboo* is online."

"All right," Xi said, finally able to increase speed as her mech crawled out of the water. *"Fledgling Phoenix, Razor Bamboo,* you're with me. We'll take up a position two klicks east of here and lend fire support to Colonel Jenkins.

"Yes, ma'am," the duo replied as she forwarded target coordinates, toward which the pair of damaged but combat-worthy mechs began to move.

"If my guess is right," Xi continued, increasing *Elvira's* speed with each step, "that Poltergeist is going to countercharge in the next ten minutes to prevent us from securing the cargo. Commander Ulbricht, return to base camp ASAP and transfer your cargo. With the Poltergeist currently moving west, this is our best chance to get that salvage secured."

"Aye, Major," Ulbricht replied promptly. "We'll breach the surface in thirty seconds."

"Cargo transfer will take three minutes once the subs are on the haulers, Major," Koch reported confidently. "There's no faster way to get the job done but to drag the boats up on shore first."

"You're the man, Captain," Xi agreed deferentially. "We'll get out there and provide cover."

"Bamboo and *Phoenix* are rearmed with missile intercept rockets," Koch added. "We can rearm *Elvira* as well, but it would take six minutes to swap the torpedo launchers out."

"Negative." Xi shook her head. Finally, *Elvira* was able to stomp through the water at flank speed. "My fifteens will do the job as long as the Nuggets remember their intercept protocols."

"I checked them out with simulations twelve minutes ago, Major," Koch said confidently. "They're green but steady."

"Good enough for me," she said approvingly as she left the last puddles of water behind and drove her mech to join the Nuggets to the northwest. "Let's see how they do with fifteens," she added, forwarding target packages to the Nuggets.

"Remember to account for recoil on the second shot by—" she began, only to be cut short when Giles' *Fledgling Phoenix* cleared both fifteens down-range on the indicated target set ten kilometers from their position.

Surprisingly, both shells exploded within ten meters of their targets, which was at least as good as Xi had managed with her first live-fires.

"Forgetting that I never gave you the order to fire, *Nugget*," Xi growled, "you didn't account for the recoil of your first gun when you fired the second. This surface is half chalk, so the first shot drove your stern legs at least ten centimeters into the ground. You might have bullseyed the mark if you'd listened instead of going off half-cocked!"

"Sorry, Major," Giles apologized with seemingly genuine remorse. "I got a little overeager."

"When have I heard that before?" Lassiter asked rhetorically.

"Can the chatter, Squeakers," Xi snapped. "Reload your ordnance, and this time *wait* for my order before firing. And *what* are we accounting for before we fire, Premature Pete?"

"No, *please*," Giles pleaded with unmistakable horror. "Don't make that my callsign!"

"A little close to home, eh? Callsigns are like Zodiac signs, Corporal." Xi grunted as *Elvira* took up position between the Razorbacks. "You don't get any choice in the matter. So unless you want it to stick, you'd better impress the hell out of me by—"

"Recoil," Giles blurted urgently. "We're accounting for recoil, planetary rotation, windage, gravity, atmospheric density—"

"Nobody likes a smartass, Giles," Xi interrupted as she identified a fresh set of targets that she forwarded to the Nuggets. "All right, this time we clear our guns on *my* command. If there's a cloaked advance force moving to outflank Clover, these are high-probability ambush sites. If we outline something, each of you fires two Guandao-class SRMs at it. And we do this by the book: fifteens fire in five...four...three...two...one. On the way!" she declared, and *Elvira's* dual cannons roared a quarter-second before those of *Fledgling Phoenix* and *Razor Bamboo*.

The artillery soared through the Pearl's blistering air, falling in rapid succession on the target zone with near-perfect precision. None of the shells missed their targets by more than five meters, and one of them was lucky enough to outline a hidden Spectre.

"Lock missiles!" she urged, though both of the Nuggets had already unleashed their ordnance on the briefly-revealed vehicle. She watched with satisfaction as the Jemmin hovertank tried to flee. The missiles were much faster, and the Jemmin's camouflage systems were inoperable following the shower of shrapnel from the artillery near-miss.

The quartet of missiles streaked toward the fleeing vehicle, which sent up a tepid swarm of interceptive fire that scrubbed only one of the SRMs. The rest struck true, cratering the target and notching the Nuggets the first half-hashes of what Xi hoped would be long, productive careers in the Metal Legion.

"Yahoo!" Giles whooped while Lassiter squealed wordlessly with excitement. Following the Nuggets' successful barrage, the four-mech Joker platoon (consisting of *Sargon*, *Cyclops*, *Murasame,* and the patched-up *Black Widow*) currently attached to Jenkins' command unleashed coordinated fire on the area surrounding the cratered Spectre. A handful of enemy vehicles were outlined by a well-placed Purgatory missile fired by *Sargon*.

"Keep your pants on, you two," Xi barked. "You're about to learn the hard way that it's *much* better to give than to receive."

The Jemmin hovercraft located just nine kilometers from her ad hoc platoon suddenly surged toward Xi's three-mech formation with murderous intent while launching fifty SRMs at the base camp.

"Launch interceptors," Xi commanded, sliding *Elvira* from side to side as the Nuggets authored a volley of a hundred micro-rockets, "and take evasive maneuvers. Our priority is to protect the base camp, not ourselves. Is that clear?"

"Yes, ma'am," the two replied, and for that brief moment, they *almost* sounded like they belonged on the battlefield exchanging fire with the enemy.

Almost.

Xi loaded HE shells into *Elvira's* fifteens and sent them into the path of the hovercraft. Two Spectres and four skimmers made up the small, fast-attack group, which was attempting to sneak closer to the Terran base camp before unleashing their ordnance. Xi was aware that the lucky strike by her Nuggets' artillery might have just saved the entire operation by exposing the would-be backstabbers before they could execute their objective.

But the time for back-patting was a long way off.

The interceptor rockets streaked out toward the enemy missiles, and thanks to Xi's charge to her platoon's new position, those rockets had gained a vital pursuit angle on the Jemmin ordnance. Had she not spurred her people out here as fast as she had, their rockets would have been only half as effective.

And the ripple of mid-air explosions confirmed the value of her decision to sprint wide of the base camp as forty-four of the fifty-four missiles were intercepted by her small unit's counterfire.

The remaining ten fell toward the base camp, where Koch's people were already transferring the precious cargo from the American subs to the more heavily-armored mechs of Koch's Repair & Recovery team.

And those mechs proved themselves more than just glorified

tow trucks as they sent a fresh wave of interceptor rockets to meet the remains of the incoming enemy ordnance. Another wave of explosions rippled across the sky and Koch's people neutralized all ten of the remaining enemy weapons, showing themselves to be up to the challenge of protecting Deep Dive's prizes.

"All right, Nuggets, weapons free," Xi ordered as she loaded fresh shells into *Elvira's* guns and targeted the six oncoming Jemmin hovervehicles. "Smoke 'em."

All six of her mech's fifteen-kilo mains thundered and *Fledgling Phoenix's* lone railgun roared as the trio of Metal Legion vehicles delivered concerted fire on the approaching Jemmin vehicles. The railgun scored a bullseye on one of the Spectres, scattering it into pieces no larger than a human torso, while the volley of artillery only managed to claim one skimmer.

The remaining four Jemmin hovertanks sped toward them at nearly two-hundred kph. Given the relatively light fire from the enemy vehicles, Xi suspected they were on suicide runs (if such a thing could be said of remotely-operated or fully-automated vehicles) aimed at her makeshift platoon.

"Put those fuckers *down*," Xi shouted, reloading and firing *Elvira's* mains while the Nuggets on either side of her did likewise.

The remaining Spectre fired a trio of missiles, one aimed at each of Xi's mechs, and she didn't bother checking the Razorbacks' inventories. She knew they had already emptied their interceptors at the first wave of fire. All they could intercept these smaller missiles with was chain- or coil-gun fire.

"Evade and intercept at knife-range," she commanded as the low-flying missiles streaked toward her formation. "Coil guns hot!" she declared, turning her starboard flank to the approaching weapons and firing her two starboard chain guns into the rapidly-shrinking space between the missiles and her hull.

The Nuggets followed her lead, discharging their coil guns in a rapid-fire stream in a last-ditch effort to intercept the inbound missiles. Their crisscrossing spray of slugs managed to take one of the three missiles down, but the rockets aimed at *Fledgling Phoenix* and *Elvira* scored.

Elvira lurched hard to port as warning alarms rang throughout the cabin. Despite her mech's ablative and shock-absorbing armor, the impact was so violent that it knocked Xi's neural link offline. Temporarily disoriented, she fought through the vertigo and momentary confusion that always accompanied such abrupt disconnects from the system.

"Report!" she barked after quelling the sudden urge to ralph all over her chair.

"We've lost all motive power on the port side, along with our port heat sinks," Lu reported grimly. "Penny's down and unresponsive, and we've got a coolant leak I'm working to clamp off."

"How's the reactor?" Xi pressed as her neural link reinitialized, feeding her a briefly-overwhelming stream of new data.

"I've powered it down to minimum until I can clamp this gusher," he grunted. "But even if I get it back up, we're stuck."

Xi looked at both *Fledgling Phoenix* and *Razor Bamboo*, finding that the former had been hit so badly that one of its legs was gone. But *Razor Bamboo* was still standing tall, firing shell after shell down-range at the approaching Jemmin vehicles. Surprisingly, just two of the Jemmin remained: one skimmer and one Spectre. Lassiter must have pulled off some sharp shooting in the last few seconds to knock two more skimmers out of the fight.

"Lassiter," Xi called, struggling to reorient *Elvira* so that her guns could lock onto the fast-approaching enemy, "put the last skimmer down. Let me deal with the Spectre."

A brief but pointed delay preceded the reply. "Yes, Major."

"*Sargon*," Xi growled, raising the missile-mech on a direct P2P, "put a gun up this Spectre's ass and pull the trigger until it goes 'click.' Then move to the indicated coordinates," she continued, knowing that technically she was violating the chain of command by superseding Colonel Jenkins during a maneuver. But she also knew that it was the right call, because sometime in the next few minutes, that Poltergeist was going to come about and finish what its stealthy backstabbers had begun. "Colonel Jenkins will need us all in optimal positions when that Poltergeist comes back."

"Copy that, Major," Sargon acknowledged before sending an MRM in fast pursuit of the Jemmin Spectre.

The MRM soared through the air, taking a ballistic trajectory before descending toward its target. As it accelerated toward the ground, it looked to Xi like a hawk diving toward its prey. While it pursued the suddenly-juking Spectre, Lassiter's artillery and coil guns worked in perfect harmony to stagger and scratch the last suicidal skimmer.

The Spectre bobbed and weaved at the last second, hoping to evade the MRM, but the missile exploded ten meters above the Spectres' position and sent a shower of molten debris down in a cone-shaped spray. The concussive force alone was enough to flatten the hovertank against the deck, but the superheated shrapnel blew dozens of holes in the hovercraft's roof, and soon after its capacitors failed and the vehicle exploded with a thoroughly satisfying crack that sent visible shockwaves across the Pearl's blackened, chalky surface.

"Thanks for the assist, *Sargon*," Xi said, finally accepting that *Elvira* was down until it could get seen to by Koch's people.

"Any time, Major," Sargon acknowledged before his four-mech platoon raced toward the patch of ground she had indicated.

"Lassiter," Xi continued while forwarding *Razor Bamboo* fresh coordinates to the west of their current position, "proceed to the following point at flank speed. That Poltergeist is bound to come back for the base camp, and I want a kill chute up and running when it does."

"Roger," Lassiter acknowledged, though the tension in her voice made clear that she was less than thrilled about heading off to a wide-open patch of ground all by herself.

"You'll do fine, Corporal," Xi assured her as Jenkins' *Warcrafter* sped across the Pearl's surface in unerring pursuit of the still-fleeing Poltergeist. "The colonel's not going to let his white whale get the better of him...or you," she added pointedly.

"Yes, ma'am," Lassiter said as she spurred her mech toward the indicated patch of seemingly unimportant ground.

But if Xi was right, *Razor Bamboo*'s contributions to this particular engagement would end up being of vital importance.

One of the more distressing alarms on her virtual HUD finally went silent, after which Lu declared, "I've got the leak under control and the reactor's stable. Penny took a bad hit to the head, but it looks like she'll make it."

"Good work, Chief." Xi breathed a short sigh of relief, both for Penny and her mech, before raising her Company XO. "Captain Koch, this is Joker," Xi grunted, forwarding damage reports from both *Elvira* and *Fledgling Phoenix*. "After you've secured the cargo, *Phoenix* and I have boo-boos that need some TLC."

"Copy that, Major," Koch replied. "*Apple of Argon* is en route with repair crews."

As *Razor Bamboo* sprinted to its new position seven kilometers to the northwest, Xi felt a surprising degree of calm despite having been functionally knocked out of the fight.

And, she was more than a little interested to see what Colonel Jenkins had in store for the Poltergeist.

16

PREDATOR VS. PREY

"At its current speed, the Poltergeist will evade our railguns in two minutes by falling below the horizon," Alice reported, seamlessly sliding into the workstation Jenkins had come to think of as belonging to Styles while he was aboard *Roy*. "Lieutenant Hao's mech is the only vehicle that will remain in firing range after we have fallen out of it, and she will only maintain lock for forty seconds beyond us."

"I see it," Jenkins grimaced, having run the same calculations a few seconds earlier. He had to slow that Poltergeist down.

Now.

"Clover Actual to *Red Hare*," he called the P2P while forwarding fire coordinates. "I need a full spread of weapons on the following targets. Everything you've got."

"We have one Starburst missile and six tactical nuclear warheads," Captain Guan replied in his usual, disdainful manner. "We do not anticipate the Starburst would survive Jemmin counterfire, but we will fire it on your command, sir."

"Do it," Jenkins acknowledged, knowing that he was emptying the last of the task force's ship-to-ship arsenal by calling down this strike. "The sooner, the better. I need to slow that thing down by hook or by crook, and we're bingo missiles down here."

"Fire order received," Guan replied intently. "Adopting attack posture and firing on my mark...mark."

High above the fleeing Poltergeist, the *Red Hare* unleashed the last of its secret armaments. The dropship was disallowed by at least nine Republic regulations from possessing the missile launch capability it had previously demonstrated.

Jenkins suspected he would soon be deprived of the versatile warship as both it and its parent government came under intense scrutiny regarding its existence. This might well be the last time it fired in support of a Metal Legion operation.

The seven missiles burned toward the planet's surface, preceded by bowls of angry fire as they tore through the Pearl's relatively thick atmosphere. The fleeing Poltergeist never faltered in its flight, moving at two hundred fifty kph.

Which was well over double the top speed of Jenkins' pursuing mechs, which consisted of *Warcrafter* and six other flank-speed-capable Razorbacks, the rest having fallen behind due to previous damage.

Among those six Razorbacks were both Chao and Hao, who seemed determined to show one another up by pushing their vehicles well past the redline. By doing so, they managed to keep pace with *Warcrafter*, which Hammer drove across the terrain with a predatory focus on the fleeing Poltergeist.

While the Razorbacks gave chase, the *Red Hare*'s last barrage of missiles fell closer to the planet's surface. "Missile impacts in twelve seconds," Jenkins called as the flight of ordnance dropped toward the optimal firing range for the Starburst missile. Designed exclusively for use in the void of space, the Starbursts' range was severely limited within an atmosphere as thick and water-rich as the Pearl's. As a result, they had to be at near-point-blank range before they were tactically-viable.

Unfortunately, Jemmin knew this as well as the Terrans. Stabbing skyward with its powerful laser beam, which swept north-south through the missile formation, the Starburst was scrubbed a half-second before it would have broken apart and fired its individual beams. While disappointed, Jenkins was not surprised by Jemmin's expert counterfire.

What he was surprised by was the fact that the Poltergeist also took down two of the six nuclear warheads with the same beam.

"Dammit!" he barked as the remaining four missiles sped toward their target, adjusting mid-flight to address the targets in order of their priority. He nodded in silent thanks to the *Red Hare*'s gunnery team, which had maintained textbook vigilance during the flight of their ordnance.

The Poltergeist adjusted its course and speed, slowing and pulling skyward two seconds before the missiles impacted.

It was a desperation move, one Jenkins and his people were ready to capitalize on.

The nuclear warheads splashed down, unleashing a combined four hundred kilotons of energy and spawning a trapezoidal arrangement of mushroom clouds.

But even before those clouds had begun to darken the Pearl's skies, the six pursuing Razorbacks opened fire on the briefly-exposed target. Two Terran railguns lanced out, those of *Warcrafter* and Lieutenant Hao's mech, managing direct hits on the Poltergeist's stern.

The Jemmin command vehicle faltered mid-flight just as the nuclear shockwaves slammed into its hull. The enemy hover-tank tilted ponderously to port before stabilizing, coming about, and making due south in an effort to flank Jenkins' pursuing mechs. The Poltergeist's speed was considerably diminished now, achieving only one-hundred-sixty kph. While that was still considerably faster than the Terran mechs pursuing it, it was unlikely that fleeing at that speed would be a survivable course of action for the Jemmin commander.

Lowering to the deck, the Jemmin command vehicle made clear its intention to destroy the base camp to the southeast no matter the cost. Jenkins had knowingly overextended his Clover Razorbacks in pursuit of the command vehicle. Judging from the furious fire being exchanged on the northern edge of his formation, between combined Clover-Joker mechs and the northern remnants of the Jemmin support vehicles, he had made the right call in driving the Poltergeist out of rendezvous range with its supporting hovercraft.

He had successfully divided the enemy forces in two, with ten Jemmin craft to the northeast of his position and the Poltergeist to the northwest. He would never get a better chance to take down a Poltergeist than this, and he intended to take full advantage of it.

"Come to papa," Jenkins grunted just before the Poltergeist unleashed its devastating laser beam on Captain Chao's *Fourth Leaf* on the western-most edge of the pursuit team's formation. The *Fourth Leaf*'s tactical icon flickered dangerously for several seconds before stabilizing a sickly shade of yellow, and an all-digital damage report showed that Chao's railgun had been taken offline and his front left leg was now useless. His mech fell out of formation while the rest of the chase team continued on an intercept course with the southbound Poltergeist.

"All hands," he called, knowing that just three more of his five still-mobile Razorbacks in the chase team had functioning railguns. "Railguns hot; fire at will. Take that beast down!"

In reply, Lieutenant Hao's railgun was the first to fire, stabbing a bolt of tungsten across the Poltergeist's bow and missing by less than thirty centimeters. Hammer followed, sending a bolt just above the ducking command tank, which had begun to bob and weave and zig and zag erratically in order to neutralize the Terran railguns' accuracy.

The other two railguns stabbed out with similarly-frustrating results as the Jemmin commander deftly maneuvered the Poltergeist through the sporadic Terran fire.

Emphasizing its tactical superiority, the Poltergeist lashed out with another devastating beam. This strike split its target Razorback in two, carving through the mech's badly-damaged forward hull and skewering its capacitors. The mech died in a violent series of explosions that threw its constituent parts in a flaming and sensational arc, a fireworks display to honor the dead crew.

The Poltergeist was fifty-four kilometers from Jenkins' mech, which put it just at the edge of artillery range under ideal circumstances. Those circumstances included stationary or near-stationary targets, not hovercraft that seemed capable of bending the laws of physics in subtle but important ways mid-flight.

Just three of Jenkins' pursuit team had functioning railguns, including *Warcrafter*. After another staggered barrage of tungsten came up dry, the Poltergeist fired its powerful beam on the next target in the queue.

Which turned out to be *Warcrafter*.

Jenkins' mech lurched violently to port with such force that Jenkins was afraid his vehicle would roll onto its back. Razorbacks were among the only mechs in the Terran Armor Corps incapable of self-righting from a prone position, but Hammer proved his worth by somehow splaying the mech's left legs out and keeping it upright.

"Railgun's offline," Hammer snarled, belching fire from the mech's fifteens in reply to the Poltergeist's insult.

"He's not trying to kill us." Jenkins grimaced as he

forwarded fresh orders to the last two Razorbacks in the chase team with functioning railguns. "He's just trying to scrape our railguns off."

The Poltergeist continued burning southward, and as it did so, the Razorbacks unleashed staggered artillery barrages against it. While their supply of fifteen-kilo shells was not unlimited, they had enough to finish the job if they could only get the Poltergeist to sit still—something it had no intention of doing.

Now was the time to put them on-target, even if that meant they were nothing more than a Hail Mary.

To the north, Lieutenant Staubach's *Cyclops* scored a devastating near-miss with his plasma cannon. With the following barrage of artillery fire from his flanking mechs, the picture-perfect volley scratched a Spectre and a skimmer. Heavy plasma cannons were capable of delivering multi-kiloton charges, though doing so was risky and expensive. Blinky had expertly bracketed a trio of Jemmin vehicles, which had come about to escape the blast zone only to run headlong into a furious barrage of Terran artillery that destroyed all but one of the vehicles in the tight formation.

With just six Jemmin vehicles left to the north and only one of those a Spectre, the smaller Jemmin hovercraft would soon be scrapped by the Metalheads.

"Lieutenant Hao." Jenkins raised her on a P2P link. "I need you to adjust course and sprint due west."

"I'll fall out of intercept on that course, Colonel," Hao replied tersely, although she did as commanded.

"Yes, you will," Jenkins agreed, "but you'll also fall into chase trajectory. If we let this Poltergeist skirt us with its superior speed and maneuverability, this becomes a game of bullets vs. beams. I don't need to draw you a picture of what that means, do I?"

"No, sir," Hao replied, driving her mech on a flat two-hundred-seventy-degree course that would bring it well behind the Poltergeist if both vehicles continued on their current courses for another twelve minutes.

"Captain Chao," Jenkins continued. "Re-target your artillery in the Poltergeist's path. Stay ahead of it at least two hundred meters and keep the shells falling as fast as you can load them."

"Copy that, Colonel," Chao acknowledged.

"*Yellow Winds.*" Jenkins switched over to the only other mech in the formation that still had a functional railgun. "Set new course south-by-southeast. I need you to—"

Yellow Winds was suddenly hammered by the Poltergeist's beam, which carved through both of the Razorback's starboard legs and sent the mech crashing to the deck.

"My apologies, Colonel," growled the mech's Jock. "*Yellow Winds* is down."

"Hao, that just leaves your railgun." Jenkins grimaced, knowing that if they didn't slow the Jemmin commander down it would be a simple matter for it to destroy the salvage they had bled to retrieve from the Pearl's underwater cache. "Make it count, Lieutenant."

"I will," she declared confidently, sending a tungsten bolt roaring through the air. The bolt slammed into the Poltergeist's port flank, knocking the surprisingly nimble vehicle off-axis for several seconds before it stabilized and resumed its previous course. "Direct hit, Colonel," Hao reported viciously as the rest of the nearby Clover mechs unleashed a storm of artillery on the Poltergeist's position.

A dozen fifteen-kilo shells soared on ballistic trajectories, moving toward the wounded Poltergeist as it slowly resumed its southern course. All they needed was one lucky strike to harry the hovertank long enough for another to land, followed by another and another. It wasn't a pretty kill, but at this point, any kill was a good kill.

Unfortunately for the Terrans, the Poltergeist wove its way through the field of fire that erupted around it, avoiding all but a pair of near-misses, neither of which seemed to affect its flight as it resumed its southern course and at a speed the Legion's mechs couldn't match.

The Poltergeist spun, orienting its beam emitter on Lieutenant Hao's mech and opening fire. Hao's Razorback crouched into as tight a ball as a mech of its proportions could manage, and its forward momentum sent the vehicle skittering across the soft stone beneath its roller-feet.

Amazingly, the Jemmin beam appeared to have failed in destroying her railgun. That was confirmed ten seconds later when Hao's mech sent a hypervelocity railgun bolt at the southbound Poltergeist.

Slowly but surely, Jenkins' trap was closing on the Jemmin command vehicle. It wasn't an airtight trap by any means, but it had enough teeth to deter the Poltergeist long enough for the northern mechs of Clover and Joker to eliminate the smaller Jemmin craft. After the Metalheads finished there, they could resume a defensive posture in support of the base camp where the American Navy personnel worked to transfer their cargoes.

If the Poltergeist continued fleeing south in an effort to skirt the Clover mechs while scraping their railguns, Jenkins' people could probably hold it off long enough to thwart a direct assault on the base camp.

But if the Poltergeist shifted course in the next few minutes and drove east-by-southeast for the base camp, there would be a corridor of Terran mechs waiting for it.

The southernmost edge of that corridor had been smartly completed by Major Xi Bao, who had maneuvered one of the Nuggets in a hastily-repaired Razorback into optimal firing position after intercepting a stealthy strike team before it could attack the base camp. Even after several hours submerged beneath the Pearl's scalding waters, the youngest major in Terran Armed Forces history had demonstrated her tactical acumen to a degree few commanders, no matter their age, could have bettered.

"Any time now..." Jenkins said, having placed *Warcrafter* precisely in the center of the trap. In anticipation of what he considered an inevitable development, Jenkins began broadcasting a somewhat controversial musical number over the local frequencies.

When the first heavily-synthesized notes of Rob Zombie's *Superbeast* pumped out over the airwaves, the Jemmin Poltergeist did as Jenkins knew it had to. It took a direct course toward the Terran base camp.

"Atta kid." Jenkins smirked. "Let's do this. Hammer, put us in that hole three hundred meters to the south. Now!"

Warcrafter was the only mech in the Poltergeist's new path —which was precisely how Jenkins wanted it—but the Poltergeist would easily destroy his mech with its ultra-powerful beam if he didn't get out of its line of sight. The crater to the south was the only place the battlewagon could take refuge.

Hammer adjusted *Warcrafter's* course, pivoting the mech so hard that its legs briefly lost footing on the chalky surface. As *Warcrafter* fled to the safety of the crater, Lieutenant Hao's railgun fired another tungsten bolt. Unfortunately, the bolt missed by a handful of meters after the Poltergeist leapt high above the weapon's arc.

While *Warcrafter* moved into the shallow crater, the Poltergeist continued its skyward climb. Its commander meant to neutralize *Warcrafter's* shelter, but this move rendered it increasingly vulnerable to railgun fire.

Seizing the advantage, a pair of railgun-hot Clover mechs

opened fire on the high-flying target. Those mechs' drive systems had suffered serious damage, but their railguns worked well enough to put bolts into the Poltergeist's path.

Strangely, the higher the Poltergeist went, the less agile it appeared to become. While it rolled and twisted mid-flight, the Jemmin hovercraft was unable to juke and zigzag. It maintained a relatively ballistic course.

With a predictable trajectory.

Unfortunately, with just a handful of railguns remaining and the rest of the Legion's arsenal consisting of artillery, the Jemmin commander had made the wise choice in surrendering evasiveness in favor of neutralizing ninety percent of the Terran guns locked onto it.

The Poltergeist inverted, flying roof-down for a pair of seconds as it swept its beam across the hull of a railgun-hot mech to the northeast. The mech did not explode, but its virtual damage report showed that the Jemmin attack had cost it its most potent weapon. The Poltergeist righted itself and resumed its climb, which would bring it into a firing angle on Jenkins' mech in plenty of time for its system to recharge. Even if *Warcrafter* remained huddled against the crater's edge, cowering like a frightened rabbit, the Poltergeist would still have him locked in its sights when it could once again fire.

"Fuck that," Jenkins growled. "Hammer, take us into the middle of this crater and send artillery up at that thing. I don't care about the odds. All crews," Jenkins broadcast over an open channel, "there's a bottle of two-hundred-year-old Scotch in it for anyone who can land a fifteen on that Poltergeist mid-flight."

Artillery roared as shell after shell went skyward, criss-crossing all around the Poltergeist as it climbed to an altitude of nearly two kilometers. Asking his people to hit that thing with artillery was like asking a kid to hit a flying sparrow with a bb gun, but if he was going down, he would do it his way.

And that meant defying the odds.

Fifty-six shells screamed through the atmosphere, with not one coming closer than fifty meters from the target. A railgun stabbed skyward, missing by eight meters, while the tentative fire clock showing the Poltergeist's expected recharge cycle slowly wound down past T-minus ten seconds.

Another twenty shells arced over, under, and all around the still-climbing Poltergeist, none coming closer than seventy meters from the target. The fire clock wound down to five seconds remaining, and Jenkins couldn't help but marvel at the dedication and focus of his people. Everyone on the field knew *Warcrafter* was next in the Poltergeist's sights, and the solidarity in their efforts to defend him filled him with pride.

When the clock hit four seconds to go, *Warcrafter* sent a pair of shells skyward. With two seconds left, it was clear that both of them had missed. Lieutenant Hao's railgun stabbed skyward with one second left, and when it landed on the Poltergeist's stern Jenkins did a literal double-take at the tactical plotter before fully comprehending what had just happened.

Hao had knocked the Jemmin off-course, and the enemy commander was suddenly on a gravity-driven date with the Pearl as the flying craft plummeted toward the ground.

"Pour it on!" Jenkins roared, forwarding the Poltergeist's drop trajectory and optimal fire solutions to the rest of the Brigade.

Artillery thundered across the part of the Pearl's surface that had been chosen for this battle, and this time the first dozen shells came within thirty meters of the enemy vehicle. The next dozen saw a pair scrape so close that they might have chipped the thing's paint.

And then, a lone HE shell from the south bullseyed the falling Poltergeist just as the Jemmin vehicle began to flatten out its descent and resume moving under its own power.

Even a bullseye with an explosive fifteen-kilo shell was unable to scrap the mighty war machine, but what it did was send the hovertank into a flat spin. After a few seconds, the Jemmin regained some measure of control over its descent, pulling out of the flat spin and setting a dangerously steep descent course.

As fate would have it, that course would bring it within a half-kilometer of *Warcrafter*.

"Let's see it, Flake," Jenkins urged his Jock, referring to Hammer by his status as a fresh inter-branch transfer. Nuggets were pulled from the ranks of would-be recruits, while Flakes were less charitably referred to as leftover bits of rust cast off by the war machines of other branches.

"With all due respect..." Hammer grunted, belching iron-wrapped death from *Warcrafter's* dual fifteens and drawing a broad grin from Jenkins as he finished, "Fuck you, sir."

The shells were airbursters, and both of them exploded directly in the approaching Poltergeist's path. One went off so close to the Poltergeist's bow that it blew a three-meter section of armored paneling clean off, while the other merely showered the Jemmin's roof with shrapnel and knocked it into a corkscrew.

Warcrafter's coil guns erupted, stabbing into the Poltergeist's nose as the vehicle plummeted to the ground under what could only charitably be deemed its pilot's control. Dozens of depleted-uranium slugs slammed into the Poltergeist's bow as its descent leveled off a hundred meters above the Pearl's surface. The Jemmin was moving much slower now, barely over eighty kph, and seemed incapable of its previously physics-defying evasive maneuvers.

With just one more hit, the thing could be brought down, and just when the Poltergeist began to accelerate past a hundred kph, another lucky strike landed on its hull.

This time it was the barely operational *Black Widow* in the Joker platoon to the north who scored the hit on the Jemmin commander. The armor-piercing shell skewered the Jemmin hovertank's stern, punching clean through the massive craft, whose size was comparable to the lost *Bahamut Zero*. The Poltergeist lost seventy meters of altitude in the ensuing seconds while slowing to less than sixty kph.

That was when the Metalheads finally bracketed the deadly hovertank.

Another shell fell from the north, this one striking the Poltergeist's bow. Two near-misses sent up showers of rocky debris to the Jemmin's starboard. Another direct hit slammed into the thing center-mass, while Warcrafter added a pair of direct hits on its stern quarter that knocked it to the ground for a brief moment before it resumed hovering less than five meters above the Pearl's surface.

Shell after shell landed on the battered Poltergeist's hull, with thirty-two direct hits registering in twenty seconds before, finally, the enemy vehicle collapsed and lost motive power.

Another forty shells fell on the dying Poltergeist in the following ten seconds, including HE shells from *Warcrafter*. Under such a devastating barrage of Terran fire, the Jemmin Poltergeist lurched upward, lifting itself off the surface for one last charge at the base camp before its fusion reactors went critical and the vehicle exploded in a fusion-powered nova that bathed *Warcrafter* in a deadly rad-wash that marked the last gasp of defiance from the now-dead Jemmin commander.

It was impossible to know before reviewing the Brigade's data recorders whose shell had proved fatal, but what was beyond the shadow of a doubt was that the last Jemmin commander on the Pearl was dead.

During that minute, the northern Metalheads finished off the suddenly-stupefied handful of smaller vehicles. With those targets cratered, the Terran guns fell silent. The board had been swept clean of enemy contacts.

Jenkins breathed a short sigh of relief. "This is Colonel Jenkins to all Terran Armed Forces personnel on the Pearl. Good work, people," he congratulated them while forwarding new patrol coordinates to the still-mobile vehicles in the battered Brigade. "Secure our position and prepare for extraction. Let's get off this rock."

17

WHEELS UP

"Glad to see you made it, Chief," Podsy greeted Styles as the containers were unloaded from *Kochtopussy*.

"Likewise, Lieutenant." Styles nodded before gesturing at the Vorr containers. "The Vorr instructions were explicit: we're not to conduct *any* kind of scans on those storage pods."

"Did you learn anything about them while you were down there?" Podsy asked as the first of eight Vorr pods were carefully transferred by forklifts to a specially-prepared drop-can that would be used in their transfer.

Styles shook his head grimly. "I didn't want to risk any active scans, and the passives didn't show anything of note. Those boxes were made to resist our level of tech, so I doubt that even with active scans, we'd be able to see anything inside."

"What was the dig site like?" Podsy pressed.

"A tomb," Styles shook his head grimly. "Whoever lived down there had a thriving culture and probably knew more about dealing with aquatic environments than we do. There were remnants of...well, *beautiful*," he said after a moment's hesitation, "underwater structures that were like stalactites made of a porcelain-style material. Our guess is those structures were living quarters of some kind."

"Why were they down there?" Podsy pressed.

"Our best *guess*," Styles said pointedly, "is that it was some kind of environmentally-controlled research station. The depth would have protected the facility from ambient radiation interfering with highly-sensitive instrumentation, and would have also made it impossible to access without vehicles capable of withstanding the pressure."

"A secret military facility?" Podsy hazarded.

"Maybe," Styles allowed as the first of the eight crates was secured in the drop-can on the far side of the *Vercingetorix's* relatively cramped drop-deck. "But it's more likely that it was a purely scientific facility. There was no evidence of military hardware anywhere, and the facility's layout was far from defensible. Then again," he shook his head irritably, "it was just *one* chamber. It looks like the Vorr collapsed the two passages that led deeper into the facility."

"Whatever they had us get," Podsy nodded knowingly, "the Vorr didn't want us learning any more about the facility than we did."

"What does Jem think?" Styles asked as the last of the containers was extracted from *Kochtopussy.*

"Jem thinks that whatever we plan to do, we need to hurry," Podsy urged, drawing an approving nod from Styles.

The *Vercingetorix* had only a single retrieval cable, which it had first used to bring *Kochtopussy* and its precious cargo aboard. It would take nearly nine hours to retrieve all of the Legion's mechs from the Pearl's surface, including the battered Razorbacks of the *Red Hare*'s Clover Battalion. Although the *Vercingetorix*, with its eleven surviving mechs and haulers, would be finished with its part in that process in just over three hours if all went according to schedule.

And since no Jemmin surprises had prevented the *Kochto-pussy* from returning to the *Vercingetorix*, there was little reason to believe the enemy had some clever ambush planned for the next few hours.

Podsy and Styles helped the team secure the last of the Vorr salvage pods in the drop-can and then sealed it before placing an armed guard around it to keep it secure. With that task complete, they turned their attention to the stack of containers Styles had loaded while retrieving the Vorr salvage.

"Fifteen crates." Styles nodded grimly after checking the stack of containers. "We lost sixteen and seventeen to enemy torpedoes."

"Let's move them to the machine shop," Podsy urged, gesturing to the drop-deck's adjacent shop space. Styles nodded, and the team carefully transferred the crates to the shop. Podsy had left Jem within that compartment while he had helped unload *Kochtopussy*, and once all fifteen crates were inside the shop, he sealed the door using his command authorization. "Colonel Moon has authorized us to use this compartment," he said urgently after shouldering the satchel containing Jem and plugging the hard-wired earpiece into the interface that permitted him to hear the alien construct. "But he wants us to finish up before the Vorr rendezvous in the event the Vorr want to inspect the ship during transfer."

"Sounds good," Styles agreed as he popped the lid on the first trio of crates, each of which was a standard half-meter by half-meter by one meter. Podsy looked inside the water-filled boxes and saw a handful of objects within each. "These first crates," Styles explained, "had what looked like the same writing as some of the ceramic shards we found near the stalac-tites." Podsy peered down at the shards as Styles picked one up with a pair of tongs while warning, "The water might still be hot enough to burn."

"Ok…" Podsy said, taking the tongs and placing the twenty-centimeter-long curved shard of white ceramic on a nearby workbench where he took a series of visual images with a camera attached to Jem's interface. "What are you seeing, Jem?"

"These markings are consistent with Jem'un records for this species," Jem replied. "There appears to be very little linguistic deviation in this fragment's inscriptions, which should help expedite our inquiry to the nature of the facility's purpose."

"Good," Podsy said in relief while Styles carefully laid out all of the shards in the first three containers on the workbench. "We're on the clock here. Let's get to it."

"Welcome aboard, Major," Lieutenant Commander Stravinsky greeted her crisply as soon as Xi Bao stepped off her battered *Elvira III* and onto the *Vercingetorix's* drop deck. The older woman, who had spent twelve years in the Terran Republic Fleet, appeared to have no great affection for Xi.

Which was good, because the lack of love was mutual.

"Report, Commander?" Xi asked as Dr. Fellows' team took the half-conscious Penny down *Elvira's* boarding ramp. It seemed Xi's latest Monkey would survive with little more than a concussion and some burns to her upper chest, which meant she was in good company in suffering severe burns during her inaugural deployment under Xi's command.

"All Joker vehicles secured, and their crews have completed their preliminary medical examinations," Stravinsky replied. "The *Red Hare* is on schedule and will complete retrieval of Clover Battalion in five hours and twelve minutes."

"Where's Lieutenant Podsednik?" Xi asked, prompting Stravinsky to gesture to the closed machine shop doors, outside which a pair of armored security personnel stood vigil.

"Lieutenant Podsednik and Chief Styles are conducting material examinations, Major," Stravinsky explained. "Will there be anything else?" she asked with clearly-forced courtesy. It was more obvious than ever that Stravinsky chafed at being subordinate to a woman more than a decade younger than her, and in a way, Xi could understand. Stravinsky's Fleet career had seen her rise to her current rank much faster than most, and Xi suspected it was the opportunity to accelerate her career's upward trajectory that had prompted her to transfer to the woefully-undermanned Terran Armor Corps.

Xi resisted the urge to scoff in annoyance before shaking her head. "No, that will be all, Commander."

"Very good, Major," Commander Stravinsky said, snapping a Fleet salute, which Xi returned in Legion fashion. The blond woman then turned smartly on her heel and made her way off the drop deck, presumably en route to the bridge.

"What a stuck-up bitch!" Xi snorted before making her way to the machine shop.

The security officers outside the shop saluted her before opening the door and permitting her passage. She returned the salute, still nowhere near comfortable with receiving the respect her rank required. It seemed like just yesterday that she was fist-fighting with Lieutenant Ford on Durgan's Folly in an attempt to wrestle some kind of control over a single company.

The thought of the ever-gullible Ford, who had made the ultimate sacrifice on Luna during Operation Antivenom, hit Xi with such unexpected force that she actually stopped mid-stride and felt a wave of unease suddenly wash over her.

She had done her best not to think about her fallen comrades, believing that to wallow in their loss was to dishonor their memories. But deep down she had known that she was just kicking that particular can down the road. There was no escaping grief, no matter how hard one tried, and it seemed Xi would have to face her own sooner rather than later.

A tear rolled down her cheek at the thought of not just Ford, but also Sgt. Major Trapper, Sr., who had lost his life in the final moments of Antivenom. In what she was confident had been merely a childish impulse, she had hoped the Sergeant Major would become a fixture in her life in the same way that Colonel Jenkins and Podsy had.

Born in an artificial womb, and having her father die when she was still too young to remember much of him, Xi understood better than most just how deep a void the lack of family could create in a person's life. She had spent most of her prepubescent years thinking she didn't need family, and much of that stubborn belief had persisted even after she had been thrown in jail for her 'crime' of exposing certain politically-incorrect information.

But in her later teens, she had come to realize that while she had no real idea what could be *gained* by having a fully-functional family in support of a person as they made their mark on the universe, she had a pretty good idea of what was *lost* by *not* having one.

After wiping the irritating tear from her cheek, she resumed her walk toward the bench where Styles and Podsy hunched over a handful of metallic objects that stood out among the mostly-ceramic shards surrounding them.

"What have we got?" she asked after the pressure doors swished shut behind her, their mag-locks clamping shut.

"It's hard to say, Major," Styles said in open frustration. "Jem thinks we've got their language worked out, and we're confident that the facility was not a strictly military installation, but beyond that, we're having trouble coming up with what purpose it served."

Xi quirked a brow in surprise. "I thought Jem would be able

to deduce its purpose in less than the three hours it took me to get up here."

"So did we," Podsy said heavily. "But there are inconsistencies that have thrown a few kinks into Jem's theories."

"Well, let's hear it," she urged, leaning down to more closely examine one of the smaller, finer metallic fragments in the neatly-arranged line of artifacts.

"At first," Styles explained, "we thought this was some sort of a listening post, probably used to collect stray cosmic rays or the like. You know, like the ones we still use on interplanetary listening posts to catalog distant large-scale stellar phenomena."

"Supernovas and the like." Xi nodded in understanding.

"Right," Podsy agreed, pulling up a holo-image on a nearby tabletop projector. "Except the debris you found down there doesn't mesh with that theory." Xi examined the slowly rotating holo-image and recognized it as part of the collapsed pile of rubble at the end of the cavern opposite the white 'stalagmite' ruins. "This system," Podsy explained, gesturing to a virtual reconstruction of the broken panels that took the visible pieces in the debris pile and began rearranging them into their previous, spherical shape, "makes no sense for such a collector."

"Why not?" Xi asked with a furrowed brow.

"Because it's omnidirectional," Styles explained. "If you're looking to capture interstellar radiation in a subsurface facility, you wouldn't build your receptor with the goal of trapping particles that passed all the way through your entire planet."

She briefly gritted her teeth in irritation at missing such an obvious point. "Ok." She nodded. "Go on."

"This detector, if that's really what it was," Podsy continued, "was designed to monitor omnidirectional effects or fields. That cuts the list of possible phenomena way, way down."

Styles nodded. "It wasn't built to detect radiation, and we can probably even rule out EM fields. At the time of this thing's construction, this species possessed the ability to launch inter-planetary probes that would have been orders of magnitude cheaper while offering higher-value data than anything you could put so far underground. Make that 'underwater,'" he amended offhandedly.

"What does that leave as the top possibility?" She cocked her head in confusion.

Styles and Podsednik gave each other meaningful looks before Jem's voice unexpectedly came from a nearby data-slate to speak a single word. "Gravity."

"Gravity?" Xi repeated, both alarmed and intrigued by Jem's first utterance since her arrival.

"Yes," Jem confirmed. "There are other possibilities, of course, but gravity seems the most likely phenomenon this facility was built to observe."

"Why would the Vorr be interested in a gravity detection system that was thousands of years old? Isn't there a formula for calculating gravity that's as old as dirt?" Xi asked.

"I lack sufficient data to confidently devise a theory at this time," Jem said. "However, while they required your assistance to retrieve their salvaged artifacts, it is also highly likely that the Vorr do not want their motives to be understood by anyone but themselves."

"Which suggests they're looking for something they think this system's data might help them find," Podsy said grimly.

"And that they're on a timetable." Styles nodded in agreement.

Xi found herself nodding along with the others. "And what-ever it is, it's important enough to cause a *major* battle here. But what?" she asked in mounting frustration.

"I don't want to step out of line here," Podsy said with an unusual lack of confidence, "but...I mean, just for the sake of argument, what would happen if we 'lost' a couple of those Vorr crates?"

Xi shook her head, but it was Jem who replied first. "That would be inadvisable. The Vorr have already deployed significant resources against Jemmin on this planet. The *Red Hare* and *Vercingetorix*, even at full armament, are ill-equipped to combat even a single Vorr cruiser. In fact, the *Dietrich Bonhoeffer* would have been woefully inadequate against a Vorr warship."

"I know that," Podsy insisted. "But...this is probably our only chance to learn whatever it is the Vorr are extracting from down there. We've gone over this other debris," he waved his hand over the broken bits of artifacts scattered on the workbench, "and I just don't think we're going to get much of use from it."

"That is likely accurate," Jem agreed. "Faced with a binary choice between completing your mission and maintaining the Vorr-Terran alliance, or willfully failing to complete that mission while earning Vorr hostility in the process, the optimal course is self-evident."

"Jem's right," Xi said, casting an appraising look toward the satchel bearing Jem's peculiar crystalline 'body.' "We can't gank the deal at this late hour just because we *think* we have an inkling what the Vorr want with this stuff." She looked at Podsy and Styles. "We should present our findings to Colonel Jenkins as soon as he's back aboard the *Red Hare*. That gives us just five hours to glean whatever we can. And by 'we,' I mean you." She pointed with her chin toward the scattered artifacts on the workbench.

"My real concern," Podsy said heavily, "is that it didn't take the three of us long to indirectly figure out what the Vorr probably want with this salvage. That means Jemmin probably already knows, and it won't take the eggheads back home very long to triangulate on it once they've gone over our after-actions.

We're not operating under General Akinouye's Black authority anymore; most of what the Legion does is on the record from this point on."

"If the Vorr are as smart as they claim," Styles started slowly, rubbing his creased forehead, "whatever they're planning might go off sooner rather than later."

"Which brings me back to the idea of 'losing' a few of these crates," Podsy reiterated forcefully. "I know the risks, and I'm not saying we *should* do it, but we might not get another chance to derail whatever it is the Vorr have planned. And frankly? I'm not all that convinced that their 'benevolence' toward us is anything but self-serving."

"Neither am I." Xi shook her head. "But that doesn't change the fact that Jem's right. We can't risk angering the Vorr. Of the factions at war in Nexus Space, I hate to admit it, but the Terran Republic is in last place in terms of firepower. And we suck by a *long* ways, which means we need to cozy up to the Vorr and the Zeen, however distressing that might be." She let her hair down, shook it loose for a few seconds and enjoyed the momentary relief she felt at releasing the pressure of the tight bun she normally wore while inside her mech. After running her hands through her hair, she pulled it into a ponytail and asked, "How can I help?"

"Grab that spectrometer." Styles gestured to a handheld scanner on the far end of the bench. "And help me examine these fragments. I think they were part of some kind of temporary data storage system. With any luck, we might get a few useful bits and bytes out of it."

"On it," she acknowledged, and the trio worked for the next five hours.

18

LOOSE THREADS

"Major, a word?" Podsy beckoned after Xi had stood up from her hunched position over the metallic shards. Five hours of constant focus had put a serious crick in her neck, so she was glad for any kind of diversion.

"What is it, Podsy?" she asked, moving to the far end of the workbench where he stood. It was unusual to have her former Wrench (and, she would admit only to herself, her best friend) calling her by her rank rather than any of the hundred nicknames he had tried out during their time together.

"Major," he said heavily, once again using her rank instead of something less formal, "I've got a theory that I think Colonel Moon needs to hear before Colonel Jenkins is back aboard the *Red Hare*."

Xi cocked her head warily. "What is it?"

"Lieutenant Podsednik." Jem's voice pulsed out from the tabletop speaker Podsy had plugged into the gestalt intelligence's core unit. "We discussed this—"

"Yes we did," Podsy interrupted, "but I have to go to him. I've already wasted too much time."

"What is it, Podsy?" Xi pressed, eyeing Jem uncertainly.

"Jem thinks, and I support the theory," Podsy explained, "that whatever is in those crates out there is going to end up being vital to restructuring the balance of power in Nexus Space. But more importantly, we think the Vorr aren't looking to *remove* Jemmin so much as *replace* it as the dominant power in the known galaxy. I've asked for information supporting Jem's calculations, but Jem has thus far been reluctant to provide me with them."

The first bit had been nothing unexpected to Xi. She had already thought that both Jemmin and the Vorr were committed to controlling whatever information was locked away down on the Pearl, so it was of vital importance to the budding Nexus Wars. That the Vorr would become the dominant race if the Jemmin were defeated also wasn't a revelation.

Sometimes, the lesser of two evils was the best choice. Xi could think of no other options on the grand scale on which Jemmin and the Vorr operated.

But the last bit of his confession was nothing short of shocking. She had stood there on the Zeen world ship, surrounded by Zeen insectaurs while the Vorr ambassador had passionately declared the three species to be in alliance with one another. To suggest that it was simply using the Republic and the Zeen to further its own ascent to power was hardly voicing an unprecedented thought, but it also represented a near-worst-case scenario for humanity going forward.

She wanted to deny it. To argue with Podsy and tell him what she had seen. The unfortunate truth, however, was that she had learned during her brief but intense military career that deception was often (if not *usually*) key to victory in a given contest.

The Vorr could have painstakingly crafted their entire series of interactions with humanity, stretching back decades or possibly even since the human race was first inducted to the Illumination League.

Operational variables changed in the blink of an eye, and it was usually the quickest to adapt who survived those sudden shifts.

"All right." She nodded, her mind working quickly but calmly through what Podsy was telling her. "I'll need access to whatever calculations you've got, Jem," she said urgently. "If you're really interested in helping humanity survive this war, I need as much information as you've got."

"Understood, Major," Jem replied serenely. "I have already prepared a full briefing for your perusal; Lieutenant Podsednik can find it attached to this data storage device."

She made pointed eye contact with Podsy. "I don't know how Colonel Moon will feel about you keeping this theory from him, but for what it's worth, I think holding onto it was the right call. Muddying the waters before now wouldn't have helped anyone, and despite Moon's seniority, he doesn't have operational command of Watery Grave. This is ultimately Colonel Jenkins' call, though I'd expect a pretty severe reaction from Moon once he's brought in the loop. Even if he agrees with us, he's unlikely to appreciate your stepping out of the chain of command."

"I understand," Podsy acknowledged with a firm nod before sliding a microchip into the data slate attached to Jem. A few seconds later, he detached the module and handed it to Xi. "Is that all of it, Jem?"

"It is, Lieutenant Podsednik," Jem replied calmly. Xi tucked the chip into her breast pocket.

Xi's wrist-link chimed, and a quick check confirmed its message was the one she had been expecting. "Colonel Jenkins is back aboard the *Red Hare*." She waved at Podsy and Styles and hurried from the machine-shop-turned-archaeology-lab.

"I'm not going to say any of this surprises me," Jenkins said after Xi had made her report. "Send Jem's data packet over now, and let's bring Lieutenant Podsednik into this before we go any farther."

"Yes, sir," Xi affirmed before summoning Podsy, who made his way through the cramped conference room's doors a few seconds later, having waited outside at her suggestion.

No, she thought with a start, *that wasn't a suggestion. It was a* command.

That particular thought drowned out all others until she managed to shake it off a few seconds later when Podsy came to attention at her side. "Colonel," Podsy greeted him.

"At ease, Lieutenant," Jenkins said, flitting a glance to the pickup while he pored over the data on a separate terminal. Several minutes of silence ticked by before, finally, Jenkins affixed his gaze on the two people in the conference room and said, "If Jem's right about these changed variables, I don't think I need to tell either of you just how vital it is that we keep this theory, and our actions related to it, compartmentalized."

"We agree, sir." Xi nodded in assent. "That's the primary reason Lieutenant Podsednik didn't take this to Colonel Moon earlier—"

"The lieutenant can speak for himself on that matter, Major," Jenkins interrupted, and for a few seconds, Xi Bao felt like she was nine years old again. "Lieutenant?" Jenkins urged.

"My reluctance to share this with Colonel Moon was based on three primary factors, Colonel Jenkins," Podsy said, his posture stiff and his voice hard. "Firstly, Operation Watery Grave is under your command, not Colonel Moon's. Since this theory had no bearing on ship operations aboard the *Vercingetorix*, I chose not to report it to Colonel Moon. Second, I could not envision a scenario where acting on this intel prior to this moment would have produced a net gain for the Republic. And third...frankly, I don't trust Jem, sir."

Xi's eyebrows rose in surprise at hearing that last bit. Jem had risked as much as any Metalhead during Antivenom, and in a very real sense, the survival of the human race had been due to Jem's assistance. If providing that kind of help wasn't enough to secure Podsy's trust, what could?

"The first point might hold water," Jenkins said dubiously. "The second represents the kind of insubordination that could get you hauled in front of a court-martial. Put bluntly, it wasn't *your* call to make regarding whether or not this was actionable intel, Lieutenant. Is that clear?"

"Yes, sir," Podsy acknowledged stiffly.

"But your third point..." Jenkins mused, "is probably what will keep you on the high side of the airlock after I bring Colonel Moon in on this."

"Sir?" Xi blurted in alarm.

"Jem has made invaluable contributions to human interests, Major," Jenkins said, fixing her with a hard look that was somehow magnified by the video feed. "But it is still an unknown variable. We don't know if any of this information will check out." He gestured to his terminal off-screen where he had previously perused the file Jem provided. "But I am seeing a few things here that suggest there's something to Jem's concerns regarding the Vorr. Let me be as clear as I can be on this point, Major, Lieutenant." His eyes swiveled back and forth between them. "Jem is inextricably linked to Jemmin in ways we don't fully understand. Even if Jem sincerely believes it is acting in our best interests, it is possible, however unlikely, that its actions have been part of an incomprehensible plot to manipulate us for Jemmin gain."

"You don't actually believe that, do you, sir?" Xi asked with forced neutrality.

"Frankly?" Jenkins let the question linger for a long moment before shaking his head. "No, I don't. I think Jem is what it says, and that it hasn't substantially misrepresented its motives to this point. But the fact that any of us even has to *consider* the possibility should make clear to everyone on this call that Jem represents a potentially catastrophic failure point in our intel stream. We need to widen our stance in that department, and we need to do it ASAP. Agreed?"

"Yes, sir," Xi and Podsy acknowledged in near-unison.

"Colonel Moon?" Jenkins asked, prompting the display to split and show both Jenkins' and Moon's faces.

"I concur," Colonel Moon said with a nod, causing the pit of Xi's stomach to plummet as she wondered just how much of the call Moon had listened to. "The data Jem provided shows several tactical anomalies in the Nexus, with the most striking discrepancies regarding the destruction of two Jemmin gate-crashers near their gates of emergence. We should calibrate both the *Red Hare's* and *Vercingetorix's* sensors to go over that region in exacting detail when we return to the Nexus, but we should do so as clandestinely as possible. We don't want to alert the Vorr or Jemmin to our interest in the exchange. I'll have my people begin going over the ship's logs from our previous trip through the Nexus. It would be wise to have Captain Guan's people do likewise, Colonel."

"Agreed," Jenkins acknowledged, "though that does bring the issue of the Vorr transfer to the fore. Your thoughts on that front, Colonel Moon?"

"There is no gain to be had by antagonizing the Vorr," Moon replied, slicing a brief but pointed look Podsy's way. "And, frankly, we don't want them coming aboard where they'll learn what we brought back from the Pearl. If we want to learn what they were after down there, our best option is to proceed with the handoff on schedule and without deviation from our mission directives. We'll have to content ourselves with the salvage Chief Styles and the Americans brought back."

"I agree." Jenkins nodded. "Pull whoever you can use to analyze that salvage, but be prepared to destroy it in the event the Vorr insist on inspecting the *Vercingetorix*. Our top priority at this point has to be maintaining the Vorr-Terran alliance, even at the cost of potential intel. Is that your opinion as well, Colonel?"

"It is," Moon agreed. "Our objective at the Pearl was to provide the Vorr with operational support, which is what we should do."

"Good," Jenkins said before turning his gaze to Xi. "We've got a couple of stray Nuggets over here, Major. Do you want them transferred back to the *Vercingetorix* before we break orbit?"

Xi grinned. "I'll defer to you on that decision, Colonel. Though if the *Red Hare* has any especially filthy heads in need of scrubbing, I'm sure they could use the practice."

Jenkins returned the grin. "Loud and clear, Major. We'll berth them over here until we return to HQ. Colonel Moon, how long until we break orbit?"

"The *Vercingetorix* is ready on your command, Colonel," Moon replied promptly.

"Captain Guan says the *Red Hare* will need another hour before we hit the couches," Jenkins said. "Start your clock."

"Acknowledged." Colonel Moon nodded before cutting the comm. Colonel Jenkins' visage remained for a moment, during which he eyed Podsy before he, too, cut the line and vanished from the display.

Podsy exhaled a long sigh, but there was nothing contented

or relaxing about the sound. Xi placed a hand on his shoulder and said, "You'll get through this, Podsy."

He nodded, but his face showed a lack of confidence as he turned and left the conference room.

"Corporal Lassiter," Jenkins greeted her five minutes after ending the call with Xi, Podsy, and Moon. "Have a seat."

The diminutive woman released her salute and sat down in the chair opposite Jenkins'. She had a keen look in her eyes that reminded him of Xi Bao's during their first face-to-face meeting. Xi had been hotheaded, razor-sharp, and in-your-face from the first moment. In fact, it had been a close-run affair to get her through basic training without her getting the boot for repeated insubordination.

This woman had the same sharp look in her eye, but she was far more reserved than Xi had ever been (or, in all likelihood, would ever be).

"Colonel, I just want to say—" Lassiter began, only to be interrupted by Jenkins as he threw a video record up on his office's two-dimensional display.

"Do you recognize this scene?" Jenkins asked, gesturing to the image.

Lassiter turned and promptly nodded. "It's *Warcrafter's* combat recorder data, Colonel. It shows the Poltergeist as it moved to gain a firing angle on your vehicle after you'd taken cover, sir."

A sudden flash on the Poltergeist's hull prompted Jenkins to pause the recording a few frames later and ask, "What happened there, Corporal?"

Lassiter squirmed in her seat before replying, "The Poltergeist was struck by a fifteen-kilo shell, Colonel."

Jenkins nodded approvingly. "Normally that would be a rare enough event since the Terran Armed Forces has only ever officially engaged three Jemmin Poltergeists in all of its recorded history." He held up a trio of fingers. "As it happens, the Metal Legion has earned all three of those hashes. But this particular shell," he gestured to the still image on the display, "struck a highly-mobile target mid-air and ended up being the decisive blow that brought that command vehicle down. It was a hit that I wanted to land for purely selfish reasons, but I was denied the opportunity to notch this hash by that shell's author. Do you know who fired that shell, Corporal?" he asked with a growing hint of threat in his voice.

Lassiter went red from the collar up, but her features remained stoic as she nodded. "Yes, sir, I do."

"Who fired that shell, Corporal Lassiter?" Jenkins leaned across his desk, lacing his fingers together and pinning her to her chair with an iron glare. "Who robbed *me* of *my* victory down there?"

"Colonel..." She faltered briefly before rallying. "Sir, I did, Colonel Jenkins, sir."

"You did?" He scoffed, working hard to keep his true emotions from breaking the act. "You're trying to tell me that during your first ride as Jock aboard a battlewagon, you landed a kill-shot on the most valuable target the Terran Armor Corps has ever engaged? Do you *actually* expect me to believe that?"

"Sir..." Lassiter regained her composure, and thankfully she made no attempt to back down. "Your own combat recorder shows where that shell came from. There is no doubt."

Jenkins kept up the glare for a long, silent moment before shaking his head contemptuously. "Even if that data is accurate, Corporal, it would only mean that you got lucky."

The diminutive, strong-willed woman jutted her chin out defiantly. "Frankly, sir, I'd rather be lucky than good."

Jenkins rubbed a hand over his jaw to cover the grin that fought to break through his stony glare. As he did so, he reached beneath his desk and wrapped his fingers around the glass neck of a bottle he'd held onto for far, far too long. "Frankly, Corporal," he said, allowing the restrained grin to overtake his features. "So would I." He set the bottle down on the desk and slid it toward her, causing her to recoil warily. "I've been saving that bottle for a long, *long* time," he explained after sliding it over to her side of the desk. It was the same bottle he had carried with him since sobering up in the wake of his wife's death. The one he had looked at every single day as a reminder of what his weakness had cost the most important person in his life. "It's two hundred years old, and I've lugged it around for more of those years than I care to remember. And honestly, I can't think of a better use for it than to commemorate your first kill." He stood from the desk, prompting her to do likewise as he proffered an open hand. "Congratulations, Corporal."

She shook his hand and hesitantly replied, "Thank you, Colonel." She picked the bottle up from the desk and turned it over before asking, "Where are the glasses? I'd be honored if you'd share the first drink with me, sir."

Jenkins shook his head, and his smile waned fractionally. "You'll find no shortage of takers for that offer aboard this ship, Corporal, but I won't be among them," he said before gesturing to the door. "You've got fifty-one minutes before we hit the couches, and Captain Guan probably won't look too kindly on a full bottle of contraband on the loose aboard his ship. Do I make myself clear?"

Lassiter seemed uncertain why Jenkins had refused the offer to share a drink with her, but she took his meaning clearly enough and gushed, "As a Solarian's conscience, sir. Thank you, Colonel."

"Dismissed, Corporal," he said with a nod, and a moment

later she was through the door with the bottle tucked under her arm.

"At some point," Jenkins said under his breath, echoing the words of his late wife, "You've got to let go of the past, Lee."

Those words were both wise and true, but he wondered if he could ever truly move on. Her death had come to define him in ways he did not fully understand, but something he did know was that he had searched for meaning, purpose, and even redemption since that day.

He knew he could never undo his past errors, nor could he overcome them. But he also knew that he needed to stop looking backward and start moving forward. Hundreds of people relied on him day-in, day-out to make tough calls on their behalf. People like Corporal Lassiter who were just starting to make their mark on the universe needed him to keep his eye on the ball and not the scoreboard.

He had found meaning and purpose for his life in the Metal Legion, which needed him more than he had been needed by anyone or anything since his wife's death.

But redemption?

Jenkins thought he was ready to stop worrying about that part, which was equally liberating and terrifying.

19

THE HANDOFF

"Event horizon in five seconds," the *Red Hare*'s helmsman reported as the ship neared the wormhole gate. Jenkins was secure in his couch, like most of the *Red Hare*'s crew, as the ship traversed the last few meters ahead of the murky darkness that loomed off the ship's bow. "Four...three...two...one. Mark," declared the ship's pilot as the ship slipped through the ripple in space-time.

The ship's sensors quickly populated with nearby contacts, and Jenkins was both relieved and surprised to find the local board was almost completely clear of Jemmin icons.

In fact, the nearest ship of note was one he had never previously seen. Its design appeared to be that of a Vorr warship, but its size rivaled the gatecrashers or a Republican-class dreadnought.

Measuring four kilometers from bow to stern and nearly a full kilometer at the widest point of its beam, the Vorr dreadnought hung less than a quarter light-second from the *Red Hare*. The roughly squid-shaped mega-ship, with a cluster of what appeared to be engine modules affixed to its stern that looked very much like squat tentacles, was surrounded by a fleet of forty smaller warships ranging in size from corvettes to cruisers. One of those corvettes was just a few thousand kilometers from the gate, and it began to accelerate in their direction immediately upon the Terrans' arrival.

Any one of those ships could have stood off and annihilated the Armor Corps dropships with their superior-range beam weapons. Despite that self-evident fact, it was the sheer *size* of the previously-uncatalogued Vorr dreadnought that dominated Jenkins' thoughts as he pored over his limited slice of the *Red Hare*'s sensor feeds.

"Vorr capital ship identifies as the *Broken Tide*," Sensors reported with tight professionalism. "It's squawking valid Watery Grave idents and is requesting a secure comm link with us."

"Colonel Jenkins?" Captain Guan urged.

"Request permission to disembark our couches and open a channel with the *Broken Tide*, Captain," Jenkins said.

"Permission granted," Guan acknowledged, causing Jenkins' couch to drain away its shock-absorbing gel before the lid popped open.

Jenkins stood from the couch and wiped off the small handful of gel that clung to his collar while removing his helmet and making his way to the ship's comm station. He was joined there by Captain Guan and Alice, who had previously requested permission to observe the exchange.

"Initiate link," Jenkins commanded after finally removing the last of the gel from the helmet and collar.

Captain Guan nodded affirmatively, prompting the holodisplay to spring to life with the image of an octopus-like Vorr floating in a green-blue pool of liquid.

"This is Tranquility of Abundant Oxygen, Primus of the *Broken Tide*," said what Jenkins presumed to be the *Broken*

Tide's CO. "We are prepared to receive the transfer as stipu-lated by our delegate, Deep Currents of Radiant Warmth."

"This is Colonel Lee Jenkins of the Terran Armor Corps," Jenkins replied. "We are prepared to conduct the transfer at your earliest convenience."

"Proceed to the coordinates indicated in the sub-transmis-sion attached to this link," Tranquility of Abundant Oxygen said, which sounded suspiciously like the command of a supe-rior rather than a formal request made by an ally.

"Acknowledged," Jenkins said, having expected such a reception. He glanced at Captain Guan, who silently held up ten fingers, followed by another six, and added, "We'll deliver the package to the drop coordinates in sixteen minutes."

"Tolerable," the Vorr said before cutting the line.

"Jesus..." Jenkins muttered as the ship slowly pulled away from the wormhole gate and made its way to the nearby patch of space indicated by the Vorr.

"They are becoming increasingly arrogant," Guan observed.

"Can you blame them?" Jenkins asked, inclining his chin toward the holo-image of the colossal *Broken Tide* that loomed well within firing range. "What happened to the Jemmin warships that were harassing the Vorr here?"

"It does not appear they were destroyed," Guan reported, poring over sensor data streaming down a pair of monitors. "However, it *does* appear they have withdrawn to the Jemmin gates, where they currently remain."

Jenkins silently examined the sensor feeds, while Alice did likewise at his side. Captain Guan was right; the Vorr and Jemmin forces appeared to have broken apart, with each side opting to hunker down beside its own gates rather than continue the complex engagements that had filled the Nexus during the Legion's previous visits to the all-important star system.

"They could still be engaged," Jenkins mused, pointing to a handful of Vorr formations that stood just outside striking range of the Jemmin, "but they've opted to pull back. Why?"

Alice narrowed her eyes contemplatively. "It could be that their primary goals have already been satisfied. Perhaps all they wished to accomplish at this stage was to push Jemmin back from Vorr gates?"

"That doesn't mesh with what we saw here previously." Jenkins shook his head.

"It does not," Guan agreed. "The engagements we previously saw here were designed to transfer total control of this star system from Jemmin to Vorr hands...or tentacles, as it were." He smirked. "Something significant has changed. But what?"

"Who blinked first, the Vorr or Jemmin?" Alice asked, drawing an approving nod from Captain Guan.

"It will take the *Red Hare*'s analysts several hours to examine this information and present a credible hypothesis on that matter," Guan explained. "But judging from what we previously knew of the two fleets' postures, I would guess that Jemmin's unexpected withdrawal prompted the Vorr to do likewise."

"So if Jemmin blinked first," Alice remarked. "The next obvious question is why?"

"I might have a lead on that," Jenkins said. He gestured to a nearby screen that displayed the relatively covert sensor data being collected by the *Red Hare*'s scanners as they scoured the sites where the two Jemmin gatecrashers that were the foundation for Jem's increasing concern regarding the Vorr and their intentions had been destroyed. "But I can't go into details just yet."

"Understood." Guan nodded, although Alice seemed less than understanding as she gave him a quizzical look.

As she did so, Jenkins noticed that the skin surrounding the subtle One Mind implants at the base of her neck was red and swollen. He gestured to the link ports. "Are you having trouble with your implants?"

"Trouble?" Alice shook her head. "No. But their deactivation has caused...uncomfortable immunological responses. I have already spoken to Dr. Fellows, who will complete the removal of the offending implants upon our return to Terran space."

"Removal?" Jenkins repeated with unexpected concern in his voice. "I wasn't aware you wanted them pulled."

"It seemed to be a meaningful gesture in the interests of fostering improved relations between our governments." She shrugged indifferently. "You have correctly, albeit subtly," she added with a trace of annoyance, "observed that the One Mind network, for all its obvious merits, bears many features your people consider to be undesirable. My new role is to facilitate trust and communication between Sol and Terra, which I will do to the utmost of my abilities. If the cost is some discomfort and a disconnection from the One Mind, it is one I will gladly pay."

Jenkins was simultaneously concerned and impressed by her decision. If she removed her One Mind implants, it was unlikely to have an immediate effect on her mind or body since Solarians were perfectly capable of disconnecting from the One Mind for significant intervals. But the prospect of not returning to what must have been the comfort of the One Mind network was one which he suspected he would never fully understand.

"I don't know how to respond," he said after a moment's consideration.

"You need not do so," she said dismissively, though he

suspected she was putting up a bold front to cover serious concerns. "As a student of individuality, I have long wished to directly experience an abrupt disconnect for purely scientific reasons."

They spent the next ten minutes in relative silence as the *Red Hare* moved to the drop point while the *Vercingetorix* emerged from the event horizon off its stern. The precious Vorr cargo was aboard the *Vercingetorix*, and Captain Guan had factored their delayed arrival into his sixteen-minute ETA.

"The *Vercingetorix* has arrived at the coordinates, Colonel," Captain Guan reported. "Colonel Moon reports that the package is secure and ready to drop."

"*Vercingetorix* Actual, this is Colonel Jenkins. Drop the package," Jenkins ordered as a Vorr corvette sped toward their position. Accelerating at nearly fifty gees, the fleet-footed warship was moving several times faster than the *Red Hare* or *Vercingetorix* could match. Peculiarities of Vorr neurophysiology made them especially adept at surviving high-gee burns, which meant that, even without augments, their bodies could withstand even greater accelerative force than the most extensively-augmented humans.

"Dropping the package," Colonel Moon acknowledged, and the specially-prepared drop-can containing the precious Vorr salvage was ejected from the launch tube.

The drop-can drifted out from the *Vercingetorix*, which adjusted course away from the cargo and toward the New America gate. It would take them several hours to reach Terran space under ideal circumstances, which these were not.

"The Vorr should collect the package in eight minutes," Guan reported a few minutes later. "We are experiencing minor fluctuations in our drive's fuel delivery system," he said, prompting Jenkins to hide a grin as the ship's CO played a card they hoped would buy them time in Nexus Space.

Every senior officer assigned to Watery Grave agreed that they needed to gather as much intel as possible while in the Nexus, so if that meant sandbagging so they could keep their scanners live for another hour or two, that was precisely what they were going to do.

"Understood," Jenkins acknowledged. "I'll inform the Vorr."

"Channel open," Guan declared.

"This is Colonel Lee Jenkins of the Terran Armor Corps," Jenkins said. "We're experiencing minor issues with our drive system. It will take us at least twenty-eight minutes to conduct a full diagnostic of the system, during which time we'll be limited to auxiliary propulsion en route to our home gate. Acknowledge."

Tense, silent seconds ticked by one after another as they awaited the Vorr reply. Seconds stretched into a minute, during which time the Vorr corvette on approach swept them stem-to-stern with active scan pulses.

Eventually, the dreadnought *Broken Tide* broadcast an audio-only reply. "Transmission acknowledged. Terran safety cannot be guaranteed if further delays are experienced. Proceed with all possible haste to your home space."

"Message received, *Broken Tide*," Jenkins replied through briefly-gritted teeth before cutting the line. If he had previously harbored doubts regarding the growing hostility he saw from the Vorr, those doubts were all but erased by that last communique.

Which only made their covert information-gathering operation during in-Nexus transit even *more* vital to securing Terran interests.

"It is possible," Alice interjected into the taut silence that followed, "although unlikely, that the Vorr are simply projecting hostility for diplomatic reasons."

Jenkins and Guan both turned toward her with surprised expressions. "Explain," Guan urged.

Alice shrugged. "The Vorr are a natural prey species, and as such, they are not naturally equipped to interact with predators in a social manner. Their intelligence and high degree of social cohesion permit them to not only survive in the presence of predators like humans or Jemmin but to stave off such predators. Still," she said pointedly, "they are not natural predators themselves, and as such they must approximate certain minimum levels of hostility in their efforts to be in charge."

"They do offer bits of their own bodies as part of a greeting ritual..." Guan mused. "Though that is a less meaningful gesture than one might imagine since it is in their species' natural arsenal of predator-avoidance adaptations, and they regenerate lost appendages in a matter of weeks."

"Lizards pop their tails off while being pursued by predators," Jenkins agreed, "just to buy a few extra seconds of confusion while the thing wriggles around in their wake. But they also grow new ones."

"Exactly." Alice nodded. "And nearly all human social gestures from the simple smile to handshakes, even including certain sexual acts, incorporate our innately predatory aggression as fundamental components upon which the relevant meaning of those gestures is built."

"Which sexual acts might you be referring to?" Guan asked dryly, drawing a withering look from Alice.

"I am certain that even *your* imagination is equal to the task of answering that question, Captain Guan," she riposted before easily returning to the subject at hand. "I think it is possible that the Vorr are simply projecting hostility, and that they do not understand the full impact of that projection, given their relative inexperience with it. What we read as cold and openly hostile might be intended as little more than a tooth-filled smile. I find it unlikely," she allowed, "but I also think that xenopsychology is one of the many fields with which my familiarity might be of some use when it comes to dealing with non-human species."

Jenkins chuckled. "I'm starting to think there was a lot more to your reassignment than you initially suggested, Alice."

"Then you are perhaps more astute than I initially suspected, Lee," she replied easily. "For a Neanderthal."

It seemed that every time Alice unexpectedly opened her mouth, she made a key observation that Jenkins had not previously considered.

But despite his newfound attraction, he remained wary and wondered if her reassignment was part of some grand plot to subvert him.

Stop jumping at shadows, Lee, he silently scolded himself. *Not everything's a conspiracy, and even less is about you.*

Still, he suspected that the Alice situation would come to a head sooner than he would have liked.

All things being equal, he was looking forward to that particular moment.

With the transfer completed and the *Red Hare*'s "repairs" made to its drive system, the ship's crew returned to their grav-couches and remained there while the pair of TAC dropships headed into the New America gate.

The *Red Hare* slipped through the event horizon, returning to the comfort of Terran space where Jenkins received a coded message addressed to Major Xi.

He scanned the message's brief contents while awaiting the *Vercingetorix's* arrival in the New America 2 system. The Zeen worldship stood sentinel opposite a quartet of Terran dreadnoughts commanded by Admiral Wallace.

As soon as the *Vercingetorix* arrived in New America 2, Jenkins raised the major on a secure P2P line.

"Go ahead, Colonel," Xi acknowledged, her voice muffled within her couch's helmet.

"Don't let your hair down just yet, Major," Jenkins advised in code. "It looks like you've got a blind date here in NA-2."

She hesitated before replying in the same code, "Will I need lipstick, sir?"

"It probably wouldn't hurt," Jenkins replied. "The *Vercingetorix* will hold position at the NA-1 gate, but the *Red Hare* needs to see to these drive malfunctions. Let us know how it goes, Major."

"Yes, Dad," she replied irritably.

20

XI BAO, DIPLOMAT

As her shuttle drifted silently through the near-vacuum of New America 2's interplanetary space, Xi Bao was given a rare opportunity to reflect on recent events.

Foremost among those were the deaths of her fellow Metalheads. It seemed both strange and wholly inappropriate that she felt more at peace (if such a term could ever be truthfully employed when dealing with loss) with the more recent losses sustained during Watery Grave than she did with those from Antivenom.

She still had difficulty accepting wholly and without lingering doubt that men like the sergeant major and Lieutenant Eugene Ford were gone from the universe. Was it because she felt closer to them than she did to other more recent losses? That was possible, and if it was true, it seemed to suggest that she had succumbed to the same process that had stripped men like Colonel Moon of some small but significant facet of their humanity. The rule was, Don't get too close to your people.

And that, to her mind, was the most concerning part of all.

She didn't *want* to be fine with the deaths of men and women under her command. She didn't *want* to learn how to treat them like entries in a database. She wanted to remember them in excruciating detail so that even if no one else did, she would carry some part of them forward as she played her part in the epic drama that was the universe.

Fatso, Ford, Trapper, General Akinouye, and the others who had fallen before deserved no greater portion of her respect and sorrow than Corporal Cervantes, who had given her last full measure of devotion in Watery Grave just like those who had gone before. But try as she might, she couldn't even muster the basic human decency to recall the face of the latter, while visages of the former remained crystal clear in her mind's eye.

Corporal Cervantes had fought and died under Xi's command. If that wasn't enough to earn someone a place in her CO's memory, nothing ever could.

A clang on the hull outside startled her from her musings, and her hand reflexively went to her hip, where a high-powered, chem-driven hand cannon rested. If she had learned one thing when dealing with the Zeen, it was that their approach to diplomacy could very easily be mistaken for wanton aggression.

"Better to have a gun and not need it than to need one and not have it…" she muttered as the already-dim lights in the shuttlecraft suddenly winked out. "What the hell?" she gritted her teeth before moving toward the tiny craft's cockpit, where all of the previously-powered-down instrumentation now seemed completely dead.

Something had not only killed the shuttle's central power supply, but it had also even killed the local backups built into each of the hardened, independently-powered terminals that made up the shuttle's control systems.

There was a faint but unmistakable triple-knock at the shuttle's outer airlock door, and Xi tightened her grip on the hand cannon before forcing herself to relax. If the Zeen wanted her dead, they could have very easily blown her shuttle apart from a full light second out.

Still, it was difficult to dismiss the thought of being eaten alive by a ravenous insectaur, but she had to leave those thoughts behind as she made her way to the airlock's manual crank-driven system. The crank was there to allow disembarkation in the event of total power failure, and after a few seconds of removing the panels that covered the crank bar, she began the slow process of manually opening the outer airlock doors.

When she had finished, there was a second triple-knock, this time much louder, from the other side of the inner airlock door.

Cranking the outer airlock door closed, she did her level best to make sure it was as tight as possible before manually cranking open the inner door.

And, just as she had expected, a single insectaur was standing on the other side of that door once she had pried it open.

Its arms were splayed wide in the symmetrical gesture she had come to think of as an inviting or greeting one. She did her best to approximate the gesture, and when she did so, the Zeen produced a Vorr auto-translation device.

Unlike the previous units Xi had seen the Zeen use, this one had undergone significant modifications, the likes of which she could only guess at.

"Greetings, Captain Xi Bao," the Zeen greeted her in a decidedly masculine tone that replaced its predecessors' synthetic, genderless one. "We are harmonious with the mind-union achieved together here."

Xi cocked her head in confusion. This didn't sound anything like her previous interactions with the Zeen, whose speech had been so badly fractured that it was nearly incomprehensible at times.

These utterances, while still falling well short of fluent, sounded significantly more complex and clear.

"I am happy to be of service to the Terran-Zeen alliance," Xi said, momentarily caught off-guard by the unexpected change in communicative style. "But it's Major Xi Bao now," she added, feeling like an ass as soon as she did.

"Human hierarchies unstable to mind of Zeen Home Three," the Zeen replied with what sounded like something approximating exasperation.

"Yes, they certainly can be," she agreed.

"Major Xi Bao capable fulfill previous designation?" it asked expectantly.

She nodded. "I am. The change from captain to major is an...increase in hierarchical standing and authority among my people," she explained after a moment's thought.

"Zeen Home Three comprehension sufficient," the Zeen acknowledged before casually dropping a proverbial bombshell on the meeting. "Zeen Home Three confidence of Vorr inadequate to sustain harmonious alliance. Termination appropriate."

She was pretty sure her heart skipped several beats in the taut seconds that followed that declaration. If the Zeen-Vorr alliance broke, there was no telling how the Vorr would react. And with Zeen Home Three sitting on the Terran Republic's front doorstep, Xi was genuinely uncertain if the Terran Republic could neutralize the threat it posed if it suddenly turned hostile to humanity.

Her mind briefly raced in search of a productive reply in the face of such a staggering revelation, and eventually, she settled on a question. "Why is Zeen Home Three's confidence in the Vorr no longer adequate to sustain a harmonious alliance?"

"Inadequate to reply," the Zeen said simply.

"What does that mean?" Xi's brow furrowed in confusion.

"Zeen unable to respond to query."

Xi suddenly felt very, very small in the grand scheme of things. She would never believe herself stupid, but conducting inter-species diplomacy had never been an ambition of hers (in no small part because she knew her short temper was ill-suited to it). So she had never considered how to craft and execute a conversation tree along the lines of what she now faced.

Eventually, she managed to compose her thoughts and ask the previous question in a slightly different way. "Why did Zeen Home Three agree to the Zeen-Vorr alliance in the first place?"

"No Zeen-Vorr alliance," the Zeen said adamantly. "Only Zeen-Vorr-Terran alliance."

She suddenly narrowed her eyes. "Wait a second, are you telling me that you wouldn't have allied with the Vorr without Terran inclusion?"

"Symmetrical."

Xi recoiled in alarm. "Why not?"

"Zeen Home Three observes asymmetrical Vorr behavior," it explained, sending a chill down Xi's spine. "Observation one: Vorr are prey species; Vorr are strong fighters. These features asymmetrical. Observation two: Vorr states Zeen equal to Vorr in Zeen-Vorr-Terran alliance; Vorr battle strategies feature unacceptably high proportion of resource commitment and loss from Zeen. Vorr statements asymmetrical with Vorr behaviors. Strategic assessment based on these observations: Vorr use Zeen to protect Vorr, not to protect Zeen-Vorr-Terran alliance."

Xi's wariness grew with each passing second. Either the Zeen were suddenly becoming much, much better at communicating or the Zeen were dramatically better at elucidating their thoughts on tactical and strategic matters than they were on anything else.

Which seemed to support a lingering doubt she and the rest of the Metal Legion's command staff had quietly discussed; the possibility that the Zeen were not, in fact, a naturally-occurring species, but were instead purpose-built weapons or, at the very least, a soldier caste of some long-dead civilization that eschewed the synthetic in favor of the organic wherever possible.

To buy herself some time and to keep the conversation moving, Xi asked, "What modifications did you make to that translation device?"

"Device insufficient to Zeen needs," the Zeen explained. "Vorr supplied device with stated goal to facilitate Terran-Zeen communication. Device's design is flawed. Zeen correct flaws. Device improved. Device's design flaw asymmetrical with Vorr stated goal of facilitating Terran-Zeen communication."

She closed her eyes in disbelief. If the Vorr had purposely given the Zeen flawed translators, the only logical reason for such diplomatic sabotage would be to minimize, or outright prevent, Zeen-Terran interactions that did not include the Vorr.

Which brought a sudden, concerning thought to Xi's mind. "Where is the Vorr ambassador assigned to Zeen Home Three?"

"Vorr ambassador alive," the Zeen replied, although the way it said it did little to allay her worst fears. "Vorr ambassador objected to Zeen removal of concealed Vorr surveillance devices on Zeen Home Three. Zeen consider surveillance devices violation of Zeen-Vorr-Terran alliance. Vorr ambassador failed to persuade Zeen otherwise. Concealed surveillance devices asymmetrical with stated nature of Zeen-Vorr-Terran alliance."

"Listen to me," Xi said urgently. "No matter what Zeen Home Three chooses to do regarding the alliance, you absolutely *cannot* mistreat the Vorr ambassador."

"Clarify."

"Regardless of what happens between the Zeen and the Vorr," Xi explained anxiously, "the Terran Republic would prefer to maintain some sort of working relationship with *both*

Zeen and Vorr. But if Zeen Home Three starts killing Vorr ambassadors, even under objectionable circumstances like the ones you describe, it's going to be nearly impossible for the Terran Republic to justify diplomatic relations with you. There could be no symmetry."

"Safety of Vorr ambassador symmetrical with Zeen Home Three-Terran alliance?" the Zeen asked.

"Yes, definitely." She nodded eagerly. "Without a doubt, maintaining the safety of the Vorr ambassador is one hundred percent symmetrical with a Zeen Home Three-Terran alliance."

"Major Xi Bao's position in Terran hierarchy sufficient to form Zeen Home Three-Terran alliance?"

"Unfortunately, no." She shook her head measuredly. "But if it was up to me, I would absolutely support such an alliance. When Zeen Home Three helped destroy that Jemmin gate-crasher, you saved hundreds of millions of Terrans from being slaughtered by Jemmin. We will *never* forget that," she said passionately.

"Human hierarchies unstable," the Zeen said skeptically. "Unstable hierarchies create unstable behavior patterns."

"That's true," she allowed, "but some things last longer than living memory. And if my read of human history is accurate, I think the assistance you provided against the gatecrasher will be remembered for *at least* as long as the Terran Republic survives." Another thought occurred to her as she belatedly realized that this particular Zeen was only referring to Zeen Home Three when discussing a potential alliance with the Terran Republic. "What do the other Hives think of this proposed alliance?"

"Unknown," the Zeen replied. "Contact broken with other Hives."

"Broken? How?"

"Zeen Hives separate," it explained. "Communication

between Hives limited to regular status updates delivered by courier. Last four Zeen Home Three couriers destroyed before reaching Zeen Home Two."

"Let me guess." Xi grimaced. "No couriers have survived since you helped fight off the gatecrasher."

"Incorrect," the Zeen replied. "One courier was sent to Zeen Home One and one was sent to Zeen Home Three with update regarding Zeen-Vorr-Terran alliance."

"But after that," Xi pressed, "no couriers have made contact with any other Hive?"

"Symmetrical."

Xi couldn't believe what she was hearing. From what this Zeen was telling her, the Vorr had actively manipulated them into being fodder for the front lines with promises of equality in a three-species alliance. The Zeen had apparently sustained losses greater than they had anticipated, and this had given them sufficient reason to question the validity of the Vorr's promises regarding equality within the alliance.

And then, to prevent the disparate Hives from making a unified decision regarding how to proceed, the Vorr were either directly or indirectly destroying whatever couriers normally served as lines of communication between the Zeen Hives.

It was looking like a nearly-worst-case-scenario from Xi's perspective, and the longer this conversation went on, the more valid Jem's concerns about the Vorr's true motives seemed.

"How closely aligned were the Zeen Hive-homes prior to losing contact?" she asked.

"Zeen Hive-homes have distinct gene-tracts," the Zeen explained. "Inter-tract genetic differences create behavioral variability, with inter-tract behavioral symmetry maintained by couriers. Behavioral predictability decreases significantly without regular communication between Hives."

Xi shook her head sourly. "So without the couriers, you

don't know what the other Hives are thinking or how they consider the situation with the Vorr."

"Symmetrical."

"Do you think the Vorr are directly interfering with inter-Hive communication?" she pressed.

"Zeen Home Three calculates a ninety-four percent probability that Vorr interference responsible for broken communication between Hives."

Xi thought she was finally getting her brain wrapped around what she was hearing. She knew that much of humanity's future likely depended on maintaining productive (or at the very least, not directly antagonistic) relationships with both the Zeen and the Vorr. And it seemed that she, Xi Bao, a can-kid-turned-Tier-One-felon-turned-military-icon, was in a key position to make that happen.

To say it was humbling would have been the understatement of the century.

"What can I do to help Zeen Home Three strengthen its relationship with the Terran Republic?" she asked.

"Answer our query without deception or asymmetry."

She felt a storm of butterflies erupt in her stomach, but she managed to swallow the suddenly dry knot in her throat before declaring with conviction, "I will. Even if I think you won't like what I have to say."

"Does Major Xi Bao predict the Terran Republic will support a symmetrical alliance with Zeen Home Three?"

"Yes, I do," Xi replied unflinchingly. "But you need to understand how different Terran society is from yours. We have hundreds of interdependent social structures that help govern our society. We write laws to help guide our actions. We regularly elect leaders who direct appointed bureaucrats, who in turn coordinate organizations of at-will employees who do their best to carry out the directives issued by the populace to the elected leaders. It's a fractured, contentious system where nothing happens without debate, or sometimes even violent protest," she warned before declaring without reservation, "but for all its flaws, it's the best system humanity has ever devised for itself. And I'm confident that, after more than a little heated argument, the Terran Republic will support a mutually-beneficial relationship with Zeen Home Three."

"Terran hierarchies unstable," Zeen warned.

"Efficient, no, but unstable?" she started. "There's a certain measure of guaranteed *stability* in the way we arrange our society. And while I can't speak for every Terran on every subject, there is one area in Terran society where you'd be hard-pressed to find dissent from the following statement: the Terran Republic has precious few friends out here, which makes us value true allies more highly than most. You fought and bled to kill that gatecrasher, where just a few years earlier even our Solarian cousins watched us suffer and die from wave after wave of Arh'Kel aggression without lifting a finger," she said with fiery feeling. "You helped us when even our own family wouldn't...and we will *never* forget that."

She believed each word with every fiber of her being, which filled her with a clarity of purpose she had rarely known. She was in a position to make a difference in the course of Terran events, and even though she knew the Zeen was right to urge caution regarding the predictability of Terran society, she also had faith that her fellow Terrans would do more than what was in their own best interests.

But to do what was *right*?

The Zeen *had* fought, bled, and died for Terra. They *had* expended an inconceivable amount of energy to make Operation Antivenom possible by transporting the *Dietrich Bonhoeffer* to Lunar orbit. And now, like the Terrans, the Zeen of Home Three felt cut off from the only support they had ever known.

The galaxy seemed fit to burst with scheming, backstabbing factions convinced of their supremacy.

These Zeen needed honest, forthright friends, just like Terra did.

And fortunately, Xi thought she might have a way of expediting that friendship's formation.

"Major Xi Bao's statements symmetrical with Zeen Home Three's priorities," the Zeen finally declared after several long, silent seconds. "Zeen Home Three advises Major Xi Bao against informing Vorr regarding Zeen Home Three-Terran alliance. Vorr behavior asymmetrical with prior statements. Vorr unpredictable."

"Agreed." Xi nodded firmly. "But I'd also strongly urge Zeen Home Three to reconsider withdrawing from the Zeen-Vorr-Terran alliance."

"Clarify."

"If Zeen Home Three withdraws now," Xi explained, careful not to reveal any of the Metal Legion's post-Pearl theories regarding the Vorr's true plans for Nexus Space, "the Vorr will become suspicious. It is a drastic change, and that will make them even more unpredictable."

"Zeen Home Three will not support asymmetrical arrangements," the Zeen said flatly.

"I'm not asking you to," she said, though for a moment she wondered if that was exactly what she was suggesting. "I'm just saying that it's probably best to move slowly. If there is to be a Zeen Home Three-Terran alliance, we'll need to make sure we strengthen our position before doing anything that might anger the Vorr. They are too strong for us to fight, at least right now," she said grimly.

"Zeen Home Three will consider Major Xi Bao's advice," the Zeen replied before producing a spiral-shaped shell-like device from beneath the folds of its armored carapace. It was nearly identical to the one she had received on Shiva's Wrath, and she felt a sudden thrill as it proffered the strange token. "Major Xi Bao is now Terran ambassador to Zeen Home Three."

"I'm honored to accept," she said, taking the token.

"Pursuit of symmetry between Zeen Home Three and Terran Republic is of vital tactical importance," the Zeen declared, once again demonstrating remarkably clearer speech while discussing tactical issues. "Reciprocity is essential to symmetry. Major Xi Bao assists Zeen Home Three with her friendship, therefore Major Xi Bao will receive reciprocal demonstration of Zeen Home Three's assistance."

She nodded, knowing from experience that the device represented a token to the Zeen. She suspected it was the same type of token the Zeen Hives used to convey some or all of their inter-tract communications, which in a very real sense meant that they considered her as trustworthy as one of their vital couriers.

"I understand," she said sincerely. "I look forward to working with Zeen Home Three."

"Symmetry," the Zeen replied, spreading its arms wide and adopting a perfectly symmetrical stance that Xi did her best to mirror before it wordlessly returned to the airlock.

A few minutes later, she had manually closed the airlock's inner door before opening the outer door and letting the Zeen back onto its own ship. An hour later, the *Vercingetorix* moved in to collect her dead shuttle. She had not expected the meeting with the Zeen to be so impactful, but despite its ominous revelations, she felt reinvigorated in a way she had not known since her last voyage aboard the *Dietrich Bonhoeffer*.

She tucked the Zeen token into her flight suit as the shuttle came to a rest on the *Vercingetorix's* hangar deck, feeling a stream of tears run down her cheeks as the deck crew worked to manually open her airlock from the outside. And for perhaps the only time in her military career, those tears were anything but unwelcome.

Because for the first time since going wheels-up from the Pearl, in what she suspected was a more meaningful development than she had time to ponder, she could recall with excruciating detail every last line of Corporal Cervantes' face.

21

DEBRIEFING THE GENERALS

"Congratulations, General Moon," General Pushkin declared, shaking Moon's hand after replacing the other man's beret with his new single-starred hat. "It has been a long time coming, but you have definitely earned this promotion."

"Thank you, General," newly-promoted Brigadier General Moon replied while shaking the other man's hand. To Jenkins, it was one of the most meaningful moments in the Metal Legion's recent history. For the first time since Akinouye's death and Kavanaugh's removal, the Metal Legion once again had more than a single flag officer on the rolls. "Frankly I'm surprised the committee didn't hold my confirmation process up longer than it did."

Pushkin made a dismissive gesture. "The committee is the least of our concerns these days. In fact," he turned his gaze to Jenkins, "I hear you also had a little trouble with the Terra Han transfers during Watery Grave?"

"I've got a disciplinary meeting scheduled for Captain Chao later today," Jenkins assured the Legion's top-ranked officer.

"Good." Pushkin nodded before somewhat surprisingly adding, "My advice is to go easy on the young man."

Jenkins quirked a brow in surprise. "You're afraid of his father's retribution?"

Pushkin snorted. "Certainly not. Besides, Admiral Zhao's focus is presently elsewhere…and I doubt he would look favorably on showing his son preferential treatment during a disciplinary review."

Jenkins allowed his confusion to show. "Then I'm not sure I understand, General."

"I'm hearing whispers." Pushkin gestured to a conference room adjacent to the Metal Legion's main war room. Jenkins shared a brief look with General Moon and then Major Xi before the trio silently followed Pushkin into the conference room. When the room's doors shut, Pushkin made his way to the head seat at the short, narrow table and indicated for everyone else to be seated while he lit a cigar.

"What kind of whispers, General?" Moon was the first to ask.

Pushkin took a long, deep draw before exhaling and turning his gaze on each of the Metalheads in turn. "Something big is happening behind the scenes," the general replied with uncharacteristic seriousness. "I don't have many details, but I've heard rumors about something called 'Project Leviathan,' and I'm starting to think it had something to do with Admiral Zhao's… let's call it 'impassioned' defense of Antivenom during your court-martial."

Xi leaned forward intently. "Do you think the admiral was doing more than setting the stage for a political run, General?"

"Possibly," Pushkin allowed before turning to give Jenkins a long, appraising look. "How close are you to Jonathan Villa, Colonel Jenkins?"

Jenkins cocked his head dubiously before deciding to give the most direct reply possible. "Outside of the Metal Legion, he's one of only two men I consider a friend. He stood up for me in front of a review board led by Admiral Zhao."

Pushkin nodded knowingly. "Then you would be most disheartened to hear that he died during a recent shuttle malfunction over Durgan's Folly."

Jenkins' eyes narrowed. "I don't think 'disheartened' is the word I'd use at hearing that particular news, General."

"What then?" Pushkin urged.

"'Disbelieving' is the first word that comes to mind," Jenkins replied with a firm shake of his head. "And not just because denial is the first stage of grief," he added with a smirk. "I first met Johnny Villa when he was a captain in the TFMC, and I was a Fleet lieutenant. His quad got downed by an unexpectedly heavy EMP following their spike of an Arh'Kel anti-orbital placement. He knew the risks of going that far behind enemy lines, but I was five klicks away when he went down and wasn't about to sit back and let four of the Republic's finest be torn apart by Arh'Kel." He snorted as some of the more vivid details of that particular ride sprang to the fore of his mind. "I took an old Armadillo-class APC armed with just a chain gun, and burned through a formation of at least three thousand Arh'Kel."

"The way I heard it," the newly-minted Brigadier General Moon observed, "you rode out against the explicit orders of your CO and earned your callsign in the process."

Jenkins shook his head wryly. "It's possible that, in the heat of the moment, I forgot to request permission to render aid, but I steadfastly reject the suggestion that I ever heard anything resembling an order precluding the possibility."

"A charming story," Pushkin said neutrally, "but what does it have to do with 'disbelieving' Colonel Villa is in fact dead?"

"Being shot down behind enemy lines isn't any fun," Jenkins said, meeting and holding the general's gaze. "Some of us crumple afterward, and some of us get up and try to pretend it never happened. And some of us, like Johnny Villa, reshape their entire lives to make sure it *never* happens again. To say he became fastidious about checking the onboard systems of every shuttle, dropship, or power suit he rode after that day would be a colossal understatement. I've seen him spend six hours running diagnostics on a power-suit's knee servo because he couldn't figure out why it had a zero-point-eight percent diminished power output." Jenkins shook his head firmly. "And even if his shuttle *did* go down, there is absolutely no way he wouldn't have been geared up and ready to make an emergency drop. If he's dead from a flight accident over Durgan's Folly, there's a more or less intact body on the ground somewhere. Until I see it, he's *not* dead."

Pushkin eyed him for a long moment before nodding in approval. "I agree. Which is why, when my sources suggested he was somehow involved in this Project Leviathan, I started covertly connecting dots. Shortly after I began doing this, Admiral Zhao was called away on urgent business and has not set foot off his flagship since."

"You think Admiral Zhao and Colonel Villa are running some kind of off-the-books operation?" Moon asked.

"If they are," Pushkin allowed, "it involves a lot more than just them. I have reason to believe that one Major Brighton of the Terra Han Colonial Guard is also involved in Leviathan."

Jenkins' brow rose in surprise. "I met Brighton on Terra Han. He was in charge of covertly training Orchid and Lotus Battalions."

"Both of which are now *here*," Pushkin said grimly, jamming a fingertip onto the oak conference table, "along with their crews and commanders...all except Major Brighton. It seems Brighton is well-connected in the Terra Han Colonial Guard, which has recently been making inroads with not just TAC but also with certain admirals in the Fleet."

Jenkins' brow lowered grimly. "Do you think Admiral Zhao, and by extension Project Leviathan, is somehow related to an attempted takeover of the Metal Legion by Terra Han?"

"On that front, I have more questions than answers." Pushkin grunted irritably. "Your latest readings from the Nexus suggest that two of the Jemmin gatecrashers we previously thought the Vorr scratched there were not, in fact, neutralized by the Vorr, but rather by some third faction that left no trace of itself and the Vorr are keeping quiet about. The Jemmin fleet largely withdrew from the running firefights against Vorr-Zeen forces in the Nexus shortly after those gatecrashers were destroyed." The general scowled. "I do not believe in coincidences, so it is difficult for me to ignore the possibility that Project Leviathan is unrelated. And if it is, it could signal that Fleet has some kind of super-weapon that Colonel Villa and Major Brighton are, or were, assigned to in some capacity."

Moon cocked his head uncertainly. "You think Leviathan is that big, General?"

"I do." Pushkin nodded firmly. "I have seen many dark ops in my career, both during and following their execution, and this one looks bigger than anything but Antivenom. If Leviathan is indeed a super-weapon, as I suspect, it could restructure the balance of power within the Terran Republic...and possibly within all of Nexus space. Admiral Zhao would seem to be in a key position to take advantage, which raises further questions regarding his trustworthiness."

"It doesn't seem to fit..." Xi began, drawing the attention of all three men.

"You have something to add, Major?" Pushkin asked pointedly.

She silently nodded as her quick, intelligent eyes snapped back and forth in contemplation before focusing on Colonel Jenkins. "*Vercingetorix.*"

Jenkins cocked his head uncertainly. "Go on."

Xi turned to Pushkin. "We all think Admiral Zhao was trying to tell us something by pushing the *Vercingetorix* to the head of the repair queue. We thought he might have been trying to demonstrate his superiority by comparing himself to Caesar, but what if he wasn't doing that at all?"

A look of comprehension fell over Moon's features, while Pushkin's expression remained unreadable. "Continue, Major," Moon urged.

"What if Admiral Zhao," she said eagerly, "was trying to tell us that *he* was our ally and that we should avoid Vercingetorix's fate by not getting overconfident in our internal preparations? When Caesar laid siege to Vercingetorix's fortress, he did it by building inner- and outer-facing walls to deal with both internal and external threats to his efforts. By the time Vercingetorix understood what was going on, it was too late."

"That would make us the Romans and the Terra Han Colonial Guardsmen the internal threat," Jenkins mused. "If so, what's the external threat?"

"Leviathan?" Moon suggested.

General Pushkin shook his head. "I don't think so. In fact, it is only due to my discovery of Project Leviathan that I was able to learn the source of our recent antagonism," Pushkin said, his stony expression finally cracking to reveal his trademark broad grin. "Well deduced, Major. Only two days ago did I come to the same conclusion as you just did. I was curious how each of you would react to this new information, and none of you disappointed. For extra credit, can you tell me why I arrived at the same conclusion you did?"

"You discovered that it's definitely *not* Admiral Zhao," Xi declared confidently, "but rather some other Fleet officer who is working with the Terra Han Colonial Guard in the attempted takeover of the Terran Armor Corps. Whatever Project

Leviathan is, or was, it looks like it's pitted Admiral Zhao against someone else in the Fleet."

"Correct." Pushkin nodded. "And I have reason to believe the Fleet officer in question is none other than Admiral Fitzgerald."

Silence hung over the room. Admiral Henry Fitzgerald III was the former High Commander of the Terran Armed Forces during Operation Deliverer, which saw the Terran Fleet drive every last Arh'Kel from New Australia following the massacre there. He was a living legend, and, after General Akinouye's death, he was the longest-serving member of the Republic's Joint Chiefs of Staff.

If he was against them, the Metal Legion's future had just taken a bleak turn.

"What reason do you have, General?" Jenkins asked into the growing silence.

"Our latest influx of supplies and financial donations has begun to lose its way en route to our bunkers and coffers," Pushkin explained. "I've traced some of the diversions high enough up the ladder to know that only Admiral Fitzgerald could have instigated them. Soon enough, we'll also find our supply of fresh recruits diverted. Shortly after that, transfer requests will come down, and deployment orders will stretch us as thin as onion paper, at which point we'll have no choice but to bend the knee to Fleet and accept some form of restructuring that cuts our balls off. This," he again jabbed his finger onto the oak table, "is the external threat that Admiral Zhao was referencing. Which is why, Colonel Jenkins," he sighed, "I think it is imperative that you ensure Captain Chao's ongoing support in determining which of the Terra Han transfers are trustworthy, and which are not."

He smirked, "Frankly, it is my professional opinion that a few lost digits are an acceptable price to pay for maintaining the

Metal Legion's sovereignty in these uncertain times. But ultimately," he made a deferential gesture, "how you deal with Captain Chao is your decision, and I will support you in it."

"Thank you, General," Jenkins said, wondering just how deep the Jemmin rot must have gotten into the Terran Republic if one of its highest, most respected officers was moving in rhythm with Jemmin's beat. He couldn't believe for a second that Admiral Fitzgerald was knowingly working against the Republic, but something Admiral Zhao had said about Major General Kavanaugh's situation being 'above his pay-grade' suddenly echoed in his ears.

Had Admiral Zhao been talking about not just Kavanaugh, but also of Fitzgerald during that highly-publicized court martial? Jenkins wondered.

"How do we fight the funding and recruit diversions?" General Moon asked.

"We don't." Pushkin shook his head sourly. "Vice Admiral Zhao has already dangerously overextended himself on our behalf. With his support waning in the face of Fitzgerald's increased hostility toward TAC, we have no choice but to concede that particular field and withdraw to a more defensible location. One with allies," he added pointedly. "And I don't mean Zeen Home Three," Pushkin continued with a glance Xi's way. "With Durgan now leading the pack of presidential hopefuls by a healthy margin, the time has never been better to hand that particular baton over to him so he can gauge and shape Republic sentiment on the matter of a Zeen-Terran alliance." He shook his head adamantly. "No, this is a purely internal *human* matter, and it should be dealt with as such."

"Durgan's looking good in the polls," General Moon allowed, "but he's got zero public service on his record. A Durgan-Zhao ticket, while ruffling the feathers of the anti-military-industrial-complex crowd," He scoffed, drawing muted chuckles from around the table, "would seem to be an ideal one in the current climate and for both prospective running mates."

Jenkins was less than thrilled at the prospect of Director Durgan and Vice Admiral Zhao holding the most influential levers of power in the Terran Republic. They were both self-evidently patriotic, devoted men who cared more deeply about the Republic than the vast majority of those within it. Perhaps it was merely a case of 'the devil you know' giving him pause, but the longer he served in the Metal Legion, the more incredible the stakes became for each and every operation.

He briefly wondered if this was how it always felt at the top of a military branch, and he suspected that question would give him no shortage of material to ponder in the coming weeks.

"I agree. Durgan-Zhao is a winner." Pushkin nodded. "And I expect Admiral Fitzgerald thinks so as well, which is why he has already moved against us. Whatever Project Leviathan was, or is," he gave a nod to Xi for having previously employed a similar turn of phrase, "I get the feeling it did not go Fitzgerald's way. And given the fact that Major Brighton is still listed as 'on special assignment,' as he has been almost continuously for the past three years, I suspect the first shots have already been quietly fired between Admirals Fitzgerald and Zhao. Given the recent uncertainty regarding Vorr-Zeen relations and the apparent ease with which the Vorr have wrested control of the Nexus, this is the most uncertain situation the Republic has faced since the wormholes first went down."

Xi shook her head in frustration. "If the Vorr are making a move, why would Admiral Fitzgerald choose to stage some kind of coup now?"

"We don't know that Fitzgerald is plotting a coup," Moon said unyieldingly. "Few officers have done more for the Republic in their lives than F3," he continued, referring to the admiral by his longtime nickname. "Whatever he's doing, he has to be doing it because he thinks it's in the Republic's best interests."

"But destabilizing us at such a crucial point?" Xi argued. "How can anyone think that would be in the Republic's best interests?"

"Much as we might hate to admit it," Pushkin interjected before Moon could reply, "the Terran Republic is the least powerful faction in Nexus Space. Even if Sol and Terra suddenly united in lockstep and pooled all available resources, and even if the Vorr suffered one-to-one losses against the Jemmin from this point forward—which, judging from our latest Nexus reports, would represent a significant step back in their success thus far," he added sourly, referring to the latest reports that showed how the Vorr and Zeen forces had suffered inordinately high Zeen losses while the Vorr had suffered only lightly, "at the end of the day, humanity's total military strength would be no more than twenty percent that of the Vorr. And given their technological edge, it's probably only a fraction of that."

He swept the group with a hard look. "Humanity is at the kiddie table, boys and girls, and until something major changes, that's precisely where we'll remain. Fitzgerald knows that as well as anyone, which is why he correctly ignores humanity's tenuous circumstances in favor of consolidating our resources under what he feels is a superior configuration. What is that configuration?" Pushkin shrugged. "Who knows. But for the time being, let's not let our eyes get bigger than our stomachs. If anyone can outmaneuver Fitzgerald at his own game, it's Zhao, who seems to have already won over the TFMC to his side. Let's leave internal Fleet politics to Fleet and focus on securing TAC's future." He stood from the table. "To that end, I have an important meeting scheduled, and you two," he flitted looks at both Moon and Jenkins, "have disciplinary meetings to conduct."

The trio of Metalheads followed Pushkin's lead, standing from the table while the elder officer nodded approvingly before rapping his knuckles on the oak.

"Operation Watery Grave was yet another resounding success for the Metal Legion. It'll add another battle streamer to your burgeoning flag," Pushkin declared. "We'll reconvene in forty-eight hours to discuss the next mission. Dismissed."

22

COMMITMENT

It had been a full year since Podsy had last put his boots on New American soil. Standing there with both feet planted on the hard ground, he should have felt as much at home as humanly possible. After all, New America was one of the most Earth-like planets in the Terran Republic. From the atmospheric and soil compositions to the gravity that bound his boots to that soil—even to the azure skies—everything but the cold was so close to Earth that one could have been forgiven for mistaking one for the other.

But despite the creature comforts surrounding him, which had an undeniable appeal to his most primal nature, Podsy had never felt more uncomfortable. Part of that was due to how much this place reminded him of home. The streets bustled with activity, the people interacted with equal measures of courtesy and purpose, and he even saw a handful of retail and food service outlets that were identical to the ones he had frequented as a youth before the rock-biters had practically erased New Australia from the universe.

And yet, no matter how nostalgic he found the surroundings, it was the event taking place before him that had the most profound effect.

Wearing his dress browns and standing at parade rest beside the coffin, Podsy listened to the sermon as Chief Petty Officer Susanna Tilden's remains were gently lowered into the bosom of the world that had birthed her. She, like fifteen others aboard the *Vercingetorix*, had died during Operation Flyby.

An operation of Podsy's design.

With the sermon concluded, Podsy joined his twelve fellow armed forces servicemen (some of whom had served with Tilden aboard the *Vercingetorix*, while others wearing Fleet blues had served with her prior to her TAC transfer) in offering the traditional Terran fifty-three gun salute. Four rounds of thirteen simultaneous gunshots pierced the sky over the cemetery, leaving Podsy with the honor of offering the final fifty-third shot to in no small way commemorate the harshest truth of military service.

Fight together, die alone.

With the salute completed, Podsy and his fellow servicemen performed the duty of closing CPO Tilden's grave using hand shovels. No matter the branch, rank, or time of service, all Terran Armed Forces personnel knew how to perform this final duty without landing a single speck of dirt on their pristine dress uniforms.

With that task completed, and without an errant drop of mud on his uniform, Podsy saluted his fellow servicemen, signaling the end of the funeral service and the gradual disbanding of the four hundred attendees.

He then turned to Tilden's family, who were the reason he had requested permission to attend the service in the first place. He had no real idea why he had asked to participate in Tilden's funeral. He knew he wasn't after 'closure' or an artificial way to make him feel better about himself. He just knew he had to come here and look Tilden's family in the eye, or he would be torn apart from the inside in the coming months and years.

Tilden's husband, James, remained at his seat while the rest of the congregation dispersed. He held the hand of his four-year-old son, Josiah, beside him. Podsy knew their names from reading Tilden's file, but he had refrained from researching further into their lives prior to meeting them in person.

"Mr. Tilden," Podsy said after coming to stand beside the seated man, drawing James Tilden's tear-filled gaze from the freshly-packed dirt covering his wife's coffin. "I wanted to say that it was an honor serving with Susanna."

James gathered his smartly-dressed four-year-old son into his arms and stood from the folding chair. "You're Lieutenant Podsednik, right?"

Podsy nodded in muted surprise. "Yes, sir."

"She mentioned you in one of her last letters," the grieving widower said while his son buried his face against his father's shoulder.

"We ran into each other, though only in an official capacity," Podsy agreed, recalling the relatively minor spat over a poorly-aligned comm booster Tilden had been assigned to calibrate. "She's a strong woman."

"Yes, she is." James agreed with Podsy's use of the present tense when discussing the dearly departed.

It was something of a Terran tradition when speaking of family to think of them as though they were still with their loved ones even after death. Podsy, like most surviving Ozzies, knew better than most just how profound an impact that such a subtle change in syntax could have on the mindset of a person whose loved ones had all died.

"You're from New Australia, right?"

"Yes, sir," Podsy agreed, drawing a somber shake of the other man's head. It was the kind of gesture all Ozzies had to endure when discussing their homeworld's fate, and most of them bristled at the seemingly canned response. But Podsy knew that the human mind was ill-equipped to cope with such a devastating loss as that which had occurred in New Australia. He suspected that even as a survivor, he would never fully come to grips with what the event meant for not only his life, but for the lives of Terrans who had been heavily invested in the once-thriving colony.

James Tilden wiped his moist eyes. "Here I am, crying over the loss of one person while you probably lost everyone you ever knew when the rock-biters attacked."

"Loss is loss, Mr. Tilden," Podsy said with sympathetic conviction. "The numbers are irrelevant."

"That's kind of you to say," Tilden allowed, stroking his son's hair. "The truth, no matter how painful it is to say, is that we both knew this could happen. When she was still with Fleet, serving mostly on shipyards with the occasional deployment on a Marine dropship as a backup gearhead, I could sleep at night because I knew she would be safe. But when she saw that DIN piece about your fight on Shiva's Wrath and the opportunity arose to transfer to Armor Corps? There was nothing I could say to dissuade her. We fought about it," he added with a wan smile, his eyes flitting to her grave before his smile warmed. "Boy, did we *fight*. But the look in her eyes when she talked about how she could.make a difference there...man to man, and without an ounce of self-pity." He sighed in resignation. "In the eight years I knew her, I never *once* put that look in her eyes. Josiah did, on the day he was born and on quite a few that followed," he said, clutching his boy tightly in his arms. "But me? Never. Not once. Which is why, despite the risks, I knew I couldn't stand in her way. She died doing what she loved, Lieutenant Podsednik," he finished with conviction. "She died doing what she loved *most*. Thank you for coming, and thank you for standing with her.

Much as some of us hate to admit it, Terra needs you doing what you do."

Podsy was at a loss for words. He had never expected the spouse of a woman who had died under his command to speak as James Tilden had just spoken, especially not while in the throes of grief. So he said the only things that he knew to be absolutely true.

"Mr. Tilden..." Podsy shook his head in bewilderment. "Hearing you speak as you just did? I've never really understood what we fight for until this moment. I've always known what we fight *against*, and I've spoken the words of a dozen different oaths so many times I could repeat them backward in my sleep. But now I know, just like Susanna knew, that *you*," he said, meeting and holding the other man's gaze, "are the reason we fight. It's people like you, not soldiers like me, who shape humanity's future. It's the job of Metalheads like Susanna and me to protect you while you do it. I think she knew that better than I did."

Podsy decided to end on the only note that could possibly do the moment justice. He reverently produced the Metal Legion's newest medal, personally designed and approved by General Pushkin: the titanium Infinite Tracks, earned exclusively by those Metalheads who fell in the line of service in the now officially-recognized Nexus Wars.

The medal featured a three-word phrase inscribed on the perimeter of the triangular arrangement of infinitely-looping tread marks, and James Tilden squinted at the inscription after accepting. "Suzy hated my glasses, so I left them off for her," the grieving man apologized. "What does it say?"

Podsy knew those three words were both timely and true, so he said them with as much conviction as the legendary man who had chosen them as his last.

"Metal never dies."

"Lieutenant Podsednik," Brigadier General Moon greeted him without so much as a sideways glance as Podsy entered his office. The newly-promoted flag officer gestured to the chair across the desk from his own without taking his eyes off his monitor. "Sit."

Podsy did as commanded while Moon's eyes remained fixed to the display. He sat there for nearly six minutes of absolute silence, knowing that the time had come to pay the piper. His meeting three hours earlier with James Tilden was still fresh in his mind, but despite the surprisingly buoyant effect of that meeting, he gave himself no better than a forty-percent chance of walking out of Moon's office a member of the Terran Armor Corps.

"Insubordination," Moon declared, snapping Podsy's attention back to the present. "That's why we're here, isn't it?"

"Yes, sir."

"It's something of a recurring theme with you, Lieutenant," Brigadier General Moon said, gesturing to the monitor that had previously held his rapt attention. "And if there's one thing a chain of command cannot survive, it's insubordination from NCOs and mid-tier officers. Don't you agree?"

"I do, sir."

"If you want out, Lieutenant," Moon gestured invitingly to the door, "all you have to do is ask. I can have your discharge processed and put you on the first shuttle to whichever of the seven colonies you choose before day's end. God knows you've earned it."

Podsy hadn't expected this particular approach, but he wasn't about to turn his back on the Metal Legion. "I'm committed to the Metal Legion, sir."

"As committed as you were to your Fleet directives under Lieutenant Commander Aquino?" Moon asked casually.

Podsy winced, so he said the only thing that came to mind as General Moon's piercing gaze pinning him to the chair. "I was under the impression my file was still sealed, General."

"Oh, it is," Moon agreed. "But as a flag officer and the third-ranking member of the Metal Legion, my security privileges allow me to pierce that seal. Answer the question, Lieutenant."

Podsy drew a steadying breath. This was it. Moon had discovered his past, and it was all over. The only thing left to him was to stand by his convictions and hold his head high while he got a size-twelve up the ass on his way out the door.

"Yes, sir," he said with conviction. "My commitment to the Metal Legion today is every bit as strong as it was to Fleet during Willow Bark."

"'Willow Bark?'" Moon mused, eyeing the monitor with disdain. "A cute codename to cover up what most would consider mutiny."

Podsy flushed with anger, but he kept his emotions in check as he replied, "That's not how the review board saw it, sir."

"Oh?" Moon quirked a brow challengingly. "They gave you forty years for second-degree murder of your superior officer. You avoided spacing because of the fucked up political situation with your CO's family connections, and the murder charge got downgraded because the board found insufficient evidence that it was premeditated. The only reason you're not *still* freezing your ass off on that asteroid-mining penal colony is that Colonel Jenkins called in a few favors during his initial recruiting drive."

That last bit was news to Podsy. He assumed that his sentence had been commuted as a more or less standard application of Republican law. "I was unaware of that," he admitted before planting his feet. "But it wasn't mutiny, General."

"Explain how that could *possibly* be the case, Lieutenant,"

Moon said, his every fiber projecting a dire warning, "or I might just have you shipped back to that rock-busting station for resumption of your sentence."

Podsy knew the general had the power to do just that. He had known the risks of re-upping with TAC instead of taking the discharge after Durgan's Folly, and he had chosen to stand on the line with Xi and the others because, frankly, it was the only thing he'd ever been comfortable doing in his entire life. He believed everything that had happened to him prepared him to be a Metalhead.

But he wasn't going to squirm, and he wasn't going to beg.

"Lieutenant Commander Geovany Aquino was my CO at Silver Savannah Six, and I was his XO," Podsy explained. "We were a standard Revere-class listening post on the sparsely-populated New Africa 2 mining colony of Silver Savannah. We had thick walls, and strong enough fixed defenses to ward off a small-scale Arh'Kel ground assault for up to three days. We also had four Viper-class interceptors, eight Bloodhound APCs, and two hundred FGF pounders who could respond to emerging local threats as needed."

"I'm familiar with a Revere's standard complement, Lieutenant," Moon said frostily.

"Yes, sir," Podsy allowed. "One day we got a call from a nearby settlement saying their seismics had just gone off. The signal was consistent with a standard subterranean attack, with said attack estimated at fourteen hours from our receipt of the distress call. The geology of the colony's environment made rock-biter emergence within the colony's perimeter unlikely, so the rock-biters were expected to break the surface half a kilometer from the colony's fragile walls. The colonists had a few chain guns and a pair of mortars, but not enough to ward off an Arh'Kel attack of the scale they were detecting.

"There were six thousand Terrans at that compound and

three hundred Fleet personnel at Silver Savannah Six. I proposed to personally lead all eight Bloodhounds, with twenty pounders apiece and all the pop-up defenses we could carry, to support the colony. If we left immediately and red-lined the Bloodhounds, we had a better than fifty-fifty chance of reaching the colony before the rock-biters. Commander Aquino cited four relevant regulations that placed our facility's safety above that of the colonists' and refused to authorize the mission, preferring to fly mid-altitude sorties with the Vipers over the area. But we were reading at least three thousand Arh'Kel, and there was no way the Vipers could have scrubbed the field clean from the safety of mid-altitude sorties.

"I made that point to Commander Aquino, who continued to deny my request to lend support even after I downgraded the proposed ground force to four Bloodhounds, forty pounders, and all the pop-up hardware we could cram into the APCs. In my professional opinion, he was actively refusing to do the very job we'd been put there to do, and was clearly more interested in securing the base than he was in protecting the colonists." Podsy set his jaw as memories of that day came back to him in a flood. "So I drew my sidearm and shot Commander Aquino in the head. I then surrendered command of the base to Commander Intercept Group, Second Lieutenant Teresa Knighton before presenting my proposal to personally lead our ground forces in support of the colony again."

"Did she agree?" Moon asked.

"Yes, she did, General."

Moon's gaze bored into Podsy with the force of a Poltergeist's main beam. "What happened then?" he asked after several silent, intense seconds had passed.

"We arrived at the colony four minutes before the rock-biters broke the surface," Podsy explained. "Using the colony's light defenses, we were able to pour enough fire into their three emergence points to buy the time we needed to deploy the pop-ups. After that, it was just a matter of keeping the barrels from melting, which we were fortunate to succeed in doing. Seventy-nine hours of constant fighting." Podsy thought back to the men and women he'd been privileged to serve beside in that hellish trio of days. "And we lost two hundred and forty-six of the colonists to Arh'Kel artillery strikes, along with thirty-four of my pounders. But we held long enough for Fleet to arrive and send the Marines down the hole with enough ordnance to set off the seismics half a continent away."

"At which point you were taken into custody and ultimately charged with murder." Moon sneered. "Does that sum the rest of it up, Lieutenant?"

"In so many words, yes, sir," Podsy agreed unapologetically. "The board found my actions, while reprehensible and worthy of high censure, to nonetheless be an, and I quote, 'exemplary manifestation of the Terran Armed Forces' primary concern with duty.' The charge of mutiny was never formally considered, and even the murder charge would have been off the table if I hadn't shot him in the *head*. But Aquino's family was, and still is, politically connected and they insisted on the maximum possible punishment. He was a coward, sir," Podsy finished with feeling, "and his cowardice almost got six thousand people killed. The board agreed, but they caved to political pressure and dropped me on a frozen rock where the median survival rate is seven years."

Moon's eyes narrowed. "Let me put a hypothetical to you, Mr. Podsednik: suppose you were to serve as my XO, and you deemed *me* to have made a similarly 'cowardly' decision under roughly identical circumstances. Would you do anything differently than you did with Commander Aquino?"

"Yes, sir, I would." Podsy nodded, having long considered

that very question. "I wouldn't shoot you in the head, General. I'd aim for the heart."

"In other words," Moon drummed his fingers on a folder Podsy hadn't previously noticed laying on the desk, "you'd just try to get away with it."

"That's not how I'd put it, General," Podsy allowed, "though it's not far from the mark."

General Moon lifted the folder from the desk and effortlessly tossed it onto Podsy's lap before commanding, "Read that."

Podsy eyed the folder's header, which was over-stamped with a glaring red 'CLASSIFIED' label. He flipped the folder open and found it was a Terran Armor Corps disciplinary record from eighty-three years ago.

His eyes widened when he saw the name on that record, and he found himself quietly saying it aloud. "Lieutenant Benjamin Akinouye?"

"I'll save you the effort and direct you to page seventeen," Moon deadpanned, prompting Podsy to flip to that page while the general continued, "Back then, cowardice was more clearly defined under the TAF military code than it is today. Then-Lieutenant Akinouye stood before a multi-branch review board for the deaths of superior officers in combat. That board found him guilty of killing two superior officers while also finding him innocent of any wrongdoing. The board found that Lieutenant Akinouye's actions were, and *I quote*," he added with a smirk, "an 'exemplary manifestation of the Terran Armed Forces' primary concern with duty,' and that 'cowardice has no place in any branch of the Terran military.' They would have copy-pasted the last bit in your case's official remarks, just like they did the first, except the code no longer recognizes 'cowardice' as it once did...or as clearly as it should."

Podsy read through the transcript, where the indicated

passage was highlighted, and could not believe what he was reading. He looked up blankly at General Moon, whose formerly stormy expression had been replaced with a more somber one.

"When you first transferred to the *Dietrich Bonhoeffer*," Moon explained, "I sat down with General Akinouye and Colonel Li to discuss which of you Nuggets might turn into actual Metalheads. Out of all the jackets, including Colonel Jenkins' and then-Captain Xi's, the old man put *yours* on the top of the pile and said two things. First, that under absolutely no circumstances should you *ever* be given command of a mech. Both Colonel Li and I agreed wholeheartedly with that bit, and you've done nothing to dispel my confidence that the old man was right."

Podsy felt his heart sink at hearing that. He had come to think of his time aboard the *Bonhoeffer*, and now the *Vercinge-torix*, as temporary assignments en route to his rightful place on the ground alongside Jenkins and Xi. He leaned forward in his chair with his elbows on his knees and looked at the floor.

"Second," Moon continued, "that we fast-track you as the flagship's CO to replace Colonel Li ASAP."

Podsy sat upright and blinked four times in disbelief before blurting, "General?"

"Obviously Li was a little upset about that, given your hack of his data core during the op on Shiva's Wrath," Moon said casually. "But even he recognized you had the stuff. In the last few years, the old man came to realize two strategic errors he'd made at the Legion's helm. The first was in not cozying up to the PDFs and Colonial Guards, since their ongoing support could have strengthened TAC's political position against Fleet encroachment. Once he recognized our shortcoming there, he tried to give General Pushkin all the support he needed to fix that weakness. But it was too little, too late, and we all knew it.

The second critical error he made, in *his* opinion," he continued pointedly, "was in not putting some of his more talented officers aboard TAC warships. The old man was right to make orbital and airborne forces a supporting cast to the Metal Legion's mechs, but he overshot the mark by sliding nearly all of his best officers into mechs instead of just *most* of them. If he'd kept a few more of us up on the ships over the last half-century, TAC would have maintained tactical viability as a naval force. That would have kept more of our ships out of mothballs while also solidifying our position in the Republic's Armed Forces."

Podsy was having difficulty keeping up with the political ramifications of what sounded like purely-internal Armor Corps matters. But he thought he got the thrust of it well enough that he asked, "The general thought we needed to be less dependent on the other branches?"

"Partly, yes," Moon agreed. "Dependence is really only good when it's *interdependence*. When Fleet needs us as much as we need Fleet, we'll get along just fine. But with the TFMC's power-suits gobbling up all the headlines and press for high-profile ground engagements, Fleet quickly became aware of the fact that Armor's tactical advantages were rapidly diminishing."

"And they leveraged it against the Legion." Podsy finally thought he understood. "Why would they do that?"

"Why *wouldn't* they do it?" Moon countered. "It may seem insane at first glance, but the various branches of TAF are *supposed* to be constantly working against each other. Hell, even the various flag officers *within* a given branch are supposed to keep a knife to their fellows' femorals whenever possible. Like a wise man once said, 'Be polite, be courteous, but have a plan to kill everyone you meet.' Fleet has to antagonize Armor. Why? That's the wrong question. The only one that matters—"

"Is 'why not?'" Podsy concluded with a knowing nod.

"Exactly." Moon returned the nod before holding out his

hand, into which Podsy placed Akinouye's ninety-year-old file. "The old man saw something in you, Lieutenant, and unlike Major General Kavanaugh, I'm not going to reverse course on General Akinouye before he's gone cold. But let me be as clear as I can," he said, once again pinning Podsy with a penetrating flag-officer glare. "I'm not personally convinced that he was right about you. You've shown enough flashes, both good and bad, to keep me from making a final determination on your future one way or the other.

"So for now, I'm going to keep you where I can see you. It would be in your best interests, and more importantly, in the *Legion's* best interests," he added with a measure of severity that actually sent a shiver down Podsy's spine, "for you to do your utmost to impress the hell out of me and General Pushkin from here on out." He shook his head resolutely. "Because whatever good grace General Akinouye's opinion of you once carried has now been fully consumed following your failure to directly report your and Jem's theory to me as soon as you became aware of it. I'll be judging you purely on your performance during our next deployment, and in every one which follows. Is that clear?"

Some small part of Podsy wanted to rebel against Moon's directive. That part, which had been the devil on his shoulder throughout Podsy's life, had grown increasingly vocal in recent months as he had moved from one post to another in his time with the Metal Legion.

But to Podsy's surprise, the memory of his last words to James Tilden drowned out that conniving little devil. His duty *was* to protect the Terran people while they fought to build a brighter future for humanity, and the only way he could see to do that was by climbing the Metal Legion's chain of command as fast as possible. He knew that he had valuable contributions to make to the Legion's command structure, and after hearing of General Akinouye's opinion of him, he even allowed himself to think that maybe, just maybe, he could one day sit in the command chair of a TAC warship.

It was time to knuckle down and do the job to the best of his ability, so he nodded with a conviction he wouldn't have thought possible just a few hours earlier. "Yes, sir. I'll give you everything I've got."

"Let's hope it's enough," Moon declared before gesturing to the door. "Dismissed."

EPILOGUE: GET YOUR ASS TO MARS

Jenkins and Xi moved side by side down the halls of TAC HQ, as they had done dozens of times before. He felt good with her at his side. Complete. She had, to everyone's surprise (including his), grown into one of the most impressive young officers the Terran Republic had ever had the privilege of fielding.

And he suspected she would make a run up the ladder that would leave him chewing her dust. She hadn't become a major at the tender age of twenty by accident, or due to political winds. She was smarter, faster, and fiercer than he had ever been. The only advantages he had over her were experience and discipline; in everything else, she held the edge.

It would be an honor to serve as her mentor and CO for however long he could honestly lay claim to either post.

Wearing their brown-and-blacks, complete with custom-embroidered berets, the duo arrived at the war room's main doors, where a pair of Terran lieutenants stood vigil. One wore the same TAC colors as Jenkins and Xi, while the other wore a Fleet uniform, and the pair of administrative officers saluted before opening the doors in time for Jenkins and Xi to march through without breaking stride.

Within the war room was the same hallowed conference table that had been the site of thousands of pre-op briefings, including the majority of those Jenkins and Xi had participated in. The far end of the table was populated by TAC's General Pushkin, Brigadier General Moon and, somewhat surprisingly, Lieutenant Podsednik.

Next to Generals Pushkin and Moon was none other than Vice Admiral Zhao, whose presence was a surprise but not a shock. Jenkins and Xi, moving in silent tandem, made their way to the far end of the table, where they offered salutes. "Colonel Jenkins and Major Xi, reporting as ordered, General."

"Be seated," Pushkin ordered before gesturing to the chairs opposite Zhao and the TAC officers. "You already know Alice," General Pushkin said, and Jenkins made brief eye contact with the Solarian woman who, to his eye, looked to have largely recovered from her post-operative difficulties following the removal of her One Mind implants. "She is here with the rest of her delegation's senior representatives to request our assistance in a matter of vital importance to Sol."

Jenkins and Xi shared meaningful looks as they seated themselves opposite the Solarians. "Ma'am," Jenkins acknowledged Alice, who nodded in reply.

"First," Alice said, sending an emphatic look to Admiral Zhao, "I appreciate you all taking the time to come here. Second, I think it is relevant to report that my entire delegation has voluntarily opted to remove our One Mind implants."

"Are you sure that's wise?" Zhao asked bluntly.

"We are," Alice replied serenely. "Terra has bled for Sol, and that blood cannot be repaid. It can only be honored. We wish to foster improved relations between our governments in the hope of reuniting humanity. The only way we can do that is if we seek to understand you, and you seek to understand us.

How better to accomplish that than by trying to live like one another?"

"Good luck getting any Metalheads to go One Mind," General Moon blurted, drawing a muted look of disapproval from Pushkin.

"That would be counterproductive," Alice said dismissively. "We know the effect of introducing a human to the One Mind. What we do not know with any confidence is the effect of withdrawing from it. Which, as it happens, is the source of Sol's urgent dilemma, for which I now formally request your assistance."

She activated a holo-display built into the tabletop, and the lights in the War Room dimmed as a series of images sprang to life in the air above the table.

"Operation Antivenom." Alice gestured to one of the images, which represented a small cluster of statistical figures, "was a resounding success by any measure, specifically in terms of lives saved on Earth. Six hundred ninety-four Solar humans died as a direct result of TAC aggression, and twelve million more on Earth died from indirect interruptions to the One Mind network. Most of these were elderly or infirm, but by any reasonable measure, the safeguarding of ninety-three billion humans at the cost of twelve million was a categorical success. Earth's, however," she continued grimly, "is not the only population in Sol."

Jenkins barely had time to confront the reality that their actions had led to twelve million deaths on Earth. They had known there was a risk to using Jem's inoculation on Earth's One Mind system and they had suspected there might be deaths, but millions? Seeing Alice casually report the figures made it seem so...cold. It was difficult for him to focus on the next numbers as Alice continued with her presentation.

"Venus, in particular, has suffered catastrophic loss of life.

This is due to the One Mind's inability to maintain stability in real-time, since the light delay made for an unfortunate lag in One Mind recalibrations that included Jem's inoculation," the Solar woman explained while magnifying a second set of statistics. "Seven-point-one billion humans called the sky cities of Venus home prior to Antivenom's execution. Today, that number stands at three-point-nine billion, and it is decreasing with each passing day." She paused and swept the Terrans with a neutral expression as she let her words sink in.

Jenkins was unable to keep his jaw from going slack at hearing that figure. A quick look up the table showed that every Terran, even the unflappable Admiral Zhao, was equally stunned by Alice's revelation.

"Three billion people," Xi muttered. "That's more than live in the entire Terran Republic."

"It is," Alice agreed. "And while more sky cities fall each day, Sol is confident that Jemmin interference has been isolated, and that the damage will soon be stopped entirely. Even with this tragic loss of life, and with the losses we anticipate have yet to come, which we of Sol collectively deem to have been unavoidable," she added emphatically, "Venus remains the second most populous community outside of Earth in all of human affairs, and for all intents and purposes, it is now secure against Jemmin influence."

She minimized Venus' statistics, and Jenkins knew he was not alone in being unable to process such a profound loss of life. He wanted to hate himself for pushing the figure from his mind, but he knew there was no way he could contribute to the briefing if his mind lingered on it.

"Which brings us to the third most populous community in Sol and the fifth most populous community in the human sphere," she continued as a third set of statistics appeared, accompanied by an image of the red planet. "Mars. Home to over two hundred million humans, Mars possesses the most important military-industrial infrastructure in all of Sol. While interplanetary asteroid mining operations account for significantly more raw production than all combined Martian industrial output, the Martian orbital manufactories are unrivaled in Solar affairs and serve to produce nearly all Solar military hardware. Those manufactories," she magnified the image of a tethered space elevator, "are serviced by nine beanstalks like this one which, as of this moment, is one of just two that has survived post-Antivenom chaos."

"What's the death toll on Mars?" Pushkin asked grimly.

"So far, fewer than three million have died," Alice replied promptly, "because for all practical purposes related to this briefing, the entirety of Mars has already succumbed to what is essentially Jemmin propaganda." She gestured to her left, where a hawk-eyed middle-aged man wearing an all-white body-glove sat. "This is Commodore Kline of the Solar 5th Fleet. Mars is under 5th Fleet's jurisdiction, and he can answer any tactically-relevant questions you might have after I've completed my formal request, which is this." She leaned forward intently. "We require immediate Terran assistance to help us retake and secure those beanstalks before Jemmin's influence destroys them."

"Sol doesn't consider this an internal affair?" Jenkins asked warily.

"We do," Alice allowed, "which is why we have come to you, our Terran cousins. If we are going to make the human family whole once again, it is our opinion that we should act accordingly rather than spend weeks, months, or even years arguing over verbiage and punctuation on a prospective treaty. You already saved us from the Jemmin apocalypse once. We are now asking you to do so again. But let me be clear on an important point," she added, looking from one Terran flag officer to the next. "The main reason we seek your aid in this matter is because in the absence of a whole and unified One Mind, Sol cannot arrive at a satisfactory threshold of consensus on the Martian issue.

"Are they in open rebellion and therefore subject to the most severe sanctions, or are they suffering from Jemmin manipulation and therefore exempt from those sanctions? Should Sol consider local Martian resources to be sovereign property lost in a rebellion, or should Sol consider Martian assets as properly belonging to Sol and therefore subject to seizure? Sol has never been faced with a situation of this complexity, which we obviously suspect was Jemmin's design. We cannot seem to reach consensus on how to proceed, but what we can do is agree that we need help. That is why Commodore Kline has come here in secret to provide you with whatever tactically-relevant information you seek, should you agree to assist us in this important matter. He, and the rest of my delegation," she looked down the line of Solar delegates, who nodded confidently, "have risked their careers, identities, and even lives by coming here to support my plea."

"Let me get this straight," Xi said, making no attempt to hide her disbelief. "You're saying that Sol is so confused about what's happening on Mars that you're willing to hand over the reins to a group of Metalheads who've already indirectly caused the deaths of over three billion Solarians...and you're willing to do that because we've earned your *trust*?"

"Yes," Alice replied simply. "We commuted your death sentences because we believed that you acted with our best interests at heart."

"I'm sorry." Xi shook her head. "Am I the only one who thinks it's appropriate to suggest this might be some kind of convoluted ploy to get us into their custody so they can reverse their commutation of our death sentences?"

"That's enough, Major," Pushkin said forcefully, but Alice shook her head at the general's rebuke.

"It is a reasonable concern, General," she replied, "which is why we have arranged for however many of us as you see fit to remain here in TAC custody during the operation."

"That won't be necessary," Pushkin confirmed, shooting a hard look Xi's way and causing the young woman to sit back and look away. "You've done nothing to make us think your request is anything but genuine. Armor Corps will continue to act in the same good faith your delegation has thus far demonstrated."

"Thank you, General," Alice said with a nod before swiveling her gaze back over to Xi. "And let me be clear on another matter; while we believe we would have made valuable pre-op contributions to your plan that might have saved the majority of the people who have already died, we also believe that it would have been beyond reckless for you to seek our guidance. In short, you *have* earned our trust, Major Xi."

"I'll take you at your word," Xi said measuredly before adding, "I'm not going to lie: it sounds pretty cheesy."

"You're welcome to sit this one out if you think it prudent, Major," General Moon drawled.

"No, sir," Xi rejected, going briefly red in the ears. "I'm making the most relevant contributions I can to this briefing."

"I can't tell if it's your branch's culture," Zhao said irritably, "or your youth, but the relevance of your contributions to this point leave ample room for improvement, Major."

"My apologies, Admiral." Xi had won no favors from anyone for her outburst. As the Terran Ambassador to Zeen Home Three, she needed to practice the subtle art of diplomacy. She was failing miserably. *I need to do better. Think before you speak, dumbass!*

"Colonel Jenkins." General Pushkin gestured invitingly. "Your opinion?"

Jenkins cocked his head skeptically. "Even if we've got Solar warships in overwatch, each of those beanstalks is heavily-fortified. We'll need at least two full battalions of armor if we're going to secure them from the ground, but we'll also need precision-strike-capable aerial support, which will be tricky given the thin Martian atmosphere." He contemplated the operation, seeing the elements take shape in his mind. "If we can deliver two full battalions to the Martian surface, we can do the job of taking those beanstalks, and probably even secure a few dozen local factories in the process. But taking those assets will be the easy part. Holding them? That's a whole different story."

Commodore Kline leaned forward. "5ᵗʰ Fleet will provide the necessary resources to secure those facilities."

"How much of the local Martian arsenal do the rebels have?" Jenkins asked. While the Martian population numbered two hundred million, the actively rebellious were relatively few, so it was likely that the vast majority of military assets were under local control. So, while two battalions of armor could theoretically punch through and take the beanstalks, it was unlikely they could hold out against a concerted counterattack.

"All of it," Commodore Kline replied bluntly. "5ᵗʰ Fleet has already neutralized local orbital assets, but there are thirty-four launch-capable military installations on the surface within striking range of those beanstalks. We can provide extensive missile and fighter intercept capability from overwatch since Solar rules on orbital engagements permit us to do so even in light of the One Mind's failure, but surface targets are out of my jurisdiction until Sol reaches consensus on the so-called 'Martian Matter.'"

Jenkins cocked his head contemplatively. "I've got significant concerns about supporting a full-speed advance without a division of pounders accompanying us." He nodded with total confidence. "But this is the kind of op Armor Corps was formed for. Find us drop-capable transport for two full battalions, and we're ready to roll as soon as you give the word, General."

"Transport, you have," Admiral Zhao declared, prompting another holo-image to spring to life. "The *William Wallace* just broke her yard moorings and will arrive in geosynch of TAC HQ in ten hours. She's a Warlord-class combat carrier, armed with four railguns and a full complement of active point-defense weaponry. It's capable of deploying a full battalion of mixed armor, and it's even got external cradles for sixteen aerospace interceptors," he added. "My advice would be to fit it with Vipers."

"Agreed, Admiral." General Moon looked pleased even though it hadn't been a revelation about the *Wallace*. "I'll transfer my flag from the *Vercingetorix* as soon as the *Wallace* makes orbit. Lieutenant Commander Stravinsky's official transfer from Fleet won't go through before we deploy, but she'll remain in command of the *Vercingetorix*. Lieutenant Podsednik will serve as my XO aboard the *William Wallace*."

"What about the *Red Hare*?" Jenkins pressed.

"I've managed to back the vultures off...for now," Zhao said sourly. "But if I were you, I wouldn't plan on retaining the *Red Hare*'s services past the upcoming op. The Terra Han government is caving to Fleet pressure, and three different Senate oversight committees are screaming to have it brought in. They want a full inspection as part of the formal investigation into whether Terra Han violated Republic law by building it in the first place, let alone secretly transferring it to TAC. Hopefully, by the time you get back, we'll have a replacement ready."

"And the Razorbacks?" Xi asked.

"Those I've had more luck keeping out of the limelight." Zhao tipped his chin to Jenkins. "But I'd recommend you keep them as far from the cameras as possible. We don't want the fact that they've got Vorr tech becoming part of the investigation into the *Red Hare.* "

"The Metal Legion owes you a debt of gratitude, Admiral Zhao," General Pushkin said heavily. "We do not quickly forget the rendering of such important assistance."

"I accepted my TAC advisory post knowing what it meant," Zhao said dismissively. "You either give everything you've got, or you go home and let someone else do it. Speaking of which," he turned to Jenkins, "how did your disciplinary meeting with my son go?"

Jenkins drew a short, quick breath before replying, "I suggested to him that he lead by example and that he not ask his subordinates to render anything he wasn't willing to render himself."

By now, Admiral Zhao had undoubtedly reviewed the results of Jenkins' disciplinary meeting with Captain Chao, along with the captain's reporting to the infirmary to address the sudden loss of his two big toes. It wasn't what Jenkins thought *should* have happened, but after several nights of debate, it was ultimately what he thought *needed* to happen.

Pushkin had been right; Chao was going to be absolutely vital to integrating as many Terra Han Colonial Guardsmen into the Metal Legion as possible. And the best way for him to do that was to appear as though he was still one of *them* rather than a dyed-in-the-wool Metalhead.

In fact, it had been Chao's suggestion that he follow in Hao's footsteps, although Jenkins had already arrived at that conclusion prior to the meeting's outset a day earlier.

Zhao's eyes locked with Jenkins', and for a long moment, it seemed like the admiral might spontaneously explode into a rage. Instead, he gave an approving nod. "Excellent. But I'd advise against letting disfigurement become a unit tradition. Armor Corps might set its own beat, but even TAC isn't exempted from basic civility. We're not a bunch of barbarians here. Bear that in mind, Colonel."

"I will, Admiral," Jenkins agreed.

"What about personnel?" Commodore Kline asked. "My understanding is that TAC was already thin on mech crews before accounting for the Terra Han transfers. Will you be able to fill out the roster in time to deploy?"

Xi leaned forward. "During our last op, Captain Winters stayed at HQ, where he's been working to assemble new mech crews from the inter-branch and street recruits. I went over the readiness reports this morning." She smiled and sat back. "We'll have two full battalions ready to rock."

"Good," General Pushkin nodded before breaking into one of his trademark grins, "because Operation War God is now officially a go."

AUTHOR NOTES - CRAIG MARTELLE

WRITTEN FEBRUARY 2, 2019

Thank you so much for your continued support for the Metal Legion! We wouldn't be here and telling these stories if it weren't for you.

This was another great story of the Metal Legion. The battle streamers hanging off the unit colors are starting to build and become a rainbow of loss and triumph! Sometimes, that ribbon or that medal is worth fighting for. We should honor those awards and the warriors who earned them.

Although we didn't have the shock of the polar vortex, we get it as a matter of course living only 150 miles from the Arctic Circle. It'll drop to -30F and then stay there for a week. The only time it warms up in the winter is so it can snow. We'll get temps about +20F for the snow days. Those are most pleasant. My dog loves that temperature. And then it'll drop back to -20F. Last year, I think we had some 130 days straight with temps below freezing (except for one twelve-hour excursion). That's right, a little over four months and that is the norm. This year, once it dropped below freezing in late October (which is much later than usual), it has not been above freezing since. That puts us at about 110 days straight as of today.

It's not for the weak of heart or weak of lung, which is me. I can go outside when it's super cold, but I can't do anything. The air in town is toxic because of the inversion layer. So I find myself more and more constrained to the house. Which is okay. The rest of the year, Phyllis the Arctic Dog and I spend a lot of time outside. There are only a few months that are prohibitive.

That's why I worked overtime to deliver a slew of new series and new stories. So much new stuff and opportunities to find more readers. If you can help me by sharing a word or two of what you liked about this book or any of my books, that would be great. You can do it on Amazon if you aren't barred from leaving a review, or you can simply share on social media or just tell your friends. Something as simple as "I liked this story," can go a long ways in helping me to get the word out. Think of the boring lives some people are leading. You can save them, but sharing a good science fiction series.

That may seem self-serving, but without readers, there can be no books. So, please, help me to find more readers.

In the meantime, I'll be up here, weathering our latest bout of cold or snow and enjoying the beauty which is the Sub-Arctic in the winter.

Peace, fellow humans.

Please join my Newsletter (www.craigmartelle.com – please, please, please sign up!), or you can follow me on Facebook since you'll get the same opportunity to pick up the books for only 99 cents on the first Saturday after they get published.

If you liked this story, you might like some of my other books. You can join my mailing list by dropping by my website **www.craigmartelle.com** or if you have any comments, shoot me a note at craig@craigmartelle.com. I am always happy to hear from people who've read my work. I try to answer every email I receive.

If you liked the story, please write a short review for me on Amazon. I greatly appreciate any kind words, even one or two sentences go a long way. The number of reviews an ebook receives greatly improves how well an ebook does on Amazon.

Amazon – www.amazon.com/author/craigmartelle

BookBub – https://www.bookbub.com/authors/craig-martelle

Facebook – www.facebook.com/authorcraigmartelle

My web page – www.craigmartelle.com

That's it—break's over, back to writing the next book.

BOOKS BY CRAIG MARTELLE

Craig Martelle's other books (listed by series)

Terry Henry Walton Chronicles (co-written with Michael Anderle) – a post-apocalyptic paranormal adventure

Gateway to the Universe (co-written with Justin Sloan & Michael Anderle) – this book transitions the characters from the Terry Henry Walton Chronicles to The Bad Company

The Bad Company (co-written with Michael Anderle) – a military science fiction space opera

End Times Alaska (also available in audio) – a Permuted Press publication – a post-apocalyptic survivalist adventure

The Free Trader – a Young Adult Science Fiction Action Adventure

Cygnus Space Opera – A Young Adult Space Opera (set in the Free Trader universe)

Darklanding (co-written with Scott Moon) – a Space Western

Rick Banik – Spy & Terrorism Action Adventure

Become a Successful Indie Author – a non-fiction work

Enemy of my Enemy (co-written with Tim Marquitz) – a galactic alien military space opera

Superdreadnought (co-written with Tim Marquitz) – a military space opera

Metal Legion (co-written with Caleb Wachter) - a military space opera

End Days (co-written with E.E. Isherwood) – a post-apocalyptic adventure

Mystically Engineered (co-written with Valerie Emerson) – dragons in space

Monster Case Files (co-written with Kathryn Hearst) – a young-adult cozy mystery series

For a complete list of books from Craig, please see www. craigmartelle.com